Only Child

Only Child

written by

ANDREW VACHSS

Alfred A. Knopf
New York   2002

THIS IS A BORZOI BOOK
PUBLISHED BY ALFRED A. KNOPF

www.aaknopf.com

Library of Congress Cataloging-in-Publication Data
Vachss, Andrew H.
Only child / Andrew Vachss.—1st American ed.
p. cm.
ISBN 0-375-41487-8
1. Burke (Fictitious character)—Fiction. 2. Teenage girls—
Crimes against—Fiction. 3. Long Island (N.Y.)—Fiction.
4. New York (N.Y.)—Fiction. 5. Criminals—Fiction.
6. Mafia—Fiction. I. Title.
PS3572.A33 O55 2002
813'.54—dc21   2002075437

Manufactured in the United States of America
First Edition

Jennifer Lynne Conti Dermody

4/7/76–4/7/02

loved always, loved forever

Only Child

I'd been gone for years. Dead and gone, the whisper-stream said. But that stream always carries more than one current.

Just past midnight, I slipped back over the border, moving downwind out of the darkness. Because Hollywood's got one part right—the dirty, scheming, heartless bitch never *does* sleep.

Especially now.

The alley behind Mama's restaurant was as immune to time as the chamber of a pharaoh's vault. A pair of dull-orange oil drums stood sentinel. I nosed the Subaru's dechromed black snout carefully into the opening between them, over to an empty patch of oil-stained asphalt. On the filthy wall above it, a square of pure-white paint. Inside the square, Chinese characters, in perfect, fluted-edge calligraphy. It was signed with the chop of Max the Silent, the Chinatown equivalent of a skull-and-crossbones on an unmarked bottle.

I slid the Subaru against the wall, not bothering to lock it. Directly across from my spot was a rust-colored steel door with no handle. I slapped my hand against it three times, hard, and stepped back, slitting my eyes against what I knew was coming.

The door opened outwards. A sudden spray of grimy yellow kilowatts framed me in place. A man's shape, backlit, blocked my way. I slowly moved my hands away from my body, keeping them down.

The man said something in Cantonese. I didn't move, letting him study me. The door closed in my face.

I heard them moving in behind me, but I didn't change position. Felt their hands going over me. Didn't react. The door opened again; no lights, this time.

As I stepped inside, I saw a man in a white restaurant apron standing to my left. He had a meat cleaver in his right hand, his left hand locked over the wrist. On the other side of the kitchen, two more men. One of them sighted down the barrel of a pistol, as if I were a piece of land he was surveying. The other flexed his hands to show me he wouldn't need anything else.

I heard the door shut behind me.

The men watching me were professionals, about as nervous as a yoga class on Xanax. More waiting. Not a problem for me; it's what I do best.

"You come home?" I heard her voice before I saw her.

"Yeah, Mama."

"Good!" she snapped, stepping out of the darkness. "You eat now, okay?"

My booth was the last one toward the back, closest to the bank of pay phones. It had the same look as my parking spot. Like it had been waiting for me to show.

I slid in. Mama stood with her arms folded. I hadn't heard her yell anything out to the kitchen, but I knew what she was waiting for.

The guy who hadn't needed weapons came to the booth, carrying a heavy white tureen in one hand—thumb on top, no napkin between him and the heat. He lowered the tureen gently to the table, underscoring the message he'd given me earlier.

Mama sat and took the top off in the same smooth motion, releasing a cloud of steam. No tea ceremony for her; she ladled out a small bowl of the hot-and-sour soup as quick as they ever had on the chow line back in prison. I took a sip, knowing better than to wait for her.

My sinuses unblocked as I felt the familiar taste slam home.

"Perfect," I told her.

"Everything same," Mama said, finally helping herself to a bowl.

I was on my fourth bowl—three is the house minimum— when Max materialized.

He stood there, looking down at me. Measuring.

"I'm all right," I signed to him.

He cocked his head.

"Yeah, I'm sure," I said aloud.

He bowed slightly, folding one scarred, horn-ridged hand over the fist he made of the other.

Mama gestured her order for him to sit and have soup. Max moved in next to her, never taking his eyes off me. He used two hands to show a tree springing up from the ground, then pointed where the roots would be, his straight-line eyebrows raised in a question.

I nodded, slowly. Yeah. This wasn't a visit. I was back to stay.

It was too late to reach out for the rest of my family. Not because they'd be asleep; the middle of the night was when they worked.

I gave the Subaru's keys to Mama. One of the gunmen had brought my duffel bag inside. Max shouldered it, and we hit the alleys.

The faint wash from the streetlights didn't penetrate much past the alley's mouth.

There were three of them. Too murky to pick out details, but they stanced young. I saw a glint of metal.

Max slipped the shoulder strap of the duffel and handed it to me. I pulled a hammerless .38 from its side pocket. A use-it-and-lose-it piece Mama had added to my take-out order. Dull blued steel, the butt wrapped in black electrical tape.

The three figures separated. Max moved to his left, I went to my right.

It was so quiet I could hear a rat doing what rats do.

We kept coming.

When we got close enough for them to see Max, they stopped liking the odds.

It was only a few more blocks to the building where Max lived. We went in the side door, climbed one flight up to his temple.

His wife, Immaculata, was waiting at the top. She held a finger to her lips, meant for me.

"Flower is asleep," she said softly.

"Okay," I whispered back.

"Oh, Burke," she said. "We never knew if you were—"

"I'm fine, Mac."

"My husband wanted to go and be there with you. But Mama said you were—"

"It wouldn't have been the play. And it doesn't matter now, girl. It's done."

"You are back for good?" she asked, echoing Max.

"Yeah. I don't know if this is the place for me, Mac. But I found out for sure there isn't any other one."

"Can you manage all right down here? Just for tonight? As soon as we tell Flower, you can—"

She stopped in response to Max's thumb touching the back of her hand. Max can't hear, but he reads vibrations like forty-point type.

"I already know, Mom!" Flower said, bursting into the room and running to me. I started to bend to scoop her up, but the little baby I had known from her first days on earth was a teenager now. She wrapped her arms around me, burying her head in my chest. "Burke, Burke . . ." she cried, hanging on to me like I was going to run out on her.

M ac told Flower I'd come a long way, and needed to sleep. Flower smiled sweetly and ignored her, demanding to know everything I'd done since I'd been gone, and who I'd done it with.

I fobbed her off with generalities, catching the caution lights in her mother's eyes.

"The last time I saw you was when you were so . . ." The girl's voice trailed away.

"I'm all right now, Flower. Just like I was before."

"You don't . . . look the same. Not at all."

"Hey! I paid good money for all that plastic surgery. What? You don't think I nailed the Robert Redford look?"

"Oh, Burke." She giggled.

"I didn't lose anything important," I said gently. "You understand?"

"I remember what happened," Flower said, as if reciting a lesson. "You were shot. You almost . . . died. They had to fix you. And so your face isn't the same, that's all. You look *so* much better than when you were here . . . before."

"Yeah. The doctors said I'd get better-looking every day. Money-back guaranteed."

"Mom! Make Burke be serious," she appealed to Immaculata.

"This is Burke, child. Your uncle that you missed so dearly. You know he is never serious."

The girl gave her mother a look much older than her years.

By the time I'd finished answering all Flower's questions, light was breaking through the high industrial windows. "I know!" she called to her mother, giving me a quick kiss on the cheek before she ran off to get ready for school.

Max gestured as if playing the bongos, looking from side to side. Telling me the word was going out.

I lay back on the futon. Closed my eyes, waiting for the drift-down. Wondering when I'd feel strong enough to face my hometown in daylight.

"What I tell you, girl?" the small, handsome black man crowed. "Sweet-potato pie; the roots never lie. Didn't I say it? Rhymed the poem—Schoolboy's coming home."

"Yes, Prof," Michelle said. A wicked grin played below her loving eyes. "That's what you said, all right. Every single day since he's been gone."

"My father—" Clarence stepped in to defend the Prof.

"Oh, honey, *please*," Michelle cut him off at the knees. "Everybody knows the Prof can foretell the future and all that, okay? He was just a little out in front on this one."

We were in Mama's, at the round table in the corner. The one that permanently sported a fly-specked "Reserved for Party" sign. I never knew why Mama bothered—no tourist ever tried the food twice, and no local would risk it once.

"Give it up, pup," the Prof said, his hand flashing to my shirt pocket, just like old times. "Huh!" he grunted, coming up empty. "Where's your smokes, dope?"

"I don't puff for real, anymore," I told him. "Just use them as props."

"Your ticker? From when they . . ."

His voice trailed away. Clarence bowed his head, as if the man he called his father had blasphemed in front of a priest.

"It's okay," I told them all. "My heart's fine and"—looking around, to make sure they all got it—"I don't do flashbacks. It's just that, ever since it happened, cigarettes don't taste the same."

"Not even after . . . ?"

"No, Michelle." I laughed.

"It's your call, Paul," the Prof said, reluctantly extracting one of his own hoarded smokes and firing it up.

I t took a long time to satisfy them all. Michelle was the worst. Little sisters always are. I must have told them a dozen times that I was okay. Just wanted to come home.

"What I don't know is how things . . . are," I said.

"At first, the drums really hummed," the Prof said. "But, last few months, anyway, the wire's been quiet."

"And the people who started it . . . ?" Michelle anted up.

"Gone," I said, watching her arched eyebrows so I could avoid her eyes. "*All* gone." The Prof and Clarence had been around at the beginning, Michelle for the middle, but none of them at the end. "If there's any trouble here, it's only from the cops. They may still be looking for me."

"You had a right to walk out of the hospital, mahn," Clarence said indignantly. "It is not as if this was a jailbreak."

"Yeah," I said, thinking it through. "But I'm not supposed to be missing, right? I'm supposed to be dead."

"Yes," Mama put in. "Bone hand."

"That *was* slick," the Prof acknowledged. "I would have never thought that dinosaur roller had it in him."

He meant Morales, the pit-bull cop who had hated me since forever. But he'd owed me, too. And he was the kind of man who couldn't sleep with his books unbalanced. After I'd split, he'd come around to the restaurant, told Mama he needed a surface where I would have left a print. Next thing anyone hears, somebody finds a human hand in a Dumpster. Not the flesh, just the bones. And, right next to it, a pistol. With my thumbprint on the grip.

NYPD put the pieces together. Decided it was payback for a Russian gangster who had been blown away in his own restaurant. The Russian had arranged a transfer—cash for a kidnapped kid—and for me to be the middleman. That's when I'd been shot. And when Pansy, my blood-loyal Neapolitan mastiff, had been killed trying to protect me.

Like everyone else who lives down here, my rep depends on who you talk to. And how you ask. But the whisper-stream always carries this piece of truth: Burke's religion is revenge. If you took someone of mine, I was going to take you. Send you over, or go there myself, trying.

So the cops had made me for Dmitri's killer. And they read the Dumpster's contents for how that had all played out in the end.

They were half right.

I'm listed as deceased in all the Law's computers now. Not a fugitive. Not a parole violator. No warrants, no APBs. Maybe the first time in my life the State that had raised me didn't want me for anything.

But my prints hadn't changed, and we all knew how that worked. I might look golden today, but it would all turn a sickly green in a heartbeat if I got myself into custody.

Nobody would ever be able to ask Morales. When the remote-controlled planes took down the World Trade Center, he was one of the first cops to charge the flaming ruins. If I know Morales, he wasn't looking to do any rescue work. He never made it out.

"So who am I going to be?" I asked my family.

Into the silence, Mama replied, "Still be you."

"I don't get it," I told her.

"If family alive, never die, okay?"

"Sure, in spirit, Mama. But I'm talking about—"

"Spirit? Not spirit. Not *die,*" she spat fiercely, her ancient eyes challenging anyone to disagree.

"You saying Schoolboy be Burke, with a new face, Mama?" the Prof asked her.

"No, no," she snapped. "People owe money, okay? Why pay? Burke gone. Who come to collect? Nobody. Right?" she asked, looking around the table for confirmation. "Nobody collect?"

"Not me or Clarence," the Prof said.

Max shook his head, agreeing.

"You certainly don't think *I* went into the thug business?" Michelle tossed off.

"Sure!" Mama said triumphantly. "But people come *here,* okay? Come with money. Say, 'This for Burke,' leave with me. Maybe *think* dead, but not *sure, okay?*"

"Who came?" I asked her.

"Plenty people," she said, dismissively. "Anyway, see you, now, not know, okay? You not look like, but *talk* like, okay? You know what Burke knows. Maybe you his brother. Cousin. So— same name. Maybe still you, new face. What difference? Nobody ever know. Not for sure, never know."

"Makes sense to me," I said, then handed it off. "Prof?"

"Could be," the little man said, not arguing with Mama, but not deferring to her, either. "Only one way we gonna see."

It was after rush hour by the time we split up. Michelle said she had to get some sleep. The Prof and Clarence exchanged conspiratorial looks, said something about putting the finishing touches on a crib they'd found for me. I went out through the back door into the alley. A beige Honda Accord sedan stood there, idling. I got into the front seat. Max slipped into the back.

"Burke!" the young man at the wheel almost shouted. Before I could answer, he calmed himself, asked, "It *is* you, right?"

"It's me, Terry," I said. "Damned if I didn't have trouble recognizing you, too."

"I'm a man now," he said. He'd been a boy when I pulled him away from a kiddie pimp in Times Square, way back before Mickey Mouse took over the territory. He reached his hand behind him for Max to slap, then folded his palm into a fist, tapping it twice over his heart.

Terry pulled slowly out of the alley, heading for the FDR. "This ride's okay, right? I knew you wouldn't want anything flashy."

"It's great," I assured him. "You got paper? A license?"

He gave me the look kids give to adults who should be in detox.

I'd been this way a thousand times. FDR to the Triborough to Bruckner Boulevard to Hunts Point Avenue. Past the endless ribbon of dull-gray blight that passes for residential housing, and into the badlands.

The kid slipped the Honda into a break in the fence that surrounded a huge junkyard. The opening was invisible unless you were right on top of it. And if you ever wandered that close, you'd see why the proprietor hadn't bothered with a "Beware of the Dog" sign. The pack formed before Terry shut down the engine.

Terry pulled a lever, and we drove into a sally port made out of two parallel walls of chain link. The dogs waited behind the inner wall, predator-patient, not even bothering to bark.

"Is Simba still . . . ?" I said, not realizing how fearful I was of the answer until the question was out of my mouth. The reigning king of the junkyard had to be at least twenty years old. He should have gone to be with Dog a long time ago.

"Are you kidding?" Terry said.

We drove past the second gate. The kid hopped out to close it behind us. In seconds, the car was a big rock in a river of dogs, their voices blending into a single low snarl.

Terry waded back through the dogs, knocking some of them aside with his knees. They didn't seem to mind. He had his hand on the car door when Simba made his entrance.

The monster was white around the muzzle now, but the others still gave him room. A bull-mastiff–shepherd cross, with one ear almost gone—probably a challenge from one of the younger males for pack leadership. He walked carefully. Not crippled, just conserving his energy. The next fight, that was Simba's life.

"Simba!" I called to him out of my opened window. "Simba-witz, the Lion of Zion! You remember me, don't you, boy? Old dogs like us, we don't need to see to smell."

The beast came closer. I dangled my hand out the window. Chum out of a shark cage, if Simba didn't recognize me.

He sniffed experimentally, then gave a deep-throated growl of welcome.

"That's my boy," I said softly, scratching him behind his remaining ear.

The old warrior's eyes were milky with age. A couple of teeth were missing. I wouldn't have taken him on with a machine gun.

Max climbed out. He never went through any kind of greeting ceremony with the dogs. They never seemed to care.

Terry stashed the Honda, came back with the topless Jeep they use as a jitney. Max and I climbed on. After a moment's hesitation, Simba jumped up there with us.

We rode through the moonscape, Terry piloting the Jeep around the hidden obstacles set up to slow down anyone visiting without permission. Compound fractures will do that.

"You drive like a pro," I complimented him. "Your dad teach you?"

"Right!" he joked. "Mom said she'd murder him if he even tried. No, it was Clarence. And my license—it's a hundred per-cent legit, Burke. I passed the test and everything."

The clearing was under a canopy of twisted metal formed by stacks of smashed cars waiting for the crusher to finish them off. The cut-down oil drums were arranged in a neat horseshoe— empty chairs, awaiting guests. Terry braked gently; then vaulted easily off the Jeep to the ground. He disappeared somewhere behind the rubble, leaving Simba with me and Max.

I sat down on one of the drums. The junkyard was a grave-yard, too. My Pansy was there, her body under a wreath of twisted rebar and razor wire. *Just her body,* I said in my mind. I'm not a man who visits cemeteries—Pansy was always with me.

Belle's body is there, too.

I see them, together. Waiting.

Sometimes, that comforts me. Sometimes, it makes me wish I could kill some people all over again.

Simba slowly came closer. Finally, the beast sat before me, his harsh old eyes holding me until he was sure I was paying attention.

"I know," I told him. "Thanks."

The Mole materialized from the gloom, wearing his standard dirt-colored jumpsuit. The Coke-bottle lenses of his glasses were prisms in the tricky light. He shambled forward, as awkward as a drunk.

"Mole," I said, getting up.

He kept coming until he was only inches away, then stopped.

"So?" His madman's eyes examined me, collecting data for his genius brain.

"I'm all right," I told him.

"Is there a job?"

"No, Mole. I just came home."

"To stay?"

"If I can pull it off."

The Mole turned and greeted Max with a slight bow. Simba banged his noble, scarred head against the Mole's leg. The lunatic absently patted his dog's head, muttering something in their two-creature language.

"Everything's different!" Terry said brightly. "You wouldn't believe it, Burke. I'm in college. Mom has a new job. We're all going to—"

"Nothing is different," the Mole said mildly.

The kid looked at me, then slowly nodded agreement. Learning from his father, as always.

We spent a few hours down in the Mole's bunker, catching up. Listening to Terry, mostly. The kid made sure to include Max in his narratives, using the street-signing we'd taught him. Max can read lips, but I'm never sure how much he gets, so I usually throw in a few gestures whenever I speak. The Mole never bothers; it's not like most people understand what he says, anyway.

"You need a car?" the Mole finally asked me.

"I . . . guess. I came in with one, but it's not exactly anonymous. A Subaru SVX."

The Mole grunted something.

"I don't know where it is now," I told him. I looked at Max, and made the gesture for steering a car.

Max tapped the ground with his foot, then pointed down. So the Subaru was buried someplace safe. It had good paper on it, and it was registered to a fine set of bogus ID I'd been using on the other coast. I could sign it over in blank, give the paper to a driver, let him clout the car down in Florida, maybe. We couldn't know if anyone was onto the ID, but if they were, the sale would place me a long way from home. And I could use the money.

"Which car did you take?" the Mole asked Terry.

"The Accord."

"You want that one?" the Mole asked me. "In the City, nobody sees it."

"Sure . . ." I told him. "That'd be great."

The Mole gave me a look, but he didn't say anything.

We walked back to where the Honda was hiding. Without the Jeep, it took maybe fifteen, twenty minutes. Terry never stopped talking. The Mole said about as much as Max did.

But before we took off, he leaned down to where I had the window open. "Nothing is different," he said again. Like he wanted to make sure I got the message.

We took the back way home, over the Willis Avenue Bridge. It was late afternoon, the deep shadows already dancing with impatience to take over the streets. As we came up on the Houston Street exit off the Drive, Max reached over and tapped my wristwatch. He wasn't asking me what time it was; he was saying we had a meet.

"What?" I mimed.

Max didn't respond. But when we got to Chrystie Street, he pointed through the windshield—keep going straight. We weren't headed for Chinatown, then. I stayed on Houston to the bitter end, then turned south down Varick Street. Max kept pointing me through the narrow maze of blocks that circled the Holland Tunnel like broken capillaries around a bruise.

We found a parking spot under a sign that said not to. I got out and followed Max down a garbage-filled alley. As we turned the corner, I saw a pair of center-joined doors, their frosted glass worn away enough to show a metal grate behind. On the glass, someone had painted ROOMS in once-red freehand.

Max made a "let's go" gesture and opened the doors, pushing the grate aside with one hand. To the right was a long plank with a hinged center section. Behind it stood a wall of pigeonholes. Large number-tagged keys poked out of a few of the slots. A long-handled bolt cutter stood against the wall.

Behind the plank, there was a fat man in a wheelchair, wearing a green eyeshade out of a Fifties movie, only twisted around, hip-hop style. His eyes were the color of old dimes. Between rapid blinks, they scanned, recorded . . . and erased the tape.

I followed Max up an uncarpeted flight of stairs that was a little cleaner than the alley. On the next landing, a single low-watt bulb protruding from the wall revealed only the vague shapes of doors, all closed.

Max went up another flight, checked the area briefly, then kept climbing. I recognized the top floor by its skylight. Signs were splattered randomly over the walls—EPA, Health Department, Office of Building Management—warning of everything from exposed wiring to lead paint to asbestos contamination. NO ADMITTANCE! DANGER!

In case anyone still felt brave, there was a triptych of rat posters, the kind the Transit Authority slaps up in your better subway stations. Drawings of malevolent rodents, with a POISON!! notice above. Nice places, subway tunnels. If the vermin didn't get you, what the City tried to kill them with would.

I warily eyed the cables dangling from the ceiling as we walked to the end of the hall. We came to a decrepit-looking wooden door, sagging on its hinges. Max pushed it open, stepped aside to usher me in, a faint smile on his usually flat face.

The Prof and Clarence were seated at what had once been a professional poker table—a green felt octagon, with round slots for ashtrays and drinking glasses at each station. They gave me an indifferent glance, as if I were a stranger who had just walked into a bar.

Max tugged at my sleeve and pointed for me to look around. Instead of the coffin-sized rooms you'd expect in a flophouse, the place was spacious enough to hold a corporate meeting—someone had taken a sledgehammer to the connecting walls. The windows were small and grimy, but an overhead skylight bathed the whole space in soft light.

Max gave me the tour. There was no kitchen, but someone had put in a little blue microwave, a chrome toaster, and a white enamel hotplate with two burners. Three stubby brown mini-fridges were stacked one on top of another.

At the very end of the corridor was what had once been the shared bathroom for the whole floor. Its walls had been punched out to incorporate the room next to it, and it now featured a coiled aluminum line that added a shower option to the good-sized white fiberglass tub. There was a skylight above that room, too.

Retracing our steps, Max pointed out the new layer of rubber flooring, a tasteful shade of black. Fresh drywall had been used to form a sleeping room, furnished with an army cot, a wooden chest of drawers, and four stand-up steel lockers.

"What you think, Schoolboy?" the Prof asked, coming up behind where I was standing.

"It's beautiful," I told him, meaning it.

"Yeah, bro. The Mole tricked it out slick."

"The *Mole*?"

"See," the little man chuckled to Clarence, "I told you Burke wouldn't bust it." He turned to me. "Don't look like the Mole's tracks, right?"

"Well . . ."

"That's the point of the joint, son. Downstairs, it's still an SRO. One step up from a chickenwire flophouse. A pound a night, cash in hand. *Every* night, or they padlock your room. The building's marked—they're gonna make fucking condos out of it or something. You know the way the City is now, bro. Ain't no place motherfuckers won't live, because there ain't no room for all of them that wants to, right?"

"Even after the World Trade Center?"

"This is The Apple, son," the Prof said, with the bitter pride only people born and raised here ever really get right—or understand. "They'd have to do a lot more than knock down some buildings and kill a bunch of folk."

He held out his hand, palm up. I slapped it soft, no argument.

"So, anyway," the little man went on, "they don't tumble buildings no more, they rehab them. This here one, that's what it's waiting on. 'Course, with all the palms that got to be greased, it'll be years before it ever actually happens."

"And in the meantime . . ."

"Yeah. You lay in the cut. Right up here on the top floor. Off the books, complete. Far as the City know, this floor's unfit for human occupancy. Nobody goes past the third."

"The guy at the desk . . . ?"

"You don't need to worry about him, bro. The only thing Gateman's got an eye out for is his PO."

"What'd he go for?"

"He's a shooter."

"You mean, he *was,* right?"

"No, son. Gateman always worked right from that chair. Last time down, the jury hung on homicide. Gateman claimed the other guy was making his move. Self-defense. The other guy was strapped, but he never cleared leather. Gateman's a cutie. Told the DA he had to sit anyway, might as well sit on The Rock until they tried him again. They have a staredown, and the DA blinked. Kept dropping the offer. When it got down to Man Two, Gateman took the lucky seven, did his half-plus."

"He doesn't work now?"

"Just behind that desk, son. But I pity the sucker who tries to stick up the place."

If this was any city but New York, I might have raised an eyebrow at anyone holding up a flophouse. Here, I just nodded.

"Gateman, he's on the hustle," the Prof said. "He gets a free room and a little cash for managing the place. Picks up some extra fronting meets—there's a big room behind that desk. Trading post; you see where I'm going."

"He trade anything else?"

"Gateman's good people," the Prof assured me. "Time-tested. Two rides; never lied to glide. I did a stretch with him, back in the day. He gets a G a month from us. That's his lifeline; he can count on it. And, anyway, you ain't no fugitive now. No price on your head. What's he going to get from diming you?"

"Does he know who I am?"

"Maybe." The Prof shrugged. "Gateman's not the kind to show what he know. But he for damn sure knows who *Max* is, understand? Besides, he don't even have to see you come and go, you don't want him to, honeyboy. I told you the Mole was on the job. Want to see?"

"Sure."

The Prof walked over to what looked like a floor-to-ceiling closet built out into the room, walled on three sides. When he opened it, I saw a flat platform and a pair of thick cables.

"Used to be one of those dumbwaiters," the Prof said proudly. "My man Mole gets his hands on it—you know what you got now? A private elevator, bro! You got to crouch a little, but it works like a charm."

"Where does it go?" I asked, taking a closer look.

"Basement. Nothing down *there* but the furnace and the boiler. Door opens in, not out, okay? When you open it, looks like you're facing a blank wall, but it's really the back of a big Dumpster. Lever to your right. You pull it down, it unlocks the wheels. You just shove it away, step out, push it back, and you're in the alley. A phantom. Even if someone sees you, they don't believe it."

"What if there's someone waiting in the—?"

"Got you backed, Jack. The Mole hooked up one of those submarine things. You know what I'm talking about, right? You look in it, you see what's happening outside. Works at night, too. Everything looks kind of greenish, but you can still see boss, hoss."

"I stay up here three nights once, while we are getting it ready, mahn," Clarence said. "Quiet as a graveyard."

"Rats don't make a sound, huh?" I said.

Max pointed to a big box in a far corner. It looked like a stage speaker for an industrial-music concert. The Mongolian pointed at his ears, raised his eyebrows, and jerked his head around as if he just heard something. He made a mound of his hand to imitate the huge hindquarters and tiny head of the Universal Rat. Then he shook his head as if the sound was painful, and made the rat scurry away.

I nodded at him. Sure. The Mole wouldn't waste his time with traps or poison. Cats can handle mice, but they've got too much sense to mess with City-mutated rats. For those, what you need is a little terrier . . . and my family knew I wasn't ready even to think about another dog.

"Well, brother? This work for you?"

I scanned their faces, seeing what I'd crossed the country to see again.

"It's the best place I ever had in my life," I said.

I took my time settling in. Trying it on, adjusting the fit. Did a lot of dry runs through the basement: in and out, always at night. Slowly, I got familiar with the place, admiring the little touches they had added to protect me, like the acoustic tile on the walls. And the three cellular phones, all set to the same cloned number, each with a separate charging holster, so that one was always live. The electricity was bridged from Gateman's own unit, and it powered the space heaters just fine when I tested them.

No A/C; wall units would have given away the game from the outside, and central air was impossible. But the venting was superb, so the fans were able to whisper the summer days down to comfortable.

I kept the anonymous pistol Mama had given me on a little shelf in the elevator shaft. One flick of my hand and it would drop to the basement, well out of reach of any search warrant.

Each room had a large plastic disk on one of the walls. Any weight on the stairs would make the disks glow flash-fire red, bright enough to wake you out of a deep sleep.

In a room off the entrance, I found they had hooked me up with a big-screen TV. And a piece of Gateman's cable package. He was a high roller in that department—I even got HBO and Showtime.

That's when it first hit me. My old office was too small to ever have friends over—say, to watch a fight on TV together. It was barely large enough for me and Pansy, and . . . and then I understood why my people had set up my new place the way they had.

"Calls come in," Mama said. "All time, always."

"Business?"

"Maybe sometimes," she said, shrugging to emphasize the "maybe" part.

"What do you think?" I asked Michelle.

"I think maybe Mr. Burke could have an assistant," she purred.

"You?"

"Me? Honey, I am no man's 'assistant.' I was talking about *you*."

"Sure, bro," the Prof counseled. "Take the handoff and hit the line. You got to get back to work."

I don't know how the woman stumbled across my phone number . . . the one that rings in a Chinese laundry in Brooklyn and forwards to the pay phones behind my booth. That number's been part of the graffiti in certain back alleys for so long that most of the people who call it can't remember where they got it.

Michelle and I met her in a diner, somewhere around the Elmhurst–Rego Park border in Queens. She looked like a woman in her late thirties who'd kept herself pretty well . . . or like a teenager with most of her nerve endings deep-fried. If she had a problem with me and Michelle both being the "screeners" for the busy Mr. Burke, she didn't say. Maybe because she was even busier amping out her story.

"Nola—that's my genetic mother but I don't call her 'Mother' because she's not a mother because mothers don't lie to their own children about critical things like she did, like she always did, from the very beginning—Nola, she told me that my father was a one-night stand, you know, like in a movie or something," she said in one breath. The edges of her speech splintered with stress fractures. "Very romantic. He was a poet or something; I don't remember. I don't remember lies. That takes a lot of work. You try it yourself, if you don't believe me. Forgetting something, that's hard. Trying makes you remember. But I finally got it. I don't remember what she said he was. My father. She said she never knew his name, but one day she saw his picture in the paper. He was killed in a car accident, or something. I think that's what she said, anyway. I don't remember. Because it was all a lie, so I don't remember it."

I felt Michelle's long fingernail pressing into my knee, telling me to sit still. She was a lot more interested in the end of the story than I was.

"She isn't as smart as she thinks, Nola," the woman went on. "And I'm not as stupid as she thinks I am, either. I investigated her. She never thought of that. She thought I'd investigate *him*. But how could I do *that,* when I didn't know anything about him? Except lies. And I can't remember lies.

"I found my birth certificate. Her name, the Nola name, it was on it. But *his* wasn't the same name she told me. It wasn't the same name she said was *my* name, my last name, not Nola's, the name from my father, the way you get your name from your father.

"After that, it was easy. So easy. I love the Internet. You can find out anything on the Internet. You can find the truth. The total truth. It's always there. And nobody can erase it or lie about it or change it. Once it's on the Internet, it's forever. Like the runes. I searched. I used search engines. They have them, just for that. And I found her."

I lit a cigarette. Took one drag, then placed it in the notch of a clear glass ashtray with a green logo in its base. The smoke drifted up between us. I let my eyes go into it, a patience trick.

"She was raped," the woman said, a sneer in her voice. "That's what she, Nola, what she *told* everyone, anyway. That's where I came from. From a rape. She *said*. She, Nola, said it when I confronted her. It was a confrontation, like you see on television, like they tell you to do to the person who hurt you. I read that. I read that in a *number* of books. You have to confront them. Make them take responsibility. That's what I did. And not with a letter, like they say to do if you can't face them, or if they're dead, but I could, so that's what I did. I went right to her.

"'You lied,' that's what I told her. And you know what she did? She *admitted* it. Like it was something she was proud of. She said she never told me my father was a rapist because she didn't want me to think I came from anything bad. She, Nola, could have had an abortion, she *said*. But she doesn't believe in abortion, she *said*. So she went away and changed her name and had me, the baby. That was after the trial. After the man was convicted."

My cigarette had burnt itself out. I wondered when she was going to.

"What do you want Mr. Burke to do?" I asked her, earning myself another puncture wound from Michelle.

"He's innocent," the woman said. I knew what was coming then. And it turned each vertebra of my spine into a separate ice cube. "I found him," she said, reverence throbbing through her voice. "We correspond. I'm on his approved list. Not everyone can be on that list. He had to get permission. And I visit him, too. He's in Clinton; do you know where that is?"

"Yes," I said, keeping to the professional neutrality of the hostage negotiator. "It's a prison. Way upstate, near the Canadian border."

"That's right. That's true, what you said. He's up there. All the way up there, for something someone else did. For what someone else did to *him*."

I was getting a headache. Even if the guy she was talking about had gone down for Rape One, and the judge had maxed him, he wouldn't still be Inside so many years later. Not in New York, where the politicians think only drug-dealing and cop-killing should lock you down for the count.

"I don't understand," I said gently. "If he'd been convicted back in—"

"No, no, no, no," she cut me off. "He was in another place. A much nicer place. In Gouverneur. That's far upstate, too. But it's better. He was in a dormitory, not a cell. And he could have more visits, and packages, and everything. But he got *stabbed*. By an Italian. A Mafia man, I think. It was for no reason. He almost *died*. But the man who stabbed him, he told a story, and they believed it. So they moved the man Nola said was my . . . They moved *him*. For his own protection, is what they said."

"I'm still not following you," I said. "When was he first incarcerated?"

"Incarcerated? When my mother, Nola is what she says her name is, when my mother made up the story. That's when."

"But that was before you were even born, right? And he's *still* locked up?"

"He . . . You don't understand. The prosecutor, she was a crazy woman. A savage person. She got them to sentence him as a Persistent Violent Felony Offender," she said, articulating the words proudly, like a child who had just memorized her alphabet.

"This was in Queens, then?" I asked.

"Yes! Right here in Queens. In the courthouse in Jamaica. I have the whole transcript. That prosecutor, she told the judge my father was a dangerous beast, and he needed to be in a cage for the rest of his life."

Wolfe, I thought to myself. The former chief of City-Wide Special Victims, she was a blooded-in veteran of the trench warfare academics call sex-crimes prosecution.

Wolfe had been hated by Legal Aid and black-robed collaborators alike. She'd taken on all comers for years, never stepping off, fighting harder when she was surrounded. She tried all the "bad victim" cases everyone else ducked—hookers, mentally ill, retarded, elderly, little kids—risking the high conviction rate so sacred to prosecutors with political ambitions.

And then she was taken down by a party-hack whore who spent so much time on his knees that the ass he kissed had become his panoramic world-view.

After that, Wolfe went outlaw, spearheading the best info-trafficking crew in the City.

Wolfe, who I always loved from the moment I truly knew her. Who told me once, "You and me, it's never going to be." Who I once had something with I'd never had before. A second chance. And, being me, I blew it.

No matter how long you're gone, some kinds of pain are always patient enough to wait for you.

"I know who you're talking about," is all I said. "But I still can't figure out what you want Mr. Burke to do."

"My father was the victim of a false allegation," the woman said. "It was all a lie. They were all liars, all those women. But only Nola, my mother, she says, even *Nola* she says, she was the only one who was brazen enough to tell the lies in court. It was not the truth, so it was a lie. My mother, this Nola, made it all up. Because she was a slut and a whore. She didn't want to admit what she was, so she said she was raped. Like the Scottsboro Boys. Just like that. It was on the Internet. Those girls were never raped. But they knew if they pointed a finger at black boys they would be heroes, not whores.

"That's what happened with my mother, Nola, the way she says it, Nola. The big hero. For testifying. Such a brave *liar* she was. So what I want, I want . . . *DNA,*" she said, in that breathless, dramatic tone people reserve for something holy.

"You're talking a lot of money," I said, trying to stem the flow.

"Money?" she sneered, almost cackling with scorn. "There'll be *plenty* of money. I talked to a producer. And she said that we'd all be there, on national TV. They can do a remote, so my father could be on TV, too, from prison."

"A producer . . . ?"

"My agent is handling it all," she said loftily. "He says a book is a sure thing, and maybe even a movie. And if Mr. Burke can get me the test, he'd be on camera, too. You know what publicity like *that* could be worth?"

About as much as my picture on a post-office wall, I thought, but I made encouraging noises at the woman, wanting her to finish so Michelle and I could vanish from her life.

"I want a complete DNA test," she said. "Of everyone involved. Me, Nola, my mother she says, and the innocent man, my father. See"—she bent forward to compel me with the brilliance of her plan—"my father's lawyers have all given up. The . . . rape kit, I think they call it, it's not around anymore. So, *normally,* there wouldn't be anything anyone could do. But Nola, my mother she says, says my father *raped* her. And that's how I was born. You see the beauty of it?

"Will you tell Mr. Burke for me? I know he always defends the innocent," she whispered, confirming that she was a dozen shock treatments past deranged.

"**S**ometimes, I'm ashamed that God is a woman," Michelle said on the drive back. "I don't like sick jokes."

"Yeah," I agreed. "Nice logic, huh? If this guy's DNA doesn't match up, so what? Means he's not her father, that's all. Doesn't say anything about him not being a rapist. Only thing it means is that the mother had sex with someone somewhere around the time the rape occurred. Probably *after,* is what I'm guessing."

"Why?"

"Lots of kids are born at eight months, not nine. Technically preemies, but they have good size and weight. The mother probably did the math herself, figured it had to be the rapist who made her pregnant."

"Or maybe just a little before, and the guy had used a condom, so the mother thought she couldn't . . . ?"

"Sure. But there's no way the *rapist* knew her, not even slightly. Otherwise the maggot would have gone for a consent defense, guaranteed. This wasn't a homicide. The victim lived, and she ID'ed him in court. There was probably a ton of other evidence, too. Remember what she said about 'all those women'? You don't get a Persistent Violent jacket without a load of priors. Ten to one, he was a serial rapist. Probably only took it to trial because Wolfe wouldn't offer him anything off the life-top, so what did he have to lose?

"You'll notice she never said a word about blood evidence being used to convict him. Experienced freak like that, maybe *he* used a condom. That woman is stone-lunar. To her, this is all some kind of weirdo paternity suit."

"Ugh!"

"You know what's worse, girl? There was no reason for the mother to lie. Who'd *want* to make up a story like that? That freak's her bio-father, all right."

"How could a TV producer *not* see she's a . . . ?"

"Knowing isn't caring, honey. Talk shows are going through what skin mags did years ago."

"I don't understand."

"*Playboy* set the standard, right? Upscale, classy, lots of features . . . *and* all the posed pussy anyone could want. Anything successful gets imitated, but instead of trying to outclass the leader, most of the others went downmarket. The more *Playboy* carved out the niche at the top, the deeper in the sewer they went, see? That's where the competition is now, who can go the lowest. Same with TV. The target's not the penthouse; it's the basement. Did you hear her voice when she said '*national* TV,' girl? Same way some people say 'Our Lord Jesus.' There's no traveling freak shows anymore—cable brings them right into your home."

"Burke," she said, leaning toward me, "you're not going to take her money, are you?"

"She hasn't got any," I told her, placating both our gods.

I never asked the Prof or the Mole what the stuff they'd set up for me cost, any more than I would ask Max if I owed him rent. I'd left everything behind when I disappeared. I didn't know what they'd sold, what they'd destroyed, and what was still around. But I knew how to find out.

"Where do I stand?" I asked Mama.

"With who, stand?"

"With money, Mama."

"Oh. Plenty money here for you."

"Mama, a straight answer, okay? You're the bank, not the Welfare Department. I'm not coming around and asking for money that's not mine. Just tell me what's left, in cash, after everything."

"Why so important?"

"I have to know when I need to go back to work."

She regarded me balefully for a solid minute. Then she said, "Soon," her face as smooth and hard as glazed ceramic.

It took another couple of hours to pry the balance sheet out of her. I was down to about sixty grand. I took ten to walk around with, asked Mama to dispose of the Subaru for whatever she could get for it, and went looking for work.

You can't do the kind of work I do without a lot of preparation. There's all kinds of people who steal, from the stupid slugs who think 7-Elevens turn into ATMs after midnight to the slicksters who can buy themselves a presidential pardon when things get dicey. Me, I've got my own ways. And my own flock to fleece.

I never target citizens. They're easy, but they squawk. Before the damn Internet, I had a lovely business built up, regularly selling everything from nonexistent kiddie porn to mercenary "credentials." The horde of humans who bought from me couldn't go to the Better Business Bureau when their merchandise never arrived in the mail.

I also dealt in hard goods, middle-manning low level arms deals, usually suctioning a little from both sides in the process. But with the breakup of the Soviet Union, there was too much ordnance floating around. By the time I left, even the congenital defectives who commanded five-moron militias were demanding surface-to-air missiles.

I gave it a lot of thought, remembering the formula I memorized during my first bit Inside—the less time you spend on planning, the more time you should plan on doing.

When I first went down, a common scam was for a prisoner to get hold of one of the lonely-hearts magazines and write to a whole list of dopes. Admitting "she'd" been a bad girl, but now all she wanted was a good man. Between the losers with handjob habits who asked for letters about lesbian sex behind bars, and the deep-dish dimwits who sent money for the "correspondence courses" their little darlings needed to take to please the parole board, you could make a nice living.

It got so bad that suckers were showing up at the gates, demanding a visit with their soon-to-be-released sweethearts. That's when they would discover that the "D. Jones #C-77-448109" they'd been sending money orders to was in there all right . . . but the first name was Demetrius, not Darlene.

Eventually, the authorities got wise. Now they stamp outgoing envelopes with bold notices that the letters inside are from a "Correctional Institution for Men."

Every move has a counter, and it's never been real difficult to defeat the great minds who cage humans for a living. The letters started going out to the marks from an outside PO box. Little Darlene's in solitary, and she can't get mail "direct" anymore. But, don't worry, Darlene's sister (who's also real cute, but only sixteen, so she shouldn't be getting too involved with a grown *man* and all) can handle the forwarding. Fortunately, her name's Désirée, so "D. Jones" would work just as well on the money orders.

And then there's the poor tormented transsexual, who describes her absolute horror at being locked up in a *men's* prison. She has to stay in close confinement twenty-four/seven, or she'd be set upon instantly by rabid packs of rapists. All she has to sustain herself are the chump's love letters, the money he sends for things like shampoo—*so* expensive in a men's prison, you know—and the knowledge that, the minute she's paroled, she could finish the sex-change surgery she'd already started before she'd been arrested (which is why she already had such nice big breasts). And they'd live happily ever after.

But that scam plays different today. Now it's a beautiful teenager prowling the chat rooms, crying out in her desperate need to get away from her horrible home life . . . until a "connection" is made and her shined-on knight sends her the money for a bus ticket. And some decent clothes, maybe some luggage . . . you know.

It'll be a long wait at *that* depot.

But I don't like working in public. And, anyway, that ground's already been strip-mined down to the bare rock.

As long as there's contraband, there's money to be made. Sometimes, you traffic in things—like no-tax Southern cigarettes or no-questions-asked shipments of computer chips. Sometimes, the product's a lot less tangible. Like jail-phone relay systems.

No matter what the level of security a prisoner's held in, he'll have the right to call *somebody,* even if it's only his lawyer, and only collect. With three-way calling, it's no trick to put a gangster in direct touch with the people waiting for his orders. The guards can open mail, but there's way too much volume for them to monitor all the outgoing calls. More gangland hits get ordered from jail now than from outside. All you need is a live person to play switchman, and decent timing.

A nice hustle . . . but not for me. Too close to home.

Drugs have ruined the game for a lot of us good thieves. Dope fiends are the illegal immigrants of crime—a cheap, undocumented labor force that will take any job, even the dangerous ones, for garbage money. Years ago, we'd hijacked a load of H and tried to sell it back to the mob. But when I mentioned that caper to the Prof this time, he sneered it away.

"Not much chance of finding a decent-sized shipment you could take off with anything less than an army, not today. And when it gets down to the street dealers we *could* jack, it's not worth it. You can't deal with these punks. The drug boys, all they know is rock and Glock, honeyboy. You steal from a professional, he knows he's got to buy his stuff back—cost of doing business. These boys out there now, they're all mad violent. They'd load up their nines and come looking to hose you down, give you a kiss for the diss, see?"

I did. And started making new lists.

What I found out was . . . I'd been away too long. I sniffed around the edges where I used to do work. Sent word through third parties to people who dealt in stuff I used to move, checked the usual drops. . . .

But no matter where I looked, the arteries were all clogged with amateurs.

There's no new crimes, only new criminals. And I didn't know any of them.

Oh, sure, there were little jobs I could pull. Minor stings where I wouldn't need an active crew, just a little help with front. Low-risk, low-return.

That's all I wanted to do, once. Live small. Stay off the radar. I could never be a citizen, but I didn't want to be a convict again, either.

Thing is, only citizens have 401(k)s. When I was coming up, I'd always hear the crime guys I admired talking about the "retirement score." That one big job they could live off forever.

When you're young, that kind of thing's just another convict fantasy. One of the Big Three—money, sex, and revenge.

When you've put on some mileage, when you've been some places and done some things, you realize that the Big Three is down to One. Money. That key works all of the locks.

And by the time you get old enough, close enough to that time when any trip back Inside amounts to a life sentence, you know what "blood money" *really* means. This is an ugly country to be poor in. Worse if you're sick. And if you're old, you can ratchet that up a few notches more.

I knew all that. I was schooled by the best. I'd been putting money aside from every score almost since I started. But when I had to disappear, most of it got eaten up during the hunt. And I didn't have another twenty years to rebuild my stake.

When I was a young man, rep was all a lot of us had. Heart. We tattooed it on our souls, a prayer never to be forgotten. Paying with our lives for the sacramental wine poured into an "X" on callous City concrete by those who had watched us go. Whenever his brothers pooled their cash for a bottle of T-bird, the man who had proved his heart in battle always got the first taste.

I'd lost that need for a two-minute tombstone a long time ago. The reason I'd rather go out quick than rot to death on Welfare hasn't got anything to do with pride. Some pain is easier to manage, that's all.

This isn't Willie Sutton's world anymore. Banks aren't where the money is—at least, not money you can get at in a quick-hit robbery. Casinos and racetracks have tons of untraceable cash. But there's no way to *ease* it out, and it would take a military assault to take it by force. Kidnappings always come unglued at the exchange. Blackmail's hit-or-miss; mostly miss. Jewelry's easier, but it has to pass through too many hands before it turns into cash, and each one cuts a slice off the loaf.

The whisper-stream is always vibrating with rumors of open contracts. A Central American druglord is offering millions for any crew that can break him out of a federal pen. A collector is offering more than that for a certain painting under museum guard. Some shadowy zillionaire has a huge bounty out on whoever the hate-flavor of the moment is.

There's always enough shreds of truth clinging to stories like that to make some retardate act on faith. Ask James Earl Ray.

The surest proof that Ray acted alone is that nobody ever ratted him out. Ask the church bombers. Or McVeigh.

But I wouldn't go there. I've been to that school. Paid what the tuition cost.

So I knew who to ask.

"Snakeheads," Mama said.

"Is there really that much in it?" I asked her.

"Always money. Just not . . ." she said, snapping her fingers to say "immediately."

"I don't understand."

"Snakeheads like farmer with cows, okay? Cow *meat* worth not much; cow *milk,* very good. Get all over again, every day, understand?"

"The people they bring over, they pay off their debts by working? Takes a long time, but the money keeps coming in . . . ?"

"Yes. Small payment, each week. But *many* make payment, so plenty money, see?"

"Sure. But where do we come in?"

"To snakeheads, people . . . cargo, okay?"

"But it isn't cargo you can hijack, Mama. What could we do with—?"

"Plenty . . . what you call 'societies,' here. In America. They, how you say, *sponsor* people."

"Pay their way over?"

"Yes. Like ticket."

"Why?"

"Many reasons. Some good, some not so good."

If you're ever fool enough to let Mama know anything she says isn't crystal-clear, she gets offended. It's okay if you don't get it, so long as it's not her fault.

Only silence works. So I just ate a little more of my fried rice with roast pork and scallions. The minute Mama's satisfied you don't want an explanation, she always explains.

"Sometimes, family, okay? Relatives. Sometimes, just want to buy girl, like for wife."

"They wouldn't need to smuggle anyone in for that. Seems like half the women in Russia under thirty are registered with some broker. It's a big business now."

"Not like for . . . American wife," Mama said, venom-voiced. "Not like for . . . marry. To use. You understand."

That wasn't a question.

"And war," she went on. "In Vietnam. Plenty brothers, sons, fathers . . . never come home. Not dead, maybe. Nobody know for sure."

"MIAs?"

"Maybe," Mama shrugged. "Nobody know for sure," she said again, as if I'd missed it the first time. "Always rumors. People in the camps, they hear. If you say you know where American soldiers still in Vietnam, then, maybe, people *sponsor,* bring you here, so you say where soldiers still kept, see?"

"What camps are you talking about, Mama?"

"Always camps," she said, no expression on her face. "Always fighting. So—always refugees. Cambodia, Laos, Burma. On Thai border, plenty place to hear whispers."

"Yeah," I agreed. "I heard about some of those hustles. I guess, if you had one of your own go MIA, you'd listen to anyone who claimed to have seen him, pay to bring him over." I thought of Robert Garwood, a Marine who had spent fourteen years in Vietnam. He was either a POW or a collaborator, depending on whose story you bought. The smart money had it that he'd originally been grabbed by the VC, then changed sides while in captivity.

Years after the U.S. pullout, he came back, and the military put him on trial. Found him guilty of collaboration, but not desertion. Maybe because they'd never listed him as a deserter, even after returning POWs reported that he'd gone over.

One of those stories you never know the truth of, I guess. But for those who want to believe that some of the American soldiers listed as MIA are still alive, Garwood's tales of "live sightings" are precious gospel. To those folks, Garwood *couldn't* have been a collaborator; he *had* to have been a prisoner. Because, if he lied about one thing, then . . .

"Other societies, too," Mama said. "Chinese. Not want coolies. Want doctors. Scientists. Computer people. Pay very good money."

Is she talking about the Taiwan government? "But if they already—"

"No, no. Same deal. Societies never trust snakeheads. Nobody trust snakeheads. Same deal. Must *see* before payments start. Only payments *bigger,* see?"

"But why should they pay us?"

"They pay *everybody,*" Mama said, explaining natural law. "Pay for paper, like green card. Pay lawyers. Pay, how you say, political people. Always pay, what difference? Pay *whoever* has cargo, okay? Pay snakeheads maybe hundred dollar a week. Forever, pay that. But pay *you* ten thousand. One time, all done, see? Everybody happy."

"But even at . . . How many could the snakeheads possibly bring over at one time?"

"Two, three hundred."

"In one boat?"

"Sure. Not nice, but . . ."

"It might be nice for us," I finished.

When I was a kid, I'd leaped from roof to roof across narrow alleys all the time. Never gave it a thought. Played chicken, my head on the subway tracks, facing another kid as poisoned with pride as I was. Death train coming, first one to jump back loses. Charged right at a boy from a rival club, even though he was holding a zip gun and all I had was a heavy length of chain. The zip misfired—most of them did—but the chain worked fine.

I even tried Russian roulette once, with an old revolver one of the guys brought down to the damp, ratty basement we called a clubhouse. We all took a turn, but I was the rep-crazy fool who went first.

I wasn't faking then. Checking out didn't scare me. It was the one sure way to guarantee that the . . . people who had hurt me would never get their hands on me again. Damaged kids learn quick: death trumps pain. That's why some serial killers and some suicides are brothers—they were raised by the same parents.

Later, I learned. I learned to be scared. And I learned how to do a lot of damage. That's when I stopped trying to run from the people who always hurt me. I wanted to get close to them then. Close enough to stop the pain.

But even back when I was one of those "don't mind dying" young guns, deep water at night terrified me. I remember once when a whole caravan of kids from the City followed the lead car out to some beach on Long Island. It was summer. Hot and muggy. Howie, the guy who'd organized the whole thing, he told us that this Jones Beach was a ton better than Coney Island. No boardwalk, no rides, no hot-dog stands. Best of all, no crowds. Nothing to do but drink some wine, pass around the maryjane, and fuck. Like we owned the place.

Of course, that's not the picture he painted for the girls. They thought they were visiting some special spot only rich people got to use . . . the kind of rich people who would actually pay attention to the BEACH CLOSED AT MIDNIGHT signs.

I was as up for the trip as anyone. But the night ocean was so monstrously deep, only your imagination could fill it. The minute you went in, it had you—you were surrounded by things you couldn't even name, much less fight. The girl I was with, she waded in until the water got to her waist, then she just sort of lay down on her stomach and paddled around. I was too welded to my image to not go along with her, but I called it off as soon as I could.

On the blanket later, after we'd finished, I was lying on my back, finishing a joint. I should have been blissed out. My rep got me on that blanket that night. With my gang, with that girl. I was a man in all the ways we measured such things in my world. I knew how it worked.

But when I closed my eyes, I could feel that hungry black water moving. It . . . reduced me. I was a child in my mind. Back in that foster home they had sentenced me to. And every time the tide lapped up on the beach, searching, I felt the fingers probing under my covers, again.

That was a lifetime ago. Now I was standing on an outcropping of rock, overlooking the spot where Mama said the snakeheads made their landings, Max at my side. The ocean was calm as a storybook pond, preening in its finest Atlantic-gray coat.

It didn't fool me.

Max tapped my shoulder, made a gesture of turning a steering wheel, then spread his arms wide. I nodded. Yeah, they'd need some big trucks. Even if they packed them tighter than a hooker's skirt, two, three hundred head would take up a lot of space.

Mama had explained that the snakeheads didn't operate like their counterparts south of the border. Mexicans coming across paid *once,* and they paid in front. So the coyotes didn't care if their customers suffocated in the back of one of the rigs, or baked to death hoofing it across open desert. But snakeheads needed their cargo alive if they wanted to collect—no point bringing them all the way across the ocean, only to lose some at the end.

We'd already solved one part of the puzzle. The land we were standing on was private property. A desolate stretch without any real beach. I'd expected a fence. Or, maybe, dogs. But it was deserted. Part of the camouflage? No matter, we still had to figure on an armed escort any night they were due to make a drop.

Max made the first two fingers of his right hand into a swimming gesture, moving slowly toward his left, which he held flat and perpendicular. The swimming fingers crashed into the left palm, and burst into fragments. The Mongol shook his head "No." Then he put his hands in the original position, but had the swimming fingers stop and tread water, while the left clumped into a smaller ship, heading *out*.

Sure. No way to bring the cargo ship right onto the shore—they'd have to go out with motor launches, bring a few in at a time. A big operation. Bigger every time we took a closer look.

Max tapped the first two fingers of his left hand with his right index finger, one at a time. Did it again. Then spread his right hand wide, tapped each finger and his thumb. I nodded glumly. Two and two *was* coming out five, all right.

"Everything like I say, yes?" Mama put it to me.

"It looks that way," I hedged.

"But . . . ?" Michelle asked.

"Fat lady in the circus ain't got as much 'but' as there is in this mess," the Prof said sourly. "There's money there, sure. But there's money in Fort Knox, too."

"My father is right," Clarence said. "Even if we had enough men—"

"Men?" Michelle asked, sweetly.

"Personnel," I stepped in quick, before it escalated. "And it's not just numbers, it's logistics. They've got a stash house somewhere. Got to be pretty close by. We'd need one, too."

"Maybe . . . scatter. Right away. Soon as they come off boat." Mama.

"I don't think so," I said. "No way they're all going to the same place. Not in the end. I can't see them running a convoy of trucks out of there, then splitting up and going in all different directions. Their best play would be to keep them all in the same place, parcel them out a few at a time. The troopers won't be stopping every car with a couple of Chinese in it."

"That's true," the Prof said. "It ain't like running niggers through New Jersey."

Michelle raised her perfectly arched eyebrows. Caught my return look in time.

"If they were all in the same place . . ." the Mole finally spoke.

"All of the cargo, sure, Mole. But not all of the snakeheads."

"So?" he asked, mildly, eyes calm behind the Coke-bottle lenses.

"Ah," Mama said, approving.

The Prof nodded. We all knew what one of the Mole's little gas globes could do in an enclosed space.

"But when they . . . the smugglers . . . when they came to, they would know it was no accident," Clarence said.

"They wouldn't know where to *start* looking," Michelle said thoughtfully.

"Yeah, they would," I told them. "The buyers. And they'd look *hard*. Nobody ever takes a hijacking lying down. It could bounce right back on us."

"Not decide now," Mama said. "Look for place first, okay?"

Max's nod was almost imperceptible.

"M ama's got her own in this," the Prof said. It was much later that same night. We were in my place, deciding.

"Max thinks so, too," I agreed.

"What is wrong with that, mahn?" Clarence wanted to know. "Plenty of times, Burke, you have *your* own in things we do, is that not true?"

"Yeah. It is. And I'm not saying anything's wrong with it. But you see where it's going, right?"

"I do not," Clarence said, his West Indian accent even more pronounced through the formal style he always adopted when he felt the need for distance.

"One sure fact in every jack," the Prof said softly. "There's always the chance some people ain't coming home from the dance."

"I know," Clarence said, waiting.

"Only there's no 'chance' in this one," I finished it up. "Even if we *could* locate the barn where they've got the cargo stashed, they'd have guards all around. What're we going to use on them, tranquilizer darts?"

"Max could . . ."

"Max could ninja one or two, sure. But the Mole's no stealth-meister, Clarence. He'd need time and access to set up his stuff. And what if there's more guards posted inside? Or if they have dogs? This whole thing, it's nothing but a damn jailbreak. And if the wheels come off, there isn't a single hostage worth taking."

The young man went quiet. We joined him, waiting.

Finally, he said, "So the only way is to . . . ?"

"Leave them there," I told him. "All of them. Not gassed, not tied up. Permanent."

"That is insane, mahn."

"It is," I agreed. "And Mama's not. So I say we take a look."

Firirst thing, we needed a local base. A place where any of us could come and go without attracting the spotlight. You can buy some privacy just by living in certain areas. But that also buys you regular police patrols, maybe even some private security force thrown in. And, worse, the kind of neighbors who act neighborly.

Gated communities and trailer parks share the same secrets. Humans hurt their babies everywhere. Beat their wives, violate their daughters, sell their sons. But we wanted an area where people worried about the DEA, not the IRS.

Michelle rented us a house in a little village nestled between two other towns, one white and one black. I didn't know much about Long Island, but I'd done enough business with assorted racist groups from out there so that I wasn't surprised by the clear division.

Max and I made the drive out in my new ride. I'd taken the Honda back to the Mole. Told him it just wouldn't work for what I needed it for. And that was true. What I didn't tell him was that a few weeks of driving that mobile appliance was squeezing the sap out of my tree.

I got the new car for eleven hundred bucks. One grand was the finger's fee for the sweet spot he'd scoped out—an underground parking garage in a small apartment building on the East Side. Room for only about three dozen cars, most of those belonging to tenants. The open rental slots were always full by nine. By ten, ten-thirty every day, the NO VACANCY sign would be out. And the lone attendant would be having his coffee and a buttered roll, faithfully delivered by the Korean kid from the nearby deli. The extra hundred was for the kid's college fund.

By noon, the attendant would come around, probably figuring he'd just dozed off for an hour or so, big deal. I'm sure the cops hadn't arrived until the owner of the brand-new Porsche 911 Turbo came to pick up his car that evening. And started screaming.

By then, the Porsche was all pieced out. And I was driving my barter, a 1969 Plymouth two-door post that had gone through half a dozen life changes since it rolled off the assembly line as a Roadrunner. Its last owner obviously had been in the long-haul contraband business. The beast's undercarriage was a combination of an independent-rear-suspension unit pirated from a Viper, and subframe connectors with heavy gussets to stiffen the unibody . . . and let it survive a pretty good hit, too. Huge disks with four-piston calipers all around, steel-braided lines. The cavernous trunk had plenty of room, despite housing a fuel cell and the battery, but I didn't find the nitrous bottle I'd expected.

Maybe that was because a 440 wedge, hogged out to 528 cubes, sat under the flat, no-info hood. I'd balked when Lymon first told me it was a crate motor, but he'd jumped all over my objections, taking it personally. Lymon's a car guy first; thieving's just his hobby.

"That motor ain't from the Mopar factory, man," he said, contempt cutting through his Appalachian twang. "Al deKay himself built this one." I knew who he meant—a legendary Brooklyn street-racer, rumored to have switched coasts. "You got yourself an MSD ignition and a brand-new EFI under there," he preached. "NASCAR radiator *plus* twin electric fans, oil and tranny coolers—this sucker couldn't overheat in the Lincoln Tunnel in rush hour. In July. Reliable? Brother, we're running an OEM exhaust system, H-piped, through a pair of old Caddy mufflers. Costs you a pack of ponies, but it's as quiet as a stocker with those hydraulic lifters. This piece, boy, you don't need to even *know* a good wrench—you want, you could fucking weld the hood shut."

It was tall-geared, running a 3.07 rear end—which Lymon proudly gushed was "full cryo" while I pretended I knew what he was talking about—and a reworked Torqueflite off a column shifter. Oil-pressure and water-temp gauges had been installed in the dash slot that formerly housed the pitiful little factory tach. The replacement tach, one of those old black-faced jobs, was screw-clamped to the steering column, with a slash of bright-orange nail polish at the 6000 shift point.

The bucket seats had an armrest between them that you could pull up to sit three across in a pinch. What you couldn't see was the chromemoly tubing that ran from the rocker sills through the B-pillars right up under the headliner to form a rollover hoop.

The windows had a tint that looked like Windex hadn't touched the glass for years. The outside lamps of the quad headlights had been converted to xenon high-lows, like switching a cigarette lighter for a blowtorch. The inside units were actually aircraft landing lights, but you'd have to be close enough to notice the nonserrated clear glass with the telltale dot in the center to tell.

No power windows, no air conditioning. The radio was the original AM/FM. If I wanted tape or CD, I'd have to bring a portable with me when I rode.

From the outside, it looked like different things to different people. To a rodder, it would look like a restoration project—the *beginning* of the project, with the Roadrunner's trademark "meep-meep" horn more hope than promise. To anyone else, it looked like a typical white-trash junker, just fast enough to outrun the tow truck. Steel wheels, sixteen-inchers all around, shod in Dunlop run-flats, with dog-dish hubcaps on three of them. Rusted-out rocker panels. A dented grille hid the cold-air ducting on either side of the radiator. Steering wheel wrapped in several layers of padded white tape. The front end was all primer, the rear the original red, since gone anemic. The left tailpipe was trimmed so that it looked like a replacement mill—probably a tired 318—was providing the power.

It looked right at home on the patch of dirt that would have been the front lawn if the house we'd rented had been in a better neighborhood.

Michelle hung around long enough to fully express her utter and total unhappiness with the dump. Nobody was dumb enough to point out that she'd been the one who rented it. She worked her cell phone, harassing the Mole unmercifully until he agreed to drive out and pick her up. I love my sister, but it wasn't the first time I'd been glad to see her wave goodbye.

Max and I went back to our life-sentence card game as if we'd never been interrupted by my disappearance. He was into me for a good six figures, but that didn't faze him—he'd been down more than a quarter-million years ago, when he caught one of those mythical lucky streaks even the most degenerate gambler never dares to dream of. Once he felt it lock in, the Mongol kept me in my seat for hour after hour, afraid of offending the gods by changing anything. When the run finally had played itself out, he was damn near even. But it didn't take him long to get back under the gun, especially after I'd taught him casino as a break from gin. Max with gambling is like me with women—love's not the same as skill.

He even dragged out the score sheets he always carries around like a religious medal. We had long since agreed to settle up when we met on the other side, and Max figures a running tab guarantees, no matter how long I'm gone, we'll be together again someday.

Today's game was part of the proof.

Nights, we rode. Me driving, Max charting. We knew what we were looking for—a place big enough to store a couple hundred humans. Remote enough so there would be no casual traffic, and close enough to the drop point to make it a quick trip. We found what we wanted easy enough. Only thing was, we found it a dozen times in the first few tries.

Back at the house, I held my hands apart, then slowly brought them together, looking a question at Max. He shrugged, no closer than I was to any factors we could use to narrow down the search.

"It doesn't matter," I told the Prof and Clarence. "It doesn't matter where they mean to keep their stash. I know how it could be worked now. Only thing is . . . it's not for us."

"Need too many guns?" the Prof asked.

"Too many uniforms," I said.

"Let's hear it run, son."

"Like you said already, it's military-scale. But it's still a hijacking. And the best way to work one of those is to have the drivers take a little taste themselves."

"Pay them off?" asked the man who'd taught me that trick.

"The opposite," I told them. "The way to make it work is to have INS—or what they *think* is INS, anyway—roll up and take them all down. So it's a bust, right? We take possession of the cargo, and the snakeheads are all in custody."

"Here comes the *mordida,* right, Schoolboy?"

"Sure. We let the snakeheads bribe their way free. The negotiations take a few hours, maybe. . . . That works easy enough; they're not going to have that much cash on them, so they'd have to persuade us that they're good for it. Meanwhile, the cargo's on the move. We cut the snakeheads loose, what are they going to do? Go tell their bosses . . . what? Good way to get themselves killed. They're likely to stay here in America, go underground.

"Ever since nine eleven, INS isn't exactly concentrating on Chinese. But whatever their choices, they're bad ones. Main thing is, we get the cargo, nobody gets hurt . . . and nobody's going to talk."

"Except . . . ?"

"Except that we'd need fifty men. Maybe more. All uniformed, full arms, and communication gear. Marked vehicles, the whole works. We'd have to pull a dozen jobs just to put the financing together. And even if we were bankrolled, we couldn't find that many rat-proof professionals still working."

"Mama had to know that, going in."

"Amen, brother. I don't get it any more than you do."

"I do not like to say this. . . ." Clarence hesitated, looking around the circle for approval. We all gave it to him, silently. He nodded his head, as if registering the vote, then went on: "We would need many men to capture them. But, in the dark, by surprise, we would not need so many to . . ."

"That's crazy," I said. "The way I laid it out, there's nothing left to show anything happened. We leave a bunch of bodies lying around, we turn a no-case into a feast for the *federales*."

"That clue is true," the Prof agreed, putting into words what we all thought—Mama would draw the line at stupidity a lot quicker than she would at murder.

Max stood up, went into the kitchen. He came back with a box of toothpicks. In ten minutes, he had a whole scene constructed on the table. He looked up, made sure he had everyone's attention, then showed us where we'd gone wrong, his fingers drawing it as clear as a blueprint. We watched the trucks line up near the shoreline. Saw the ocean-goer sit offshore, the smaller boats go out to it to vacuum off the cargo. The cargo got offloaded, and the trucks went to the warehouse. Max tapped my wristwatch, ran his finger around the dial a couple of times to show the passage of time. Then one of the trucks pulled out of the warehouse, loaded. He put himself behind the wheel, driving. Pointed next to him, shook his head "No." Then he pointed at Clarence, touched under his left armpit, and shook his head "No" again.

Sure, he was right. Each of the cargo-haulers would be alone. And unarmed. A thin smile spread across the Prof's lips.

Max's toothpick truck motored along. He quick-built a little roadblock, spread his hands in a "Why not?" gesture.

I bowed my head just enough to let Max know he was a genius. The bow wasn't just out of respect—slapping five with Max was a high-risk move. "Max has got it," I said aloud. "There's a ton of ways to stop a *single* truck. Hell, a flat tire would do it. Taking down one driver . . . we could do *that* in broad daylight. And what's he going to do after we're gone, call the cops?"

"We couldn't *keep* dialing that number," the Prof said, deliberate-voiced. "It'd be a one-shot. And we'd need some kind of watch on the plant, to know when the right one was leaving." He took a thoughtful drag on his cigarette. "You think that's what Mama wants? All this planning and scanning just to kick *one* of them loose?"

"She's done it before," I reminded him. "And that's her style, too, swooping in from the wings. But, even for Mama, this is extreme sideways."

"So . . . ?" the Prof tossed out.

"We ask her," I said.

T he Prof rode with me on the drive back. When we got to the on-ramp for the LIE, I nailed the Plymouth, gobbling ground for the sheer hell of it. We were over eighty in a slow eye-blink, the tach laughing and loafing around three grand. I backed it off, listening to the restrictive mufflers mute the throb of the torque-monster.

"Like your old ride never died, Schoolboy," the Prof said approvingly.

"Faster, actually. Corners a *lot* better, too."

"But it don't feel the same, right?"

I thought about it for a minute, avoiding where he was going, the only father I'd ever known.

"No," I finally said. "It's sweet, but . . ."

". . . but it ain't got no holes punched in the trunk," he said, pinning me. I looked at my right hand. At the tiny heart tattooed between the last two knuckles, hollow and blue. My old Plymouth had the trunk all fixed up for her, complete with the air holes the Prof was talking about. Many's the time I popped the trunk from inside the car so that Pansy could be a surprise guest at a party people planned for me.

The last time I'd done that was the last time for her. She'd gone out the way she wanted, taking one of the enemy with her.

I always see her. On the screen inside my head. A flash of dark gray against the black night, charging across that stretch of waste ground, hell-bound for the man who'd shot me. Dropping him as he tried to run. Rearing up, a chunk of the shooter's throat in her mouth. Taking fire from the others who'd been in on the ambush. Going down. Getting up again. When they closed in to finish me off, I could still see her . . . trying. It was the last thing I saw before I went someplace else.

I had come back. Pansy hadn't.

"You evened it up, honeyboy," the Prof said softly.

"Doesn't bring her back," I told him, through clenched teeth.

"Go on *Oprah,* fool. That lame game ain't for folks like us."

Truth.

I breathed through my nose, centering myself.

It wasn't even midnight when I dropped the Prof off. Way too early to meet with Mama. I headed back to my place, figuring on killing a few hours.

If Gateman saw me come in, you couldn't tell it from his eyes; they stayed as neutral as cancer.

I poured myself a beer mug full of ice water from the fridge. New York City tap water is as clean as any of that glacier-grown crap they sell in fancy little bottles. Tastes better, too.

I fired up the TV, kicked back, and watched some of the races from the Meadowlands on cable. Reminded myself I would need to find a new bookie—if there was one guy on earth who'd know my voice on the phone, it was old Maurice.

Later, on the drive over to Mama's, I found CBS-FM, Don K. Reed's *Doo-Wop Shop.* Caught The Heartbeats' "Crazy for You" from the top. Street-corner perfect.

That was another thing I'd missed about New York—radio stations where Dion was a *first* name.

I drove past Mama's, slow and careful. The white-dragon tapestry was in the window, barely visible behind smeared-streaked glass that had collected more fingerprints than a crime lab. All clear. If the dragon had been red, I would have kept on going. And if it had been blue, I'd have known exactly what the problem was.

Mama's a patriot. Same as we all are. The country we're loyal to is the only one we vote in. And it's never much bigger than wherever we stand.

I parked the Plymouth in the alley without a second thought. Pulling out the ashtray toggles an on/off switch wired into the distributor; if it's not in the right position, the engine will crank but never catch.

And for that one spot, I had even better security. The driver's door was now a replica of the alley wall—a white square against the dull-gray primer, with Max the Silent's chop in gem-cut black inside. You'd think this would blow the whole anonymous deal, but you see quasi-Chinese ideograms on everything today, from clothes to skin. They usually don't mean anything, but people who read comics for the ancient wisdom think they look cool.

There's a tattoo artist Mama knows in a basement off Mott Street. He always has a vast display of the symbols for customer viewing. They pick the one they like, and Hop Sing or Wo Fat or whatever he feels like calling himself that day makes up a story about what it stands for: Truth, Justice, Integrity, Honor, Power, whatever. Mama says there are hundreds of different symbols for "sucker" in Chinese, and this guy knows them all.

The men on the door did their job, like always. But they hadn't bothered with the threat displays since that first time.

Mama was at the front, by her register, staying close to the only altar she truly worshipped at. And making sure any stray customers who wandered in got the message that they didn't want to eat there. She and the tureen of soup arrived at my booth at the same time.

"Damn! This is extra good tonight, Mama. You put something different in it?"

"Always something different," she said. "Not good last time?"

"No," I said, laboring. "It was superb the last time. It is never *less* than superb. This time, it was even superior to your usual standard, that's all."

"Huh! So—want more, yes?"

The soup was so hot it burned my mouth. My big mouth.

I was deep into my meal of braised beef and bok choy when Mama dropped it on me. "While you . . . gone, people still call, okay?"

"Okay."

"Not like, all right, okay. Okay, like, you understand, okay?"

"Okay."

Her eyes were black olives. I took the double-barreled scrutiny; looked back, blandly.

"Sometime, people owe money, want to pay. Sometime, want *time* to pay, okay?"

"Sure."

"Sometime," she went on, ignoring me, "want work done, okay?"

"Yeah. What did you tell them?"

"Mr. Burke not here, okay? You call back, okay?" she parroted in her best Chinese-laundry voice.

"You had a long time to be saying that."

"So sorry," she said, in the same voice. "You maybe try again, okay?"

"I get it. But most of the people I deal with, they'd want whatever they wanted right then."

"Too bad, so sad," Mama said, her voice a perfect imitation of her granddaughter Flower. "Oh well."

"So, after a while, the whispers die down. And people stop calling. Is that what you're telling me?"

"New people, stop call. Old people, not same. You understand?"

I nodded to tell her I did. Sure. Made perfect sense. My name had been in the street a long time. Someone coming up on it for the first time, if they needed what I was known for, they'd give a call, take a shot. If they kept getting sloughed by Mama, they'd give it up, go elsewhere. But *old* customers, they'd keep trying.

Like old enemies.

"Sometime, *big* job," Mama said.

I nodded again, not questioning how she could tell all that from a few words whispered into a pay phone—Mama could smell a dollar bill in a slaughterhouse.

"So! Big job, old customer, get different story, okay?"

"What story?"

"Story like I tell you before, okay? Burke not here. *Long* time. Not in country. Special thing. But somebody else do job."

"Who'd you send them to?" I asked, frankly curious.

"No, no. Not send away. Tell to wait. Can't wait? So, okay, I not know anything about Burke business. But *now* job come in, you do; like say before, okay?"

"You mean, be my own . . . brother, or whatever?"

"Not look so much like you," she talked through what I was saying. A train on tracks, rolling. "Little bit, maybe. But same voice. Just like talk to Burke, talk to brother."

"All that for what, Mama?"

"Money," she said, black eyes glowing like a Geiger counter near a rich vein. "Big, big money."

"The snakeheads?"

"Not now," she said. "Snakeheads all the time come. This business, come only once, okay?"

T hree nights after my meeting with Mama, I nudged the Plymouth through the still-thick Manhattan traffic, taking my time. This was a quicker contact than I'd expected. When Mama told me who was playing, I'd been sure they'd use foot soldiers to screen me before going face-to-face.

The upper roadway of the Fifty-ninth Street Bridge took me past the luxo highrises on my right as I crossed the river, into another country.

I found the adult-video store wedged into a concrete triangle under the bridge extension on the other side, just before where Queens Boulevard starts its long run through the borough. The store's back was crammed up against a no-star hotel. A long-abandoned gas station made up the third leg of the triangle.

They'd told me I could leave my car at the gas station, but I didn't like that option much. I turned left, up Skillman Avenue, and motored along, watchful. When I saw the white rag dangling from the door handle of an old brown Buick sedan, I flicked the lever into neutral and blipped the throttle.

It was as if the Plymouth's deep-chested snarl had knocked on the Buick's door. I caught a brief glimpse of Asian faces, at least four of them. I pulled up a few lengths, made a U-turn, and waited as the Buick maneuvered out of its spot. Soon as it left, I parallel-parked into the space they'd vacated. I settled in carefully, cranking the wheel full-lock to make sure I could blast straight out if it came to that. I wasn't worried about the decrepit station wagon parked in front of me—it would stay there until the boys in the Chinatown war wagon came back to collect it sometime tomorrow.

I still had a forty-five-minute cushion, so I did a last-minute check to make sure I had everything I needed for the meet. Which was nothing.

Then I took a walk. Up Skillman to Thirty-sixth Street, then a right to Queens Boulevard, across from the old Aviation High School. I glanced at my watch. Still early. I strolled back down toward the triangle, relaxed.

And thinking about Mama. "It don't take no crystal ball, son," the Prof had concluded. "Mama don't want the whole pot. She must have got word, her one chip ain't making this trip."

Maybe. And maybe all the money this meet promised made it worth her while to wait.

At least I was done with trekking out to Long Island all the damn time.

The porno shop was fortified as if some sleazy alchemist inside had turned gash into gold. Gun-turret windows in a slab-faced cinderblock front, the flatness broken only by a pale-blue door behind a set of bars that wouldn't have looked out of place in San Quentin. Red neon, twisted into the usual promises, glowed reptile-cold.

A pair of cross-angled cameras in weatherproof boxes were mounted at the top of the door, as subtle as a handgun pressed against your temple. I pushed the buzzer, waited, my back to the street.

The door was opened by a tall, skinny guy with a hollow-cheeked face. The forehead above the orange sunglasses he wore was an acne graveyard. In the sullen light from overhead, his crooked teeth looked like an ad for nicotine.

I stared into his mirrored lenses until he stepped aside.

The interior decorator's palette had been limited to gray and yellow. A few old posters on the walls, some half-empty video racks, one wall of limp magazines. Not a DVD in sight. No private booths, no lingerie shows. The joint was as erotic as a used condom floating on an oil slick.

The cadaverous-looking guy went back to whatever he'd been doing. I browsed through the racks, playing the role. Ignoring the two other men in the place, but not before I absorbed that they were both wearing the latest in *Sopranos*-chic.

Time passed. No new customers. I didn't look at my watch. I'd gotten there on time, and I was working flat-rate.

Finally, they glided up, one on my left, the other somewhere behind me. I kept my focus on the greasy pictures, letting the sense impressions flood in. Textures and colors. Sharp tang of too much cologne. They never touched me, just air-cushion-herded me toward the back of the store.

Nothing too fancy in the back, just a long rack on rollers, with a door behind it. A door with no knob. A hand came into my field of vision. Two-knuckle rap. A panel slid up in the door, revealing a Plexiglas window. Maybe fifteen seconds passed. The panel slid down. The door opened. I stepped inside.

The only thing in sight was a flight of stairs, going down. "Uh-huh," a voice behind me said.

At the bottom of the stairs, a man in a white lab coat pointed at a long bare workbench. I walked over there.

One of the men stepped close. He was a muscular guy, a couple of inches shorter than me, with longish, heavily gelled black hair. He made eye contact: communicating, not challenging. I opened the channel, waited for his next move.

He held one finger to his lips, making sure I got it. Then he unbuttoned the overtailored jacket to his onyx suit, carefully took it off, and draped it on the workbench. I took off my own jacket with a little less ceremony, placed it on the bench the same way he'd done.

By the time we finished, we were facing each other in our shorts and socks. Without his shoes, he was much shorter than he'd been before. His body was nicely cut and defined, but I had better scars.

The guy in the white lab coat started working on my clothes with some kind of wand.

The guy facing me held his finger to his lips again. I didn't change expression.

It didn't take long.

Then we got dressed.

The next door was much more elaborate; no way you would see it unless you knew it was there. It looked as if the stone wall of the basement had just retracted into itself. I followed the guy in the onyx jacket into a long, narrow room with a low ceiling. Each of the three walls I could see had a separate door, undisguised. In the far corner, two men were seated in padded armchairs. A third chair stood empty, facing them. I walked over until I was standing in front of the empty chair.

"You're Burke," the man to my left said. He was Italian, mid-thirties, darkly handsome, saved from pretty only by a nose that hadn't been perfectly set the last time it had been broken.

I just nodded. It hadn't been a question.

"I'm Giovanni," he said. "And this is Felix."

The man to my right was Latino, maybe a decade older than the Italian. Or maybe a generation; it was hard to tell much in that light. He was lighter-skinned than the Italian, with the face of royalty. Ruthless royalty.

"Sorry about all the . . . precautions," the Italian said. "You understand."

I nodded again.

"Sit down, please," the Latino said.

I caught the briefest flicker in the eyes of the Italian. He wasn't a man who liked being one-upped, not even when it came to class and courtesy. He made a tiny gesture with his right hand. A man came forward, put a fresh pack of cigarettes—same brand as the half-empty pack I'd carried in with me—and a heavy gold lighter on the low table in front of me. A large amber glass ash-tray was sitting there, sparkling clean.

"You'll get all your stuff back when you leave," the Italian said. "You want a watch to wear in the meantime?"

"I'm fine, thanks."

"I heard a lot about you," he said. "From a lot of people. For a long time."

"About my brother, you mean."

"Your brother, yeah. But the Chinese lady, she said you were the same."

"Like how?"

"Like you could do the same stuff. The *exact* same stuff. Dealing with you, it would be just like dealing with him. Is that right?"

"Exactly right."

"I have heard much about you as well," the Latino said, offering his hand for me to shake.

I gave him a light-pressure grip. He turned his palm up, holding my hand a second longer than he had to. Long enough to verify the tattoo. "I am sorry for your loss," he said. "To lose one so close to you . . ."

"Thank you," I said, my eyes empty. *Is he playing it straight, buying the "Burke's brother" thing? Or being cute . . . telling me he knows about Pansy?*

"Reason you're here is," the Italian said, "me and Felix, we've got a problem. A problem for both of us, maybe. Or maybe not. That's where you come in."

"I'll tell you where I *don't* come in," I said. "That's between the two of you."

The Latino smiled. "We do not want you to take sides, señor. We want your . . . advice. Your counsel. And, perhaps, your skills."

"Why me?" I asked them both.

"You'll see," the Italian said. "You're a natural for it. And you're getting five large just to listen—like we agreed, right?"

They spent the next half hour marking turf, asking me if I knew so-and-so, if I'd been Inside when such-and-such went down, like that. As they talked, their two crews drifted away from our corner. One of them watched a ball game on TV, with the sound turned way down. A few started to play cards. A couple just stared into the middle distance.

"What I'm going to tell you, it's nothing illegal," the Italian said. "I'm the victim, not the perp. But it's not nothing I'd want anyone to hear about. . . ."

"You say that to say what?" I challenged him. I wasn't any more impatient than their crews were. But you let a man warn you too many times, he starts to think he has good reasons for doing it.

"We have decided to trust Mr. Burke, yes?" the Latino said. "That was our agreement. Mr. Burke is a businessman. He has a reputation. He knows the value of things."

That last was a nice touch, telling me I better know the *cost* of things, too.

"I'm sorry," the Italian said. "It's just that this whole thing may sound . . . weird, right?"

The Latino nodded gravely, but stayed silent.

"I got a . . . position, okay?" the Italian said. "I'm not the boss, but I'm *a* boss. I don't have to spell it out for you, do I?"

"No."

"'No' because you can work it out, or 'no' because you been looking at charts?"

"Look," I said, "I don't want to be hostile. And, it's true, you bought my time. But you keep tossing these shots at me, and I don't get it. What am I supposed to say now? No, I'm *not* an undercover? No, I *didn't* get your ranking off some OC chart?"

He took a deep breath through his nose. Let it out, slow. "Sorry," he said again; a reflex, not an apology. "I've been over some rocky ground. All twists and tricks. It's hard to trust."

"I didn't come to you," I reminded him.

"Yeah. I know." He took another deep breath. Looked over at the Latino. "Fuck it. All right. Me and Felix, we've got a business relationship. A good one, for both of us. But it's the kind of thing that some people wouldn't understand. You following me?"

"Sure. Want me to spell it out?"

"A little. Just so we can be sure you—"

"You're like a salesman," I said, as casual as if I was giving directions back to Manhattan. "The boss gives you a territory. He says, You got the franchise; now go out there and make us all some money. Your franchise, say it's for vacuum cleaners. And a lot of other stuff. But not for TV sets. Those, you got no license to sell.

"Now, there's a lot of money in TV sets, but the boss doesn't *make* TV sets, and he doesn't trust the people who do. So they're off limits. But you got a crew to take care of. If you don't give them a chance to earn, they get . . . unreliable. So what you do, you find yourself a good solid manufacturer of TV sets. And you sell a few of them. Carefully, and only to the right people. This is good for you, good for your crew. Hell, it'd be good for *everyone* if your boss would just green-light it. But he's not going to do that, and you know it."

Giovanni looked bored. Except for his eyes.

"Meanwhile," I went on, "you've got a regular payroll to meet, a big nut to crack. Much bigger than the boss knows. You've got to keep those wheels oiled. Another problem you've got, you've been one of the top salesmen, *on* the books. And the way you manage that, you sweeten all the deals on vacuum cleaners. Say the boss expects a hundred a month. But you, you're handing him ten more. Keep him happy. But what that means is you've got to move a few more of those TV sets to make up the deficit.

"Now, maybe, probably, in fact, the boss *knows* you're into TV sets. He's got his rules, but so long as you're earning that strong, and he gets his taste, he might not be so heavy into enforcement. Some bosses, they're like bitches; you know what I'm saying? 'Bring me that money, honey. Buy me presents. Get me stuff. Take me places. But don't tell me *where* you get it all, that's not my problem.' Then, when you get popped for something, they go, '*Ohmygod,* I had no *idea!*' That sound about right?"

"Like you were listening in," the Italian said.

"A big boss is always a politician," the Latino said, trying to smooth over his partner's habit of playing picador. "This is the same in my business, too. A politician wants things done, but he doesn't want to touch the work with his own hands."

I nodded the way you do when you hear great wisdom, marking what the Latin was really telling me—he wasn't the boss in *his* organization, either.

"How can I help you?" I asked them.

The two men exchanged looks at the outer edge of my vision. I leaned forward, opened the pack of cigarettes they'd brought me, fired one up with the gold lighter. I took a deep drag, then put the cigarette in the ashtray, stared at the smoke, waiting.

"This gets complicated," the Italian said.

I watched the smoke. The trick is to look into it, never through it.

"You got any idea how dirty the feds play, sometimes?" the Italian asked.

"There's all kinds of feds," I told him. "Vietnam was the feds. Waco and Ruby Ridge, that was the feds. So was COIN-TELPRO."

"What's that last one?"

"Political," the Latin answered for me.

"This isn't that," the Italian said.

"Political?"

"What it is, it's personal."

"I don't know any feds," I said, to head him off in case he was talking about solving his problems with a bribe. I've got no moral problem with being a bagman, but I'd never trust strangers at either end.

The Italian did the thing with his breath again. The Latin lit a cigarette of his own, apparently used to it.

"You know the best way to flip a man?" he asked me.

"Depends on the man," I said. "And where his handle is."

"Right. But it's not true that everybody's got one. Gotti took the ride alone. And he never said word fucking one."

"Uh-huh," I agreed. "Everybody talks Old School, but only a few walk it when the weather turns bad."

"Remember the first of the super-rats?" he asked me, like a kid testing a newcomer's knowledge with a soft lob down the middle of the plate.

"Valachi?"

"Joe Valachi. He blew the covers off our thing *major,* back in the day. You know what turned him?"

"Same thing Henry Hill said turned *him.* Barbosa, Pesnick, plenty of others, too."

"'Said' is right. But Valachi, see, they *thought* he was going to roll over. So they put out a contract on him. And they missed. They didn't clip him, so *now* what's he going to do?"

"What he did."

"Yeah. You ever wonder how they got the idea that Valachi had gone rotten?"

"Who knows? Maybe some old man got paranoid. Or maybe they figured, He's doing forever, and you never know. So, what the hell, let's eliminate the *possibility*."

"What happened," the Italian said, his voice almost religious with conviction, "is that the *feds* planted that word. It's perfect. You hear you're on the spot, what're you going to do? Sit down with the boss, ask him, 'Hey, you got a hit out on me?' You got no place to run, because you been around the same people all your life and that's all you know. You know how easy it is to get someone done in prison. The only safe harbor is to make a deal with the feds. And since you got so much to trade . . ."

"Maybe so," I said.

"You don't sound convinced."

"I wasn't there. You know where I was once? In a war. That war's been over for a while. Guess which side gets to say who was in the right?"

"*Verdad,*" the Latin said. "Same as in my country."

"This isn't fucking *history,*" the Italian said, his voice tight as piano wire. "This is right now. Today. Look at how the feds use the super-maxes. Pelican Bay, they lock you down for being a gang member. Then they tell you, right to your face, you're *staying* there until you get out of the car, all right? Only thing is, you do it, you have to *prove* it. And how do you do *that*? The only way *they* accept is, you turn rat. Give some people up." He stopped talking, closed his eyes so hard the corners crinkled. The way you do if you don't know the technique to fight a headache. "So, if they want to kill a man, all they have to do is fucking put him back in population, am I right?"

"Yes," I said, waiting.

The Italian did his breathing thing again. I ground out my cigarette, stayed patient.

"There's a new twist on that game," he finally said. "The way this one works, you put word out that someone's *already* cooperating."

"When he's not?"

"When he's not; right."

"What's the gain for them? Getting someone whacked?"

"No. They don't want the guy whacked. What they want is for the rumor they planted to be true. To become true, see?"

"What you're talking about, it's too delicate. Valachi was a gift, dropped in their laps. They could never be sure a hit would miss."

"Exactly! But what if the guy got a warning first?"

"A warning *not* to rat? That doesn't make any sense. The way you're laying it out, the cops would already know he's not."

"It would make sense if the warning came from . . . people who weren't sure, maybe. But worried . . ."

"You've lost me now," I said, telling the truth.

I caught the glance between them again. Went back to waiting.

"Fuck it," the Italian said again. Not angry, resigned. "I got a daughter. By a . . . girl I knew when I was a kid. It was an outside-the-tribe thing, you understand what I'm saying?"

"Yes."

"The girl, when she told me, I didn't know what to do. I couldn't ask anybody, either. I offered her money to get rid of it, but she wouldn't. I even didn't feel right about that myself. Abortion—by the church, that's murder. I was just getting some traction then. I wasn't made or anything, but I was on my way; sure thing. What was I going to tell my people? What was my mother going to say? 'Oh, my Giovanni don't live here no more. He's over in the Village, married to a *moolingiane*. I got a beautiful granddaughter, too. Sweetest little half-breed you ever saw.' That was all the choice I had.

"The girl, she wasn't some whore I had on the side. She was . . . a very pure person. I was the first man she'd ever been with. I had . . . feelings for her, for real.

"But if I went with her, that was the end of everything. I'd end up like one of those robots from my old neighborhood. Ride the subway to work every day. Hope you get on with the union; be like every good *paisan* with a steady jay-oh-bee. Keep some tomatoes out back, some pigeons on the roof, maybe. Play some bocce, get a weekend in Atlantic City once in a while. Once a year, two weeks in Florida; do some fishing or whatever. Always making payments on something. What's all that? Just putting in time until they get old enough to go down to Florida for good. Get fucking buried there.

"I told her I could get money. I mean, even then, I was doing good. I had a new Camaro, my own place . . . but no way I was having my name on the birth certificate.

"She didn't get mad. Didn't even cry or anything. But she told me she wasn't getting rid of the kid. And if she had to go on Welfare, they'd make her tell who the father was, and she wasn't going to act like some tramp, pretend she didn't know. She had an aunt she could go live with. Her aunt could watch the baby while she went to work.

"She wasn't jacking me up for money, just telling me the way things were. If I'd thought it was a shakedown, I would have . . . I don't know what I would have done. It doesn't matter. What I *did* was, I pulled a job. Down in Jersey, with two cousins of mine. I didn't keep a dime for myself—I gave her my whole share of the take."

He looked at me. I looked back, as unreadable as rain.

"I never saw her again," he said. "But I know she had a little girl. Every once in a while, I'd get a letter. Not a written one, just an envelope with pictures in it, some little notes on the back. Pictures of the girl. Her name was Vonni. After me, I guess.

"I got other stuff. Report cards, copies of letters from her school . . . I know what you're thinking, but this wasn't nothing like blackmail. Sure, I sent money. I figured the pictures was her way of telling me that kids need things. Like . . . a school picture, okay? That maybe meant the kid needed stuff for school, you see what I'm saying?"

"Yeah," I said, just to let him know I was listening.

"They lived out on the Island. Got her own house. I . . . helped her with that. Money, I mean. But Hazel, the mother, she always worked. She never went near the Welfare," he said, completely unaware of the pride in his voice.

"And the girl, she wasn't into anything. Not in her whole life. She was an honor student. Going to college. I mean, not some *dream,* okay? She was already accepted. To SUNY. That's a very good school," he said solemnly.

He stopped and did his breathing thing again.

The Latin lit another smoke, tilted his pack toward me. I accepted.

"Some sick fuck killed her," the Italian said, his voice flat and hard, tiptoeing past emotion like a mouse around a cobra. "Stabbed her to pieces. For no reason, you understand?"

"Yes," I said, going even flatter than he was.

"What it was, it was a warning. But not the kind my people use. You see what I'm saying?"

"The kind of warning Felix's people might use," I said, no longer mechanical.

"Yeah. But whoever did this, there's one thing they never counted on."

I kept quiet, waiting.

"If Felix was warning me, then someone must have warned Felix. You see what a mess this is? Someone tells Felix I already turned. I'm wearing a wire, maybe. Who would do that? If I got scared enough that *my* boss was going to find out what . . . what we were doing to make money . . . if I got scared and made a deal with the feds, Felix's people wouldn't care. Not unless I was going to bring *them* into it . . ."

"I understand."

"You know what they never counted on? Me and Felix. That I'd go to Felix. And that I'd take his word when he told me he had nothing to do with . . . what . . . happened."

"Did the cops ever ask you—?"

"I was never in it," he said. "When I . . . heard, I . . . I called her. For the first time since we . . . She told me the cops said it was a sex maniac."

Another breath. Close to a sigh.

"That was over a year ago," he went on. "And nobody's ever been popped for it."

"And your boss . . . ?"

"Hey, *fuck* my boss, all right? This isn't about him. I'm a boss myself now. It's about me. Me and Felix. About *our* thing. Somebody was trying to send a message, wreck what me and Felix have. Who else but the feds? They spook me into going over, they get *everything,* the dream RICO case."

"It's too subtle for them," I said.

"Yeah? Who *else* would know about my . . . about her? It was so long ago. And I never told anybody. Not in my life. Not my mother. Not no priest. Not even . . . Nobody knew. There's nothing to tie her to me. But the feds, they've got everything in the world in their computers. . . ."

"I still can't see the feds actually—"

"Not *the* feds. *A* fed. Someone who hates . . . us to death. Hates us that much that he'd want to see us kill each other."

"Who's 'us'?"

He looked ice-picks at me for a few seconds, then held his finger under his nose, pinched one nostril, and snorted an imaginary line.

"You have a name?" I asked, eye-sweeping to include them both in the question.

"We do not have a name, but we have a way to the name . . . if there is one," Felix said. "What we need is the truth of what happened. And only one man can tell us."

"The killer," I said.

"Yes."

"And you want me to, what, exactly?"

"Here's the deal," Giovanni said, leaning forward, handcuffing my eyes. "I promised Hazel that I'd find out who did this. If it was some fucking skinner, that's easy. I can fix that." He paused, did his breath trick again. "But if it's a game, if it's someone trying to crush me and Felix, what we have, then I want whoever did it to talk.

"That's not your problem, getting him to talk. What we want to do is hire you. Hire you to find whoever did it. We'll take it from there."

I lit another smoke, letting them see I was thinking over what they'd told me. And I was—hard, now that I knew the relationship between the two men. The one their bosses would never understand.

"It's a long shot," I finally told them.

"We want to play it," Felix said, his eyes holding Giovanni's the way his hands never could, in public.

Round Two was all business. Giovanni talking, me listening.

"That's it," he finally said, maybe twenty minutes later. "I'm empty."

"Where are the pictures?"

"The . . . ?"

"The photos. The ones the mother sent you over the years."

"I burned them," he said, as if daring me to make something of it.

"Couple of more things . . ."

"What?" he snapped, like I'd been asking him for favors all night.

I turned to Felix. "No offense, but you can see why I have to ask you. Did you know about this?"

"After she was—"

"No. Before. Did you know there even was a daughter?"

"He knew," Giovanni said. "But there's no way—"

"I'm not asking because I think your partner would betray you," I said, sliding the words through his upraised hands like long-stemmed roses—quick, before he felt the thorns. "But you know how it works. Whatever one man knows, another man can—"

"No," Felix cut me off. "What you say is true. But if an enemy, if *anyone* knew, they could only know from listening to Giovanni, not to me."

"You mean, listening at the exact time he told you?"

"That is right. Only then. Because it was never said again,

when we were together, by either of us. And, myself, it is as if I was never told." His eyes were immortal with honor.

I moved my head a little, somewhere on the borderline between a nod and a bow. Accepting that, at the time Giovanni told him, neither man had been wearing a wire. And that it hadn't been over the phone.

"There *is* such a thing as coincidence," I told them. "But— say it's not; who profits?"

"The feds." Giovanni, saying his rosary.

"Or somebody in one of your crews," I said, my eyes including the both of them.

Both of them shrugged. Too professional to dismiss such a possibility, but not going for it, either.

"I can't go there," I told them. "You understand, right? I've got to work backwards, from the killing. I'll give you whatever I find, but if there's any Machiavelli stuff going on in your outfits, it's up to you two to sort it out."

"Understood," Felix said. He looked over at Giovanni. Something passed between them.

"Okay," Giovanni said. "You got anything to tell me, you know how to do it."

"I'm not making progress reports. And I won't be coming back to you unless there's something you can help me with."

"Like what?"

"Like a phone call," I told him. "A phone call to the mother. Tell her I'll be around. Ask her if she's willing to talk to me."

"I'll do it," he said. "I'll do it tonight."

"You knew?" I said to Mama. It only sounded like a question.

"Not what you say," she replied. "Know *something*, sure. Big people, big money."

"You knew the girl was from Long Island? That's why you sent us out there to—"

"No. Girl, whole thing, big surprise. Snakehead thing different, okay?"

"Okay," I said, remembering what I'd told Giovanni about coincidences. And not buying it any more than he had.

"**S**he's the only one for us," the Prof said. "Girl sings the no-dime rhyme, all the time."

We were in my place, making decisions. But I was having trouble with the one I didn't have any choice about.

"And she already knows about you, bro," the Prof hammered away. "You not going to spook her with this coming-back-from-the-dead horseshit."

"Me and her, we're not . . ."

"Don't matter what's between you, Schoolboy. Wolfe wouldn't know how to fucking *spell* 'rat,' am I right?"

"Yeah," I said, not arguing with proven truth. "But she might not want to help . . . get involved with anything I was doing."

"This ain't no marriage proposal, son," the Prof jabbed me again, working the open cut mercilessly. "She's just like us. Girl works for the money. And we got a budget. Fuck, off what they fronted, they *expect* us to have to pay for stuff. We got to shop, I say we start at the top."

"**A**YW Enterprises," the voice on the phone said, as warmly inviting as a "No Trespassing" sign.

"Hey, Mick," I said. "You know my voice?"

"No."

"Okay. How about I speak with Pepper, then?"

"Who?"

I breathed through my nose, reaching for calm. Said, "All right. Could I leave a number?"

"Go ahead," the voice said. In his business, leaving a number without a name, as a message for a person who didn't exist, was an everyday thing.

"**E**h, what's up, doc?" Pepper's voice. One of her voices, anyway—she had dozens of them. I hadn't heard the Bugs Bunny before, but it didn't surprise me.

"I want to see her."

"*¿Por que?*"

"Business."

"Oy vay!"

"Pepper, come on. I'm serious. Stop playing around."

"She's very busy right now," she said, in a bored clerk's voice.

"Sure, I know."

"Do better than 'business,'" she told me, her voice dropping half an octave and thirty degrees.

"I'm working on something. And I need some—"

"Are you brain-damaged? Be *specific*, understand?"

"I'm trying to solve a crime."

"Solve?"

"Solve, Pepper. For real."

"For real and for who?"

"Not on the phone."

"I can tell you this, right now. If this 'crime' is about someone taking something from someone else, and the someone else can't go to the cops, you're twisting in the wind, pal. She's not going to—"

Pepper had a professional's patience. She'd listen as long as it furthered the objective. I could feel her disengaging, said: "Listen to me. To what's in my voice. This is the truth. The crime is a murder. The victim was a child. I'm back to being me. That's what this is about, Pepper. I swear it."

I listened to the silence until she finally said, "This number I called, it's a cell, right?"

"Yes."

"Leave it on," she said. And hung up.

"**M**rs. Greene?"

"Who is calling, please?"

"My name is Burke, ma'am. I believe you were told I would be . . ."

"Yes. Yes, I was," she said. I could have been a magazine salesman for all the emotion in her voice.

"Can you tell me when it would be convenient for me to come by and—"

"Convenient?"

"My apologies, ma'am. A poor choice of words. If you can give me a time, any time at all, that would be acceptable to you, I would like to talk with you."

"Here?"

"Or anyplace you wish, ma'am. And in any company you wish, as well."

"Company?"

"If you would feel more comfortable not being alone when I—"

"Comfortable?"

"Ma'am, I'm sorry if I have offended you in any way," I said softly, treading delicately. "I have a job to do, and I'm trying to do it as best I can. You could help, considerably. My only point, all I was saying, is that I will do anything in my power to . . . minimize whatever negatives you might associate with talking to me."

"You're from the City, aren't you?"

"Yes, ma'am."

"Do you know how to get here, where I live?"

"Yes, I do."

"How long would it take you?"

"To be safe, a couple of hours."

"Safe?"

"To be certain I was on time," I said, beginning to catch the rhythm of her communication, sensing that any show of impatience on my part would be a lighted match to her gasoline.

"Can you be here by noon?"

"Absolutely," I promised her. Easy enough—it was only nine in the morning. And I was already on the Island.

She hadn't offered me directions, and I hadn't asked. I had her address nailed. Not just from the street map—I'd driven past her house twice before I'd called. The town was in central Long Island, splayed across the Nassau-Suffolk border. All I knew about it before I drove through the first time was from checking the real-estate section of *Newsday*. And that hadn't given me much of a fix on the area—houses ranged from just below six figures to several times that amount.

The commercial area was long and narrow. A single main street, with no depth to it, bisected by tracks from the LIRR commuter line. The little wooden depot was small and deeply weathered. Either nobody gave much of a damn, or some historical-preservation society wouldn't let them touch it. I can never tell the difference. The parking lot was big enough for a couple of hundred cars, but only the area closest to the station was paved. At that hour of the morning, it was as full as it was going to get. Maybe thirty cars, each parked a polite distance from the next.

The north side of the strip looked like it had been there for quite a while. The street had a gentle curve to it, and the shops were small, with storefronts laid out in compliance with some quaintness code. A patisserie, a gourmet deli, a tea shoppe, an apothecary, couple of boutiques. Almost everything was two-story. Retail operations at street level, with a plain door between every few shops, probably for access to the second-floor apartments.

The south side of the strip was string-straight, not so much modern as sterile. It felt like an afterthought. Most of the frontage was all-glass, and the individual units were wider. It boasted a discount drugstore, a tanning salon, a SuperCuts, Baskin-Robbins, Carvel, and an OTB.

From end to end, little slot-size stores. Not a single super-market, home-improvement warehouse, or chain bookstore—that size stuff would be in a mall, somewhere close by.

I was way early, so I found a spot at a meter and walked over to the Baskin-Robbins. Got myself a two-scoop cup of mango ice from a young woman with purple hair and a passé nose ring, and took it back to the Plymouth.

I killed half an hour playing with various approaches I could use. All I really knew about the girl's mother was that I'd most likely not get a second chance with her. When I'd asked Giovanni, he'd just said, "I knew Hazel when we were kids. I could tell you what she was like then. But I don't know her now."

I f I hadn't scouted the area beforehand, I would have rented a car for the meeting. Something to go with my medium-gray summer-weight suit, white shirt, dark-blue tie, and scuffed black leather attaché case.

Her house was near the middle of a short, straight block. The yards were shallow in front, fairly deep in back, but cramped tight on the sides. The street wasn't so wide that any neighbor with an interest would need a telescope.

I had to assume she'd had a lot of company back when they'd found her daughter's body, and I wanted to look like I was more of the same, a year later. Not a cop. Some kind of civilian thief, like an insurance adjuster, or a lawyer.

I parked the Plymouth on the far side of a copse of trees that divided the houses from what looked like a Little League baseball field, a few blocks down from her address. Then I went for a walk.

If anyone wanted to follow me back to the car, they'd have to do it on foot, and it wasn't exactly the kind of terrain a shadow would want to work. Every neighborhood has some wannabe cop twerp who listens to the police band on a scanner and likes "running the plates" of suspicious cars. But even if I got unlucky enough to stumble across one of those, the Plymouth would come up clean.

For that matter, so would I. Wayne B. Askew was a good citizen. The "B" was for "Burke," that's what his friends call him. An undistinguished sort of a guy. Self-employed all his life, now semi-retired. Still kept his hand in, dabbling in real estate. Never been arrested. No military service—that bad ticker, you know.

That's an extra safety feature, a bad heart. I always carry one of those Medical Alert cards. Mine says Wayne had a quadruple bypass a couple of years ago, takes all kinds of medication for it. And, around my neck, I wear a plain steel necklace holding a small metal screw-cap cylinder. The cylinder is stamped with the serpent-curling-around-the-staff symbol, and the words: "Nitroglycerin. Change Pills Every 2–3 Weeks." Inside the cylinder, I keep a half-dozen legit nitro pills. If I get busted, I know how to fake a heart attack. And when one of the cops reaches for the life-saving cylinder . . .

If that doesn't look like the right play—maybe too many of them in on the arrest—I can always have the attack in the holding cell. When they call the cardiologist listed on the Medical Alert card, the phone rings in my lawyer's office.

Wayne B. Askew will stand a lot of scrutiny. But if his prints drop, so does the mask.

T he house was an ambassador for the subdivision. Started out a basic two-bedroom, one-bath unit on a concrete slab, but the carport had been made into a real garage, and the dormer window showed that the attic had been finished for occupancy. Maybe another bedroom and bath up there, too; no way to tell from the outside.

I noticed other upgrades. Vinyl siding in a rich shade of brown, set off by white trimming for a gingerbread look. A bay window in front. Skylight above it. The lawn was neatly mowed, but not razor-edged immaculate the way some others I passed were. No fence.

Slate slabs, set in an irregular pattern, led up to the front entrance. The door was painted the same color as the siding, plain except for two overlapping glass bricks at the top right—made me think of a pair of dice.

The button for the doorbell was set into the frame on the left. I pressed it. Heard the faint sound of a gong inside, vaguely Oriental. I could see from the way the door was framed that it opened in, but I stepped back anyway, so she wouldn't feel as if I were looming over her when she answered.

Nothing. I checked my watch. A minute shy of noon. The gong sound had been very muted. Maybe she was around back . . . ?

I was mentally tossing a coin on whether to ring again, or walk around the back, when the door opened. The interior was too dim for me to make out anything more than that it was a woman.

"Yes?"

"My name is Burke, ma'am. We had an appointment. . . ."

"Appointment," she said, as if confirming.

"Yes, ma'am. For noon. Could I . . . ?"

She stepped back, not saying a word. I crossed the threshold, deliberately leaving the door open. She moved behind me, closed it herself. And stayed where she was.

To my right, I could see the kitchen. The appliances all seemed to be the same bronze color. To my left, the living room, where the skylight bent the sun into a rectangular patch on a beige carpet. I didn't move.

I heard a deep intake of breath, as if she were getting ready to lift a heavy weight. She moved from behind me over to the left. "Please come in," she said.

I followed her to the living room. She sat herself on the white twill couch, nodded her head toward a matching wingback chair. Said "Please" again. I sat down.

"I'll try to make this as easy as possible," I began.

"Easy."

"I apologize. A poor choice of words. I understand this could never be easy. My intent was to—"

"Understand."

"Mrs. Greene . . ."

"Ms."

"Ms. Greene, you know why I'm here. You agreed to see me. You know what I'm doing, what I was hired to do. I'm trying my best not to offend you, but I don't seem to be very good at it."

"Offend me?"

"Perhaps that was overstated," I said, trying for mild, not oily. "When I speak with you, I seem to always use the wrong word for what I mean to convey."

I waited patiently for her to say "Convey," but she stayed silent, not bothering to conceal that she was studying my face.

So that's what I did, too. All I knew from Giovanni was her color, and even that had been misleading—I'd seen blondes with deep tans who were darker than her skin shade. She had a narrow nose, high cheekbones, and thin lips. Her hair would have made a Filipina proud. I can't do genetics-by-sight the way Mama does, but it didn't take a DNA specialist to see there was a heavy dose of cream in her coffee.

A beautiful, slender woman in a plain blue dress. Still in shock, as if they'd just told her last night.

"You work for Giovanni?" she finally asked.

"I'm doing this job for him," I said, treading carefully.

"You're not in his . . . organization?"

"No. I'm not in any organization."

"You're not a criminal?"

"No, ma'am, I'm not."

"Yes, you are," she said, in a sterilized voice. "Some kind of a criminal. Everyone in Gio's world is a criminal of some kind."

I didn't say anything.

"What did he hire you to do?" she asked.

"To find who . . . murdered your daughter. And why they did."

"The police say *they* know."

"*What!?* They know who—"

"Not who," she said, emotionless. "Why."

"Those are guesses, Ms. Greene. Theories. The only sure way to find the person who actually—"

"Why do you say that?"

"Well, theories are generalizations. They're based on—"

"No. Not that. 'Person,' you said. The police said it was a man."

"I can understand why they might think that, ma'am. And I'm not arguing with it. Just trying not to exclude anyone until I know more."

"More?"

"More than I know now," I said, trying to catch her waves so I could surf. "Some of it, I hope you'll tell me. The rest, I have to find on my own."

"And Giovanni hired you to do that?"

"Yes, he did."

"Will you do it yourself?"

"Mostly. It depends on what it turns out is needed. I might bring others into it, if I have to."

"Needed?"

"To find the person."

"So Giovanni can kill him," she said, with no-affect certainty.

"I don't know anything about—"

"Oh, Gio will kill him," she said, mournfully confident. "Honor is so very important to him."

"Honor?" I asked, switching roles.

She smiled faintly, without warmth. "You're right, of course. I said 'honor,' but I meant 'image.' What the kids call 'face.' That is Giovanni, right there. That sums him up."

"I don't know him," I slip-slided.

"You said it might not be a man."

"Giovanni, I mean. I don't know . . . the child's father. I'm doing a job of work for him, that's all."

"Father?"

"Ma'am, I am truly sorry if I keep stumbling around. I can't seem to find the right words. I don't know Giovanni. And I'll never know your daughter. But if you'll help me know *about* her, maybe I can find who killed her."

"What then?"

"When I find whoever did it . . . *if* I can?"

"Yes. What then? Will you tell the police?"

"That's not my job."

"Will you tell me?"

"Yes," I spooled out the lie like a bolt of silk, "of course I will. You have the right to know."

"Please wait here," she said. At a nod from me, she stood up and walked out of the room.

I didn't move from where I was seated, contenting myself with a visual sweep of the room. It was neat and clean, but without that demented gleam you get under a No People, No Pets, No Playing regime. The room was clearly for company, but not the kind that kicked back with a few beers and watched a football game with their feet on the coffee table.

I'd been in homes where people had lost their child to violence before. I expected at least one photo of the girl—a shrine wouldn't have surprised me.

Nothing.

When the mother came back, she was carrying a large gray plastic box by the handle. When she opened the top, I could see it was filled front-to-back with file folders. She knelt, placed it on the floor in front of my chair, said, "I have three more," and walked off again.

I didn't think about offering to help her any more than I did about looking through the files outside her presence.

"It's all there," she said, finally. If lugging all those boxes had tired her, she kept it off her face. Her breathing was as regular as if she'd never left the couch. "The first one is everything that was in the newspapers, and everything I got from the police. The others are all . . . Vonni. From her baby stuff to just before . . ."

"I—"

"The reason they're like that," she interrupted, "is because of . . . what happened. I always kept Vonni's . . . everything. Every report card, every note from school, every doctor's visit . . . I always took pictures, too. But I didn't have them in this . . . this filing system, before. I was trying to help the police. They had so many questions, they kept coming back and back and back. Finally, I put this all together for them. But it wasn't what they were interested in, I guess."

"They wanted to know about her boyfriends, right?"

"Yes."

"And yours?"

"Yes." No reaction, flat.

"Her teachers? School friends?"

"Yes."

"Her computer?"

"Oh yes."

"Drugs? Parties? Gangs?"

"Of course," she said, a tiny vein of sarcasm pulsing in her voice.

"And they drew a blank with all of that?"

"That? There *were* no drugs. There *were* no gangs."

"They said this? Or you just know from your own—?"

"*I* said it. They didn't believe it. They didn't say so, not out loud. But I could tell. After a . . . while, after a while, though, they believed it."

"And they apologized for—?"

"Be serious," she said.

S he didn't offer me so much as a glass of water. Just sat there watching me go through the files, one at a time. I wanted to start at the latest ones and work backwards, but I could sense that would sever the single frayed thread between us.

I tried to engage her in conversation as I worked. Several times. All I got for my efforts was monosyllables. And when I suggested that I could maybe take the files with me, return them later, I got a look that would have scared a scorpion.

Okay.

Only Child

The birth certificate was strangely impersonal.

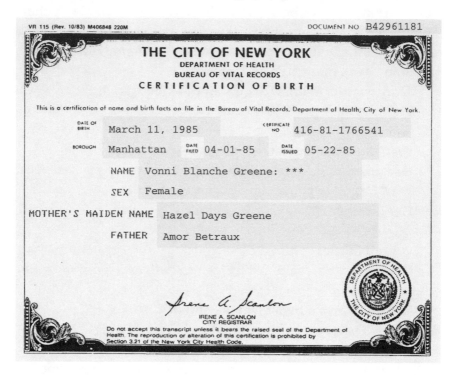

I'd seen New York birth certificates from the Fifties. They were a lot richer in detail, and a lot less socially correct. They used to give you the time of birth, the number of children "previously born alive" to the mother, the race and occupation of the parents . . . even where they lived. But I thought that even the little bit of information on this one might open a door, if I could just engage the mother. . . .

"I thought her name would be spelled differently," I said.

"Vonni's name?"

"Yes."

"I don't understand."

"I thought it was . . . a reference to Giovanni."

"Yes, that's right. But I spelled it the way it should be *pronounced*, so her friends wouldn't get it wrong. Or her teachers, when they called on her in class. Vonni might not have felt comfortable correcting people all the time, just gone along with whatever they called her. When she was little, I mean. I didn't want that. I mean, if I spelled it like 'Vanni,' they'd all think they should say it like 'Vanna' with a 'y.' Vanny. Then she'd have no connection to her father at all. No child would want that, would they?"

"No," I assured her, "they wouldn't." Thinking of my own birth certificate. The one that said "Baby Boy Burke." Time of birth: 3:03 a.m. If I ever wanted my first name to link me to my father, I'd have to change it to "Unknown."

I kept looking. A color photo marked "5/13/91" on the back showed a pretty, slightly chubby little girl, more darkly com-plected than her mother, with long wavy hair. The child had almond eyes, and a smile you could arc-weld with.

If an activity existed on this earth Vonni hadn't been exposed to, I'd never heard of it. Piano lessons, T-ball, dance, karate, gymnastics, soccer, glee club, drama society.

Only the last one had gone the distance, though. At the very end of the "Activities" file, there was a program for the school play for her junior year. Under "Cast," I found:

Amanda . . . . Vonni B. Greene

The play was scheduled for the night of May 23. They'd found the girl's body the day before.

The files looked like raw data. It didn't seem like any of it had been sanitized by a loving parent's hand, but I still had to ask.

"Ms. Greene, I apologize if this question offends you in any way. I hope you understand why I'm asking. This material, it shows an almost . . . idyllic life. I wonder if there was any other . . ."

"You and the police," she said, an ugly little twist to her up-per lip.

I didn't say anything.

"This is *everything*," she said. "I'm so sorry Vonni wasn't having an affair with a married man. Or smoking crack. Or run-ning with a gang."

"All right."

"Is it? Are you satisfied, sir? Are you going to tell Giovanni I 'cooperated'? I'm sure he'll be asking you about that."

"Ms. Greene, anything you share with me is privileged."

"What does that mean, privileged?"

"It means two things," I said, keeping the volume down, but putting some weight into my voice. "One, you have no obligation to share *anything* with me, and I'm well aware of that. So whatever I might learn from you *is* a privilege. Not a right, a privilege. A privilege I would respect. Two, anything you say to me *stays* with me. It's a privileged communication, just as if you spoke it to a priest."

"You're no priest."

"No, I'm not. I'm not a lawyer or a doctor or a social worker or anything the *law* would prohibit me from repeating what you tell me. I'm just a man. But what I am is a man of my word."

"You say so."

"Yes. I say so."

"That's all you have, your word?"

"That's all anyone has. Question is, how good is it."

"That *is* the question. How would I find the answer?"

"Watch me," I told her. "Watch me close."

"Why should I do it?" the pudgy-faced guy asked me. He was wearing a rumpled white shirt under wide red suspenders, a battered dark-brown fedora tipped back on his head. A cigar that wasn't from the same hemisphere as Havana was planted in the corner of his mouth. Dressing the part.

"I'm not asking you to *do* anything," I told him. "Like I said, all I want is the assignment. On spec. You're a journalist, right? Your whole operation, it's about investigative reporting. That's what I'll be doing."

"Solving that murder?" he asked, sarcasm smearing his thick lips. "The case is over a year old. Maybe you'll find who killed Chandra Levy, while you're at it."

"I'll solve it, or I won't," I said, matter-of-factly. "It's my time. I'm not asking you for a dime in front. Not even expenses."

"And if you *did* manage to come up with the killer . . . ?"

"It would be yours. A total exclusive."

He puffed on his cigar, trying to get the hang of it. Said, "We can't issue press credentials. Internet journalists don't get the same respect our brothers on the print side do."

"The only credential I want is, if the cops call, you say I'm working for you. On this assignment."

"What do you need us for? Just tell anyone who asks that you're freelance."

"Sure, I could do that. But I'll get treated better if I'm working on an assignment."

"You might," he conceded. "But a story like that . . . I mean, if you actually found the killer, it'd be worth a lot. Why should I trust you to bring it to us?"

"I've got references."

"Is that right?" he said, just short of snide. "Who would they be?"

"I'll have them call you," I said.

"**W**hy should I believe you?" Wolfe.

"I can prove it," I said into the phone. "If we could just—"

"Arm's-length," she said, sugarless.

"Whatever you say."

"I won't say it twice," she warned.

"**G**uy's down here, looking for you."

Gateman, whispering into the phone he kept in the room behind the front-desk area.

"Me? Or a name?"

"Burke."

"Ever see him before?"

"No. Big guy. Dresses like a fucking lumberjack. Stands like a fighter, though."

"Send him up, okay?"

"You're the boss."

Mick came up the stairs slowly, hands open at his sides, distributing his weight carefully. He saw me watching through the open door, walked in.

"I was expecting Wolfe," I said.

"After I look around."

I waved my hand to indicate he could look wherever he wanted. Giving up my address to Wolfe was the only way I could get her to meet with me. Mick was part of the package.

"You got another dog?" he asked, wary.

"No."

"Sorry," is all he said. More than I thought he would.

"Hi, chief!"

Pepper. Sporting a red beret and a white jumpsuit with a matching red belt.

"Hey, Pepper. You guys going to keep coming in waves, or what?"

"She'll be here. In a minute. I'm just picking up Mick. Today's our anniversary, and I thought we'd—"

I shot a quick glance at Mick. I'd known him for years, and I was sure that nothing that walked the earth could make him nervous. But I didn't think that bulge in his jacket was an anniversary present. And there was a definite look of alarm on his face. He disappeared in the direction of the bedroom.

"Pepper, can I ask you a question?"

"Talk's cheap," she said, then giggled to take the sting out of it.

"Wolfe doesn't really think I'd ever—"

"Ah, don't go there," she advised, not unkindly. "I'm not here for nothing."

Just as I opened my mouth to ask her what she meant, Mick came back to where we were sitting, and a barrel-chested Rottweiler strutted through the open front door. The beast came toward me, making little trash-compactor noises.

"Bruiser!"

Wolfe. In a tightly belted silk trenchcoat of pale lilac and matching spike heels with ankle straps. Her long dark hair was streaked with auburn highlights now, but the trademark white wings still flared out from her high forehead. Gray gunfighter's eyes took my temperature.

"Thanks for coming," I said.

She clapped her hands, one short, sharp sound. The Rottweiler hit the deck, never taking his baleful gaze off me.

"Bruiser has a good memory," she said.

"Then why doesn't he relax?"

"Oh, he *never* liked you," Wolfe said, no trace of a smile on that gorgeous mouth.

It took less than half an hour for me to lay the whole thing out for her. Mick went back to roaming around the apartment, but Pepper never left Wolfe's side.

All business, then.

Fair enough. Where I come from, whatever train you want to ride gets to call the price of the ticket.

"You want what, exactly?" Wolfe asked. Then added, "What do you want to buy?" avoiding a mixed message.

"Whatever you can get me on the crime that I couldn't get for myself out of the papers."

"The same stuff a defense attorney would get if they'd ever brought anyone to trial?"

"No. Not just the *Brady* stuff. McVeigh-type discovery. The whole thing. Investigative reports, suspects ruled out, blind alleys. Everything."

"I'm not sure I can get all that. Some of it, sure. But I don't have the same contacts on Long Island that I do in Queens."

"Why Queens?"

"That's where the body was dumped," she said, a faint note of surprise in her voice. "You didn't know that?"

"No. No, I didn't. So Long Island's connection with the case is only because that's where the girl was from?"

"I don't know. I took a *quick* look. Maybe there's more to that, but I can't say right now."

"All right."

"And what else?"

"Whatever you can get me on Giovanni Antrelli and Felix Encarnación," I said, not pretending surprise that she knew there was another reason for me calling her in.

"Didn't you just say they were your clients?"

"Yeah. I did."

"So . . . ?"

"So I meant what I told you on the phone. This is straight-edge. Me, anyway, I am."

"So you think your clients might have had something to do with—?"

"No. Not in the way you mean. But *they* think it's about them. That's one out of three."

"Burke . . ." she said, with just a trace of impatience.

"One," I said, holding up a finger, "it was a random thing. Young girl's out, doing whatever, runs into Mr. Wrong. Anyone from a roving tramp to a Ted Bundy. Two, it was somebody in her life," I went on, "somebody she knew. The way she was killed, it fits either one. Serial killers, it's nothing unusual for them to be in a rage when they work, right? And a boyfriend, or anyone who thought he'd been betrayed, they might get into a frenzy, too. But the third choice is what my clients themselves suspect—a professional job. Someone sending Giovanni a message. 'We know *everything* about you. And we're *very* serious people.' Killing a daughter nobody was supposed to know he even had, that would make both those points."

"And Antrelli, he thinks it's the feds?"

"That's maybe not as crazy as it sounds," I said, catching the defensiveness too late to choke it off.

"The feds hiring psycho sex-killers?" she said, the sarcasm all the heavier for its absence in her tone.

"First of all," I told her, "the feds are masters of the means-justifies-the-end strategies. How many times have they left a child molester running around loose, even when they *knew* he was doing kids left and right, because they wanted to build a case against some of the people in his ring? Or just gather more evidence, make a stronger case? They let Klansmen they had in their pockets go along on lynchings, didn't they? They stirred up that war between the Panthers and Karenga's group—a lot of bodies behind that one. I don't know about outright assassinations, but how many people did Hoover *get* dead with the games he played?"

"You're a historian now?" she said, letting the sarcasm surface. "And you actually think they'd sex-murder a teenage girl just to drive a wedge between some narco-traffickers?"

"A whole agency? No way. Even if some supervisor had an aneurysm and hatched a plan like that, they'd put him in a padded room. But Giovanni thinks it's a rogue."

"In the FBI?"

"Ask the agent doing life for selling secrets to the Russians. What's his name, Hanssen?"

"Yes. But he was a whore. This, what you're talking about, it would *have* to be personal."

"That's what Giovanni thinks, too," I said. "But if he's telling it straight, it's nothing more than a feeling—he doesn't *know* anything."

"Does he have someone in mind?"

"Not even a guess. He's . . . confused, is the best way I could put it. If someone in law enforcement hated him *that* bad, why not just take him out? Trap him in an alley, ventilate him, flake the corpse with whatever they need—pistol and powder would do it—and walk away giggling. If a beat cop guns down a homeless black guy, there's people in this city who'll get in the street behind it, raise all kinds of holy hell. But a known gangster? A made man? Where's the Al Sharpton for that? Columbo tried it years ago. And remember how he ended up."

"So it's some kind of deeper game, and the girl was a pawn?" Wolfe asked, hunter's eyes hard under skeptically raised eyebrows.

"Maybe," I said, not committing myself. "That's *if* it wasn't a random freak, or someone with a specific motive to kill her. Giovanni's big reason for believing it was aimed at him is the biggest reason for anyone else believing that it *wasn't*."

"That nobody knew she was his daughter?"

"Yep."

She shifted in her chair to face me more squarely. The Rottweiler did the same from the floor. "You said, on the phone, that this was back to being what you once were."

"I did."

"That's a long jump. What's so high and mighty about this job that gets you there?"

"I'm not saying anything like that. You know I used to . . . look for kids, things like that. I know this one's dead. So it's not about protecting her, sure. But this *isn't* crime I'm doing, right? A job like this, it's about as legitimate as a man like me could ever hope to get."

"A man like you?" She dry-laughed.

"What do you want from me?" I said.

"From you?" she said, icily. "Half up front, half when I deliver."

Every time I see Wolfe, it's always the same. And after she leaves, it's always a Patsy Cline night.

I know how to wait. It's just time, and I've done enough of it. And, now that I was home, I had plenty of things to help make it pass.

Not TV. That's the same all over. What I'd really missed was my newspapers. There's nothing like the New York tabs, especially when they're in one of their turf wars.

I hit the mute on some sit-com, improving it considerably. Then I fixed myself a rye toast with cream cheese, added a big glass of grape juice, and settled down with the *Daily News* and the *Post,* glad to be back with journalism where all murders are "brutal," all prosecutors are "tough," and all blondes are "attractive." And any lawyer who cooperates with the reporter is "high-powered."

The ex-mayor, a guy who usually had all the charm of a public housing project, had stepped up big after the World Trade Center destruction, and the papers were covering his endless divorce with a lot less intensity now.

A genetically engineered football player, whose gigantic neck made his head resemble a shot put stuck in a pool of mud, hospitalized his girlfriend.

A pattern rapist was terrorizing Queens. The DA promised "the maximum penalty" when he was caught. Sure . . . if he pleaded to it.

Two broken-synapse robbers killed four people "execution style" in a convenience store in Corona.

Some addled actor who played a doctor in one of those made-for-cable movies was giving a speech at NYU on the need for Medicaid reform.

Politicians kept "calling" for different things. Nobody ever seemed to answer.

The gossip columns were the usual mix of pipe jobs and courthouse-bin scavenging, with a little credit-card info thrown in for seasoning.

A couple of buffoons were running for some state-senate seat just vacated by the incumbent's prison term. One accused the other of being "against the Internet"—a knockout punch in a world where whole hordes of humans think better sex is a faster modem.

There were five separate heavyweight champions of the world.

The Twin Towers were gone forever, and the debate about what to put up in their place had turned sanctimonious and ugly at the same time.

Various humans called each other racists.

A rap star got arrested for keeping it real. And a comedian for child abuse.

Four more celebrities went into rehab, one for the third time.

A man, despondent over his mother's suicide, swan-dived off the Throgs Neck Bridge. Didn't even break a bone.

A fourteen-year-old got twenty-eight years in prison for shooting his teacher. Part of his sentence was he had to take anger-management classes. I hoped someone was going to teach him knife-fighting, too.

On the international front, Cambodia was still selling its children as prostitutes, and the Sudan was selling its children, period. There were anti-immigrant riots all over Europe, the swastika out of the closet. The Middle East was as stable as nitro in a Cuisinart.

The boss of the Olympics cartel said the games were the world's greatest single opportunity to advance the cause of international human rights. Which is why they picked Beijing to host them in 2008.

A five-million-dollar federal study announced that the latest stats showed crime was way down in America. I guess that's what Bush had meant by "faith-based."

"What is that, mahn?" Clarence asked the next day, pointing to the walls I'd covered with white posterboard.

"Time lines," I told him. "The stuff in red, that's what we know for sure. She left her home on a Saturday morning, around six-thirty. The cops didn't find the body until almost three weeks later. The papers were kind of vague about how long she'd been dead, so I'm waiting on Wolfe's stuff before I try to tighten it down."

"To the exact time she died?"

"Maybe not to a specific time of death, but, at least, to a time of *life,* see what I'm saying?"

"No, mahn, I do not. How does this help us to—?"

"If whoever killed her was a stranger, there's a number of ways it could have played out. Maybe he did it on the spot, and took the body with him."

"Why would anyone—?"

"Maybe he needed to clean the body, remove any traces he might have left. Maybe he wanted to confuse the cops by moving it. Or maybe he just liked playing with the corpse," I said, thinking of a human I'd done time with years ago who had that very same hobby. "Or maybe it started out as a kidnap-rape, and he killed her sometime while he had her captive. If it's random, then there's all kinds of possibilities. But if it was someone she knew . . ."

"Ah. Then maybe she was seen. While she was alive. With . . . with whoever might have done it, yes?"

"Yeah. She wasn't alive that *whole* time; not from the moment she disappeared until they found her body. But she was alive for *some* of it. The more of that we can eliminate, the narrower the time frame it had to have happened in."

"The police would do all this, no?"

"They would. A case like this, they'd have done everything *I* could think of, that's true."

"I doubt that is so true," Clarence said, reflecting what all real outlaws believe—if we ever switched sides, the crime rate would drop as quick as Sonny Liston in the Ali rematch . . . and just as guaranteed.

Clarence decided to hang around, help out. I vacuumed the information the mother had provided, while he wrote it up on the posterboard in his strict-school copperplate. We had to start over a few times when we didn't get the spacing right, but we finally finished around six.

"It doesn't look like it will tell us much, mahn."

"Not yet," I said, with maybe a bit more confidence than I felt. "But when we start filling in those blanks . . ."

"Where does it start, then? Looking for a killer?"

"The way the cops do it, they take a rock, and throw it into the pond of the victim's life. Then they work on the ripples, starting with the closest one first."

"They are not wrong, to think like that."

"Not wrong, but not always right. It's a place to start, that's all."

"You said the girl's mother told you—"

"Yeah. They've already thrown that rock. And if they're working the ripples, they're a hell of a distance from the center by now."

"The girl was . . . she was a black girl, you said?"

"Well, her father's—"

"Don't matter if her father was a blond-and-blue Swede, Schoolboy," the Prof said, strolling into our conversation and the apartment at the same time. "You know the way it play—they write the book behind how you look."

"What're you saying?" I asked him.

"It's what Clarence is saying," the Prof answered, turning toward his son. "You thinking the cops ain't going to work a little nigger girl's case as hard, right?"

"They might not," Clarence said stubbornly.

"I'm not saying that don't ever happen," the handsome little man said soberly. "But I don't think that's what we got here. That child wasn't living the kind of life where the rollers would get all smug, say she made her own bed, see what I'm saying?"

"And the cops *want* to clear homicides," I agreed. "That's a major stat for them. Unsolved murders, they make everyone look bad. The kind of thing you're talking about, if they'd gone dirty on it, they'd have popped the wrong guy for it, rather than not clear the case at all. They don't solve it, you know what happens. The TV vultures give the poor little girl an 'anniversary' date. Do the same story every year until somebody takes a fall for the kill. That's not the kind of spotlight any department wants."

"For true," the Prof said, more to Clarence than to me.

"Hard to figure out *which* department it is, for this one," I added. "I mean, theoretically, it's a Queens County case. That's where they found the body. I won't know until I see what Wolfe comes up with."

"You saw her?" the Prof asked me. "Face-to-face?"

"Yeah."

"What'd you roll, honeyboy?"

"A hard eight, Prof."

"What does it matter what I told her?" Hazel Greene asked, her eyes calm and steady in the last light of evening.

"I don't know that it matters, ma'am. I only know that it *could*."

"Give me one example," she said firmly. "One example of how what I told my daughter about her father could possibly help you find who killed her."

"Let's say you told her . . . that her father was an . . . accountant," I said, feeling my way. "And he lived in Boston. The day she . . . the day she left, it was early in the morning. She told you she was going to the City with two of her girlfriends. To look for a special hat to wear in the play, yes?"

"That's what I told you, yes. That's what she had told me, yes," the woman said. Soft-voiced and civil, but not a great distance from hostile. The way an innocent person talks to a cop.

"But you never actually saw her leave."

"I did!"

"Of course you did," I said, backpedaling fast, before I lost her for good. "You saw her walk out the door, after you had breakfast together. I just meant, you didn't see the actual car she got into."

"No. I just gave her a kiss and went back to my—"

"I know," I cut in, quick, slapping a tourniquet over the guilt-wound. "But what if what she *really* did was go to the airport?"

"What?"

"To go to Boston. To look for her father," I said, gently tugging her back to the hypothetical. "It's only an hour flight. She could have gone up there, spent the whole day, and still been back on time. You see where I'm going? You weren't expecting her until late, you said."

"Twelve-thirty. Half past midnight. That was her curfew on Saturday nights. It used to be eleven-thirty, but she'd just turned sixteen and . . ."

"I understand. She said there was a party that night, and she'd go straight there from the—"

"Vonni wanted to sleep over. At her friend BJ's house—that's a girl. But I told her she could *either* go to the City with her friends *or* have the sleepover, not both in one day. She chose the City."

"How did she seem that morning?"

"Excited! So excited. Happy and . . . just looking forward to . . . her whole life, I guess," Hazel Greene said. Her voice was hollow, walled off from the pain.

"That was normal for Vonni?"

"Normal? She was a sixteen-year-old girl, Mr. . . . Burke, is it?"

"Yes, ma'am."

"Did you change it?"

"Change . . . what?"

"Your name," she said. "Burke, that's not Italian."

"I told you I didn't work for your . . . for Vonni's father, Ms. Greene."

"I remember. I assumed you were a member of some other . . . organization. But still part of their whole thing."

"No. No, I'm not."

"Why would Gio trust you, then? You're not . . . 'family,' " she said, her lips twisting with contempt.

"You would have to ask him."

"Oh, that's all right. I believe I understand it now. If anyone has to know his shameful secret, better an outsider."

"I don't know, ma'am," I said mildly, trying to steer her back to where I needed her. "But . . . you see what I mean now? About what Vonni knew about her father?"

"I certainly never told her that her father was in Boston."

"It was just an example," I said patiently. "Of the kind of thing you *might* have told her."

"What good would it do you if I—?"

"The morning she left, she knew you wouldn't expect her until at least half past midnight," I interrupted, still working on not losing her. "If she *was* looking for her father, she might have gone to wherever you . . ."

Hazel Greene nodded, as if finally seeing where I was going, if not the sense of it. "She thought her father was dead."

"Ah."

"When she was little, she used to ask. Where I was raising her, at first, it was nothing so unusual for a father not to be in the home. But they, the fathers, they were . . . around, you know? In the neighborhood, someplace. A presence. Even in prison, they were real. I thought of telling her her father had been a soldier, killed in some war, but I could never make the dates work.

"Besides, even when she was a little, little girl, I knew how smart she was going to be. And what a heart she'd have. If I told her that her father had been a soldier, she'd want to see his grave someday. So what I did, I told her that her father was dead, and that I'd explain everything when she was older."

"She accepted that?"

"Not at first. But then we made a bargain. On her eighth birthday, I'd tell her *everything*."

"Why then?"

"I was just buying time when I said it. And Vonni never spoke of it again. Neither did I. But on her eighth birthday, she asked. And that's when I told her."

I didn't say anything, keeping slack in the line so it wouldn't snap if she made a sudden run.

"She'd just seen *West Side Story* on television. I thought it was maybe a little mature for Vonni, but she just *loved* it. So I told her that's how it had been for her father and me. A forbidden love. It felt good to wrap the lie I was going to tell her in so much truth.

"It *was* the truth. Gio's favorite song was some old thing, from the Fifties, maybe? 'Running Bear.' I'm sure you never heard it. . . ."

"Johnny Preston," I said. "With the Big Bopper doing the bass line."

"Oh! Then you know. The boy and girl, from two different tribes, on opposite sides of the river. 'But their tribes fought with each other,'" she recited, "'so their love could never be.' Gio played that song over and over for me. He said that was us. There even *was* a river between us. The East River. Do you remember how the song ended?"

"Yes. The young brave dove into the river that separated them, and the maiden jumped in, too. They met in the middle. The current pulled them down. And they drowned."

"Together."

"That's right."

"Yes. And that's what crazy Gio wanted to do. He wanted us to die together. Not in some dirty river. He wanted us to go to the top of the World Trade Center . . . that was years ago, before those crazy people, the terrorists, did that terrible . . . and jump off, holding hands all the way down. So we could be together."

"There were other ways you could be—"

"I know. We could have run away. He could have gotten a job. But none of that was real to Gio. He could never imagine leaving his . . . life. Or getting a regular job. But dying, *that* was something he could deal with."

"Not you, though."

"I had my baby inside me," she said, as if that explained everything.

I stayed quiet for long enough to understand that it did.

"I always remembered what Gio had wanted to do," she said quietly. "A couple of years after I . . . left, I saw a story in the *Post*. It was about a young man who tried to jump between two high buildings over in the Bronx. It was some kind of gang thing. Not an initiation—the young man was the leader. The story seemed to imply that he was showing the others how to do it.

"So that's what I told Vonni. How her father died. That young man? In the story? His name was Romeo. Isn't that just too ridiculous?"

Then she started to cry.

I cruised the neighborhood the way I'd case a bank, starting out way past the perimeter and working my way toward the center. Only a fool goes into the jungle without memorizing enough trail-markers to find his way back out.

When you look for kids—runaways, castoffs, missing-and-presumed—finding a body is always one of the possibilities. But this time I was starting at the other end of the tunnel. That changed the game. If I stepped out of the shadows, had the mother "hire" me, got the names of Vonni's friends from her, and tried to talk to them, I might as well dial 911 on myself.

In the past, I'd sometimes pretended to be a cop. Never flashed a badge or anything stupid-amateur like that. I'd just plant an impression and let people fall into their own assumption pits. It's especially easy when people *expect* a plainclothesman to come around, asking questions.

But I didn't look the part anymore.

Ten days of drifting with the currents didn't lead me to a way in. I didn't know much about small towns, and what I thought I knew wasn't proving out. The mall was the real city, like I'd suspected, but inside it the population was as fractured as Manhattan's. Rich and poor walked the same paths but never touched, like human railroad tracks.

Some kids lounged around the food courts, designer shopping bags stuffed with credit-card purchases, gabbing on cell phones until they drove away in their mothers' Mercedes, or their own Miatas. Other kids worked in the fast-food kiosks, earning less in a month than their better-born counterparts spent in an hour, saving every dime so they could go mobile, too.

That was the common ground. Car culture. You couldn't get anywhere without one, in every sense of the word.

The parking lot had enough diversity to make a liberal come all over himself. Cute little LOOK AT ME! roadsters stood shoulder-to-toe with hulking monster-truck imitators, Corvettes were docked nose-to-nose with minivans, and thoroughbred sportscars shared space with pro street–quarter-horses. Fundamentalists don't care what you wear to church—only attendance counts.

The cars got closer to each other than the clans ever did. Inside, a see-and-be-seen parade. Jocks in letterman's jackets. Whiggers in hip-hop gear. Cholas in tight jeans and bright-colored spike heels. JAPs in pastels. Goth kids in their bloodless black-and-white. Rich boys in stuff that showed they were.

Their jewelry was as varied as their hairstyles, but they all seemed to pack pagers.

Like a prison yard. Everyone crewed and cliqued, no mixing.

I wondered if that was how Giovanni saw it, back when he'd made his choice.

The mall seemed to be on a strict schedule: near-empty in the mornings, stuffed with adults at lunchtime, and swamped by a wave of teenagers in the afternoons. Then came hordes of married-with-children until mid-evening, after which the teens took over again and carried it to closing time.

In-store security was tight—undercovers so obvious that they must have been hired as deterrents, lots of fiber-optic cams, especially wherever they sold CDs or clothes—but the corridors and the outside grounds didn't get any real coverage. At night, they tightened up the perimeter a little. But it was mostly rent-a-cops, eye-fucking wannabe lowriders who spent hours draped over their not-much cars.

Malls are like cities; they have whisper-streams, too. But

without a native to front me, any attempt to tap in would draw way too much attention.

So I kept sniffing around the area, looking for openings. I found some places where hanging out for a few weeks could make you into enough of a regular to talk with people without drawing suspicion, but I didn't have that kind of time. Anyway, I couldn't picture Vonni's crowd spending hours in a low-rent tavern, or at the local OTB parlor.

After the Plymouth dusted off a poseur Firebird with more tire than motor on Hempstead Turnpike, a hardcore Nova slid in alongside me a few lights down. The driver looked over, raised his chin in a question I answered with the Roadrunner's cartoon horn. He cracked his throttle deep enough to let me know he was carrying heavy. I held the engine against the brake just a little past idle, quiet as a turbine.

We both left on the cross street's yellow. He got out first, but I drove around him just before the Torqueflite grabbed second gear on its own.

The Nova's driver passed me as I backed off, made a "Follow me!" gesture out his window. In the diner's parking lot, I got an invite to a not-yet-completed section of the LIE, where they were running for money.

Later that night, I stood off to one side and watched the drivers of a couple of trailer queens go at it. Negotiations first. They argued about lengths and the bust—who got to leave first—for what seemed like hours. When they finally got down to it, the race was over in less than ten seconds.

There was a lot of buzz in the crowd, but it had nothing to do with a murder. Everybody wondering if some guy named Gary was really going to show. I listened close, but all I could pick up was that this Gary was from Island Trees originally, moved to the Midwest a long time ago. Supposed to be the fastest gun on the East Coast years ago. Supposed to be coming back now. Maybe so, but it didn't happen that night.

Still nothing. When you're man-hunting, you can buy information. Lots of it's always for sale—separating the diamonds from the dirt is the trick. I knew the kind of people to ask, and I knew where to find them. But I didn't have a target. And I couldn't offer anything as good as what the cops would have already put on the table, a year ago.

I went through the motions, but I didn't lie to myself about it. I was marking time, waiting for Wolfe.

I was watching a fight on ESPN2 when my cellular buzzed.

"You want to come here?" I asked Wolfe, holding the phone to my ear as I looked out the window into the darkness.

"Once was enough," she said.

"Just say where and when."

"Right now. You're close enough." Then she gave me an address on lower Broadway.

A large office building, diagonally across from Federal Plaza, a few blocks away from what the tour operators like to call "ground zero." The man at the security guard's desk was hunched over a paperback, his back to me. I made enough noise to let him know I was there. He turned and looked up. Mick.

He walked into the freight elevator, me following. There was no floor indicator, but I could feel us going down.

Mick still had the paperback in his hand. *The Bottoms,* Joe Lansdale's long-running smash.

"You like that one?" I asked him. "Me, I like his Hap and Leonard stuff the best."

Mick pulled the lever and the car rattled to a stop. He pulled back the gate and pointed to the left—all the answer I was going to get.

I stepped out, moved toward the only light. Heard the elevator door close behind me, the whirl of the machinery as the car went back up to the lobby floor.

Some kind of storage room, near as I could tell. Wolfe was perched on a two-drawer lateral file cabinet, wearing blue jeans and a pink pullover with matching sneakers, her hair in pigtails. In that light, she looked like a teenage girl.

With a hostile Rottweiler.

"Ah, shut up, Bruiser," I said to the beast. "You know me." He snarled softly in agreement.

Wolfe pointed to a carton on the floor. Looked like it was stuffed with paper. "That's all the hard copy that's coming," she said. "The rest, you'll have to hear it from me."

"Fair enough."

"You're paying a lot of money for not very much," she said, like she was warning me against a bad investment.

"It's not my money."

"I know whose money it is. And I'm guessing there isn't a lot in here that they don't already have."

"Maybe."

"You don't sound so sure."

"I'm not. I know stuff's for sale. But, sometimes, there's no way the potential buyer can make contact without telling the seller more than what he wants him to know, right?"

"Sure. And you're saying you're just a cutout? They only hired you to get . . . what I've got?"

"If that's all they wanted, they could have used a go-between a long time ago. This town, you can find a thousand lawyers to do anything by the hour. *In* an hour. It's just like I told you it was— they hired me to find out who did it. And why."

"If there *is* a 'why,' " she said.

I wasn't going to argue with Wolfe about that one. She'd prosecuted hundreds of humans who did freakish things without a "why" that would make sense to anyone else. "Yes," is all I said.

"What do you want first?"

"It doesn't—"

"The stuff on the killing? Or on your clients?"

"Oh. The killing," I said, opting for the secondhand stuff before whatever Wolfe had dug up on her own.

"It *is* a Queens case, technically. But most of the spadework was done by the Long Island cops. That's where the girl lived, where all her friends were, where she went to school . . . you know."

"Did they form some kind of—?"

"Joint Task Force?" she said mockingly. "But of course! And it appears the feds got to play, too."

"Profilers?"

"Yep. But you know how that works. They—if they're very good—can tell you the *kind* of person who might have done it, but that's a few miles short of an ID. And, with a kill like this one, there isn't much guesswork involved. A freak or a frenzy. Or both." She took a deep drag off her smoke. "Or a cold-blooded attempt to make it look that way."

"They don't even have a guess?"

"Truly, no. Not that they didn't try. But there never *was* anybody they really liked for it."

"Because she had no one that close—?"

"She had boyfriends," Wolfe said. "Nothing super-deep. She wasn't pregnant. In fact, the autopsy said she was a virgin."

"So she wasn't—?"

"Raped? No. Or sodomized. No indications in her mouth, either. But that doesn't mean it wasn't a sex crime. Not with all that stabbing and slashing. You know how some of those maggots love their in-and-out."

"The wounds . . . ?"

"That's one of the things I got to look at, but not bring along. Ever since the slime-sheets started publishing autopsy photos, every coroner's office in the country tightened up. Good thing, too. What do you want to know?"

"The bloodwork?"

"Not all that useful, since so much time had passed. Coroner said *minimum* of two weeks since death. But, still, they went the route. Even toxed her hair. Negative on everything. Plus, she had no tracks, and there was no independent indication of drugs."

"Did it . . . the killing, look professional?"

"Professional? She was stabbed seventeen times!"

"If a pair of prison hit men cornered their target in the shower, they'd stick him that many times, just to be sure."

Wolfe lit another cigarette. Sucked in the smoke like bitter medicine. Held it down a couple of seconds, then blew a harsh jet across the room.

"I'd forgotten," she said softly.

"What?"

"How . . . tuned in you are. If you'd ever worked the other side of the street—"

"I'm working it now."

"That's what you say."

"Behavior is the truth," I told her. "We all live by that. Come up with another explanation for what I'm doing," I challenged her. "I can't be working for the killer, helping to cover his tracks. According to you, there aren't even any tracks to cover."

"You're working for gangsters."

"I didn't say I turned citizen," I said. "What I said was the truth—my job is to find whoever did it. And that's what I'm doing. It's a job a citizen *could* do, right?"

"Sure," she said.

"You believe me," I told her, sure of myself.

"Why do you say that?"

"You wouldn't have gotten me that info if you didn't."

"I'm in business."

"Bullshit. I know what you do for a living. And I know where your lines are."

"You're so certain?"

"Yeah."

I felt her gunfighter's eyes measuring me, waited for the judgment.

"She was just a kid," Wolfe finally said. "I wouldn't mind helping out anyone hunting whoever did it."

"More than one?" I asked her, not pressing the personal.

"Come again?"

"Edged weapons leave tracks, just like bullets. If more than one knife was used . . ."

"That's only true if they were used at the same time."

"And . . . ?"

"The TPO is very shaky, you know that much already."

I nodded. Time and Place of Occurrence is never more than a guess when the body isn't discovered at the original scene. "It would still help to know if there was more than one blade. Not likely two freaks would go off at the same time."

"Ask Bianchi and Buono," she said, in her diamond-cutting prosecutor's voice.

"The Hillside Stranglings weren't spontaneous," I told her. "Those two maggots had spent a lot of time together, mixing their juices, before they blended into a sex-kill unit. Felonious gestalt. Like Leopold and Loeb."

"Could have been the same thing here," Wolfe said, stubbornly. "There isn't enough information to even guess from."

"Sure," I said, trying to maneuver her back to where I needed her to be. "Let's work with what we have."

Wolfe leaned back a little, cast her eyes up as if the grungy basement ceiling had some answers. "The victim was stabbed *and* slashed," she said. "The same weapon could have inflicted all the wounds, if it was configured that way. Or it could have been more than one."

"Defensives?"

"No."

"No?"

"Her hands were clean. Wrists, too. Maybe the first thrust brought her down . . . ? I hope so."

I didn't say anything, the silence between us ugly with the thought we shared. Sure, it would be better if the first plunge had been right into her heart, so she wouldn't have died in pain and terror. But if Vonni had even so much as scratched one of them, maybe there'd have been some DNA under her fingernails.

"You see anything in the county-line thing?" I asked her.

"Oh, yes," she said, the deep contempt acid in her mouth. "There's jurisdictions known to be soft spots. A DA in charge who cares so much about a perfect conviction rate that he won't move on anything less than a signed confession.

"Rapists read the papers, especially when they're Inside, marinating in their own hate. For the child molesters, all the more so. Especially the 'boy lovers'—they've got a real underground wire, pass along information like they do photographs.

"What any freak's really looking for, with soft prosecutors, is a deal. You get a DA who's afraid of taking a case to trial, you can get him to give away the courthouse." She pulled on her cigarette, let the smoke float out her nose, ground out the butt on the side of the file cabinet, dropped it on the floor. "But that's for sex crimes," she went on. "For this, I don't see the logic. Doesn't matter how spineless the DA is—homicide like this's a guaranteed life-top, no matter where you do it."

"So the cops don't have a clue . . . whether it was a panic-dump, or part of a plan?"

"They don't even know where it happened. It's not possible she was just hanging out in the place where they found the body. She had to have been *brought* there. But that could have been from any direction. Maybe right after it was done, maybe a week later—nothing points either way, so far."

"How early can they pinpoint her, on the day she disappeared?"

"They can't pinpoint her at all," Wolfe said. "She walked out of her house and that was *it*. Nobody saw her. Nobody talked to her on the phone, and she didn't leave any answering-machine messages, either. Nobody got an e-mail from her. She didn't page anyone. She didn't have a cell phone. No letter she mailed that date . . . or after . . . ever came to anyone. Plus, not a single sighting from the minute she walked out of her house until the body was found."

"*Somebody* was supposed to meet her. She was being picked up."

"That's what she told her mother, sure."

"It seems likely to me," I said. "She didn't have a car. And the bus service around there is lousy at that hour."

"It's not so much lousy as lightly used," Wolfe corrected me, rapidly leafing through the paper until she found the document she wanted. "The police were all over that the very next morning," she said, tapping the paper for emphasis. "The driver was emphatic—no one *close* to the girl's description got on during his route. And, yes," she said, anticipating me, "there were already passengers on the bus by the time it got to her stop." She gave me a level look, waiting. When I didn't speak, she said, "They checked every car service, too. It's not like here—cabs don't cruise, you have to call them."

Wolfe held out her pack of smokes to me. I took one, fired a wooden match, lit her up first. Neither of us said anything for a while.

"I don't like this as a random," I told her. "The girl told her mother she had an appointment. And plans for the whole day, deep into the night. But, unless one or more of them's lying, none of her friends knew anything about it."

"People lie."

"That's what all those years as a prosecutor taught you. Thing is, they also tell the truth. And if someone she knew *is* lying, then either they're the person she met, or they know who it is. Doesn't sound random to me."

"The liar could be the girl herself."

"I thought of that. Off on an adventure, and she didn't know the territory. Sure. But teenagers, they don't usually go on adventures by themselves. Runaways, yeah. But you didn't see a shred in all that stuff you brought about a reason for the kid to run, did you?"

"No. But that doesn't mean—"

"I know," I said. "The mother didn't have a boyfriend?"

"There's no evidence she even dated. Why are you so big on that one?"

"I was in a case once. Mother's boyfriend, a few years younger than her, he was going at the daughter for years, since the kid was about nine or ten. Girl gets to be thirteen, she disappears one night while the mother is at work. During a big snowstorm. Boyfriend said he had a few beers watching TV, fell asleep, never saw her leave. They find the kid's body in a vacant lot, day or so later. The same snow that covered the kid covered whatever tracks there might have been.

"The cops find the girl's diary in her school locker. She thought she was having an 'affair' with the boyfriend. They were going to get married as soon as she became of age. She didn't want to wait."

"What did the boyfriend get?" she asked, eyes cold.

"Get? He never got *arrested*. They questioned him, but he was smart. Kept it very simple. Didn't admit anything. He had a prior—exact same MO, but no homicide. And he knew they couldn't even make out the stat rape without his confession, much less a killing, so he lawyered up immediately. Forensics were useless; they *had* lived in the same house."

"This isn't anything like that."

"Okay."

"You don't sound so sure."

"I'm sure the mother wasn't hiding a boyfriend in the basement, yeah. But it could have been a similar scenario . . . one of her teachers, maybe."

"Maybe. Whatever happened to that . . . case you had?"

"I told you, he never even got arrested."

"So that filthy freak and the girl's mother lived happily ever after?"

"Far as I know," I lied.

"Giovanni Antrelli has three arrests," Wolfe said, a half-hour later. "None in the past fifteen years. No convictions. He's a family man; this you knew, of course. If he were a doctor, he'd be a general practitioner. Gambling, loan sharking, bust-out schemes, labor racketeering. Supposed to be a real comer. Word is, he reports to a capo but he's actually a higher rank himself. Which means the old men have big plans for him, down the line."

"He's never been Inside?"

"In the Tombs, overnight, maybe. Or on Rikers for a week, at most. The charges were always dismissed. The court records don't say why, but I don't think we have to waste a lot of speculation on it. I guess the bosses *always* thought highly of him."

"Anything about him trafficking?"

"Funny you should ask," she said, twisting her mouth as she spoke. "His rep is, he wouldn't *touch* drugs. Too risky, he says. And the time is so high, a bust could make anyone in the chain roll over. In fact," she went on, watching me closely, "the feds *did* make a little probe of their own, a couple of years ago."

"What do you mean?" I asked.

"It was almost comical," she said. "They popped some moke with serious weight, turned him right at the scene. What they wanted was what they always want: the man at the top. A headline-size fish. But what they got was this genius running around trying to make *new* cases for them. He was wired when he approached Antrelli—on his own, the memo says—and tried to get him to go into business."

"And you think Giovanni made him?'"

"I didn't hear the tape," Wolfe said. "Just read the transcript. What Antrelli told him was, and I quote, 'Drugs isn't a game for white men. Let the spear-chuckers and the banana brains have it. The money never sticks to their hands, anyway. We always get it back from them, one way or the other.'"

"The guy the feds have, is he still under?"

"That's not part of our deal," she said, no-argument cold. "You want to protect your pal Giovanni, hire on as a bodyguard."

"I wasn't looking to . . . Never mind."

"Right. Now, Felix Encarnación, this one is another story entirely. He's never been arrested in America, but Interpol has him on file as an assassin for a Colombian cartel. Supposed to have done a half-dozen *very* professional jobs, two of them in Europe."

"Supposed to . . . ?"

"All of this was a long time ago. He was held—I wouldn't say 'arrested,' not with the system they have there—in Peru a while back. Held for about two years, until he was released. Ransomed out, that's what I'm told."

"By the Colombians?"

"Could be. Nobody's sure. Encarnación himself's not Colombian. Or Peruvian, either. Guatemala is what the money's on, but even that's just an educated guess."

"Then we know two things about him for sure," I said. "He can do *very* hard time and not give anyone up. So he's got a lot of trust going for him. And a sure pipeline to pure."

"Yeah. The rest is all gossip-level. Antrelli's supposed to have *no* temper. Pure ice. Never loses control. An old man's head, that's what they say about him."

"And Felix?"

"What they say is, he can never go back down south. And that, to him, a gun's like a hammer to a carpenter."

I spent the next three days in my place, sifting and straining the information in Wolfe's paper through every filter I had, adding to my charts until I could see bits and pieces of Vonni's life in every room.

When I ran dry, I went out to see what I could find of her death.

I started where they'd discovered the corpse. A culvert off an unpaved lane in the swampland between Jamaica Bay and JFK Airport. I could feel the hackles that must have gone up on Giovanni's neck when he'd first been told. The area's a big favorite of mob guys who have a recurring need for unmarked graves.

As I slowed to a stop, my shoulders tightened and my nostrils flared, taking the pulse of the place. It was way too long after the murder for the cops still to be staking out the dumping ground; but I'm an old dog, and sniffing for danger is an old habit.

Her body had been found wrapped in heavy plastic sheeting, secured with baling wire. "Like a slab of meat, ready for the freezer," one cop's notes had said.

You'd think that would rule out a Lovers Lane encounter that had gone wrong. What kind of man carries plastic sheeting and baling wire in his trunk?

I knew the answer to that question, so I spent an hour criss-crossing the area. But there was nothing resembling a regular spot for car sex. About the only dry land was where the body had been dropped off.

Dropped off, not buried. That meant something. Maybe the killer was in a hurry.

Or maybe he was a psycho, making a statement. Those kind never write their messages in invisible ink.

One look around was enough to show me that the site was outside New York's special two-tier recycling system. You want to get rid of something in Manhattan, you just leave it out at the curb. It doesn't matter if the Sanitation Department takes a pass. Between the scrap-metal scavengers, the flea-market restockers, and the homeless guys pushing their pirated shopping carts, nothing worth a nickel survives.

But, out there, all I could see was dregs nobody would touch, anywhere—a few empty forty-ounce malt liquors, a couple of screw-top wine bottles, a slab of tread from a truck tire, one aluminum leg from a kitchen chair, a crushed pack of Newports, strewn condoms, a torn potato-chip bag. . . .

I knew the condoms were recent—they would have been the first thing bagged and tagged by the forensics crew if they'd been there when the body had been discovered.

It was a pretty good spot for people who were too crazy, or too smart, for the homeless shelters. Close enough to the airport to make Dumpster-diving productive, with plenty of natural cover to keep you through the weather with the help of a few artfully rigged plastic garbage bags. The cops would have scoured the area. Not just for traces of the killer's vehicle, but for any signs of campfires, lean-tos, cans of food . . . anything to show people were living out there. In the jungle, the birds see everything. Getting them to sing on cue, that's the tricky part.

Nothing in Wolfe's paper showed they had found anyone to talk to, but that didn't mean nobody had been around at the time the killer had dropped off his garbage. If anyone from a homeless camp had seen a body being dumped, they would have just nomaded on out of there, quick.

But if the area was inviting enough, maybe some of the old residents would have drifted back over the past few months. . . . At least that's what I was hoping for.

It turned out like most of my hopes.

In books, the detective stands at the spot where the victim was killed and makes a promise to her—seems like it's always a woman—that he'll find the murderer.

I didn't feel anything. And I didn't make any promises.

"I know street kids," I told Michelle. "I know where they go, even *why* they go. I can tell the weekenders from the permanents. I know where they shelter up when they have to. They're like a . . . species, I guess. There's a food chain, predators and prey. They've got their own look. Their own mating habits, their own survival systems. I can always find some of them, tap into their communications."

Michelle touched one perfect cheek with a long, red-lacquered nail, saying nothing. She'd never seen her son Terry before the night I'd finessed him off a kiddie pimp in Times Square. But she'd adopted the kid in less time than it would take a sperm to merge with an egg. Terry had never seen the pimp again.

I had.

"Some things never change, girl. You drop a dope fiend into a strange city, how long's it going to take him to find a slinger? It's like that for me with runaways. I was one of them once. It's easy—*too* fucking easy, sometimes—for me to put myself right back there, in my mind."

"But . . . ?"

"But there's no street kids in that town where she came from. I mean, there's probably the equivalent of some kind, but they're not *on* the streets, see?"

"They're all in cars?"

"No. That's not it. Sure, out there, the cars are the drivers—everyone's social status rolls on wheels. But that's got nothing to do with what I mean."

"Small towns . . ."

"It's not the size, honey. I've been in little towns that make Vegas look like Amish country."

"*Border* towns, I know. But when there's money . . ."

"Not that, either. There's lots of ways to join the street-kid army, but they're not all draftees. Where you come from doesn't matter so much as why you're there . . . and what you're willing to do to hold your place. Plenty of kids of rich families are eating out of garbage cans and selling their bodies."

"My bio-parents had money," Michelle said, saying it all.

"You see where I'm going with this, then. The kids I *could* connect with, they're not still in that town. They're here. Or out on the coast. What difference? It's all the same place."

"I know, baby," she said. "You know I do."

"But even if there's any runaways from Vonni's town here, I couldn't find them," I told her.

"Her mother, she'd know the girl's closest friends, right?"

"Yeah, I think she would. I know when there's secrets, and I didn't smell any in that house. But I guess I *could* try just asking her, if . . ."

"If what?"

"If I can't figure out a way to bring them to me."

"Her friends?"

"Not just them, Michelle. The whole . . . environment."

"The police . . ."

"They've been over the ground, sure. But they don't know how to take soil samples the way we do."

"You have any ideas?"

"Not yet, I don't. I've been . . . studying them from a distance, I guess you could say. The mother gave me one place I think I could try."

"A hangout?"

"No. A woman. Vonni used to babysit her kid."

"What makes you think she knows anything?"

"Not her. The kid. The way I read Vonni's mother, no way she'd let her daughter have boys over without supervision. But when the girl was babysitting . . ."

"Kids don't miss much," Michelle said, agreeing

"**H**azel said you'd be calling," the woman said.

"Yes, ma'am. Then you know what my job is. Would you be willing to talk to me?"

"If you think it will do any good . . ."

"There's no way to tell without trying," I said. "Okay?"

The house was quite a bit downstream the status river from where Vonni had lived—a small, squarish tract house, squatting undistinguished in a tight cluster of identical boxes. The front lawn was a crabgrass-and-dandelion postage stamp. The sidewalk was cracked. A clapped-out once-blue Monte Carlo was parked out front.

The woman who opened the door was sweet-faced, with a mop of tightly curled hair the color of fresh rust, and lively blue eyes. She was about six inches shorter than me, and ten pounds heavier, wearing a bright-yellow sweatshirt and jeans.

"Hi!" she said.

"Good afternoon, Mrs. McClellan."

"Oh, please! Call me Lottie. Everybody does," she said, stepping aside to let me in.

"Is the kitchen all right?" she asked, seeing me hesitate.

"It's fine," I told her. "I just didn't want to barge in. . . ."

"Your mother raised you right," she said.

"Yes, ma'am," I said, maintaining the myth.

"Lottie," she reminded me, pointing to a kitchen table with a pink Formica top.

"Burke," I said, offering her a hand to shake.

"Irish! I'll bet we're cousins, somewhere back on the Emerald Isle."

"Scotch, actually," I told her, straight-faced.

"Ah, well. I'm not clannish. You may be Scotch, but I'll bet you fancy an Irish coffee now and then," she said, the smile so at home on her face that I knew it was a permanent resident.

"I do, that's a fact," I lied. "But never while I'm working."

"Well, suit yourself. And tell me how I can help you."

"Mrs. Greene called you . . . ?"

"She did. And I promised I'd tell you anything you want to know. So fire away."

"You understand what I'm trying to—"

"You're trying to catch whoever did it. Hazel told me."

"That's right. So if some of the questions I ask seem—"

"I'm not one who believes you can harm the dead. Let's get on with it."

"Vonni was your babysitter?"

"Sure was. And the best I've ever had. She was never late; never minded *staying* late, even if I only called to tell her at the last minute. She never went into the liquor cabinet, never had boys over—"

"I'm sorry to interrupt, but how would you know that for sure?"

"That she didn't have boys over?"

"Yes."

"The houses around here, they're not exactly estates. You probably saw that for yourself, driving over. Now, my neighbors on the right," she said, pointing in that direction, "the Feinbergs, they're experts at minding their own business. But on the left, Mrs. North, she's an expert at minding mine."

"And she'd notice if—"

"She'd notice if a new butterfly landed on a bush, never mind a young man coming around when I wasn't home. She'd be over here in a flash, that poison tongue of hers ready for work, I promise you that."

"But she's not home all the time, is she?"

"Isn't she? The woman's in a wheelchair. Never goes out, except to the doctor, to hear her tell it. Her husband's not home much, I give you that. Poor man. Between working two jobs and listening to her rant, he'd probably rather put in a third shift if he could."

"If she's in a wheelchair, how would she get . . . Or do you mean she'd call you on the phone?"

"I mean exactly what I say," Lottie said. "That husband of hers built her a ramp and a little runway. Right up to my back door, he did, without even asking. So, when I saw what he was doing, it was me who asked *him,* what did he think he was up to? And he says, well, Flo, that's the wife, he says Flo said she'd talked it over with me and that's what we *both* wanted. He was all ready to build *another* ramp so she could just roll right into my house."

"And you stopped him?"

"No," she chuckled, "I sure didn't. I took pity on the poor soul. I didn't want him to have to go back and tell that harridan she wasn't getting her little 'access road.' Ever since, whenever Flo's got anything to report, you can be sure she does it in person."

"She's got the area under surveillance, huh?"

"That's the right word," she said, laughing. "Most of the time she comes over here, it's to give me the lowdown on the rest of our neighbors. I suspect her of having binoculars, but I've never caught her at it."

"Your own Neighborhood Watch."

"Don't think for a second she isn't. And I won't pretend it isn't kind of a comfort, sometimes."

"How old is your baby?"

"Baby? Oh, you mean my son. He's no baby. But he's not big enough to be left on his own. He's only ten. And got himself some bad asthma, besides. So he wants watching."

She stood up, went over to the cabinets, moved enough stuff around to let me know she wasn't going to force me into a stare-down when she said whatever was coming next. "The reason I need a babysitter so much is, I've got a boyfriend. His name's Lewis, and he's a wonderful, gentle man. But Hugh never took to him, because of his father, so I can't really spend much time with Lewis here. And certainly not at night . . ."

"Did Hugh get along with Vonni?" I asked, before she went driving down her own road.

"Get along? He *adored* her. Told me a thousand times he was going to marry her when he got big enough. He's got a real contrary streak in him—gets it from his mother—but he minded Vonni like she was an angel from heaven. Now I guess she is. . . ."

I never know what to say to a woman who's crying, even when it's not me who made her cry. I reached over and took her hand, letting it run its course.

It took her less than a minute to get back in control. "That's the Irish blood for you. If there's one thing we know from the cradle, it's how to grieve. Nobody really dies if they're still being mourned."

"That's true," I said.

"You know that for a fact, don't you?"

"Yeah."

"That tattoo on your right hand. A hollow heart. That's for someone who's gone? Someone you loved?"

"Yes."

"Ah, I'll bet *that's* a story."

"Not one it comforts me to tell," I said. "What do you think about me speaking with your son?"

"You might not be thanking me in a little while, but, sure," she said. "He's right out back."

T he yard was mostly dirt, with a few patches of burnt grass and one wiry little tree. I admired that tree. I don't know anything about horticulture, but I know tough when I see it.

A little boy was sitting on a wooden milk crate, in the middle of a meager patch of shade the tree had wrestled from the sun. As we walked toward him, I saw he was talking earnestly to a short, blunt-bodied, mostly black dog.

"Hugh, this is my friend Burke," his mother said. "He wants a word with you."

The kid looked up at me, his left hand resting on the dog's head. "What about?"

"About Vonni, son," she said gently.

"I knew you'd come," the kid said.

I squatted down, held out my hand to shake. "I'm pleased to meet you," I told him.

He shook, gravely, not speaking.

"That's a great-looking animal you have."

"He's the best dog."

"I can see he's all class. What's his name?"

"The Brains of the Outfit."

"Uh, okay. What do you call him?"

"The Brains of the Outfit," the boy said, the way you explain the obvious to the dull-witted.

"Don't pay any attention to him, Burke," Lottie said. "Hugh loves those old gangster movies."

"What did you mean before," I asked him, "when you said you knew I'd come? Did Vonni's mother—?"

"She was killed, right?" he said, his voice hard against the pain.

"Yes, she was."

"And they never caught the guy."

"The police—"

"Those coppers couldn't find their—"

"Hugh! You watch your mouth," his mother cautioned.

"Yeah, yeah, okay. But, Mom, I know who he is."

"You know who Burke is, son? Is that what you mean?"

"I know who he *really* is," the kid said, utterly certain, letting his eyes travel over my face. "You've been in the Big House, right?"

"A long time ago," I said, trusting whatever kept me from a glib lie.

"Nah. Not so long ago. I know."

"How would you know something like that?" I asked him.

"I told you. I know who you are."

"Okay," I said. "Who am I?"

"You're Vonni's father," he said, stone-sure. "And you came for payback."

"**V**onni told me," he said, later, seated at the kitchen table, having some cookies and milk. The Brains of the Outfit was getting a disproportionate share of the cookies, but if Lottie noticed, she kept it to herself.

"Told you what?" I asked, staying near the edges.

"She was the same as me," the kid said proudly. "See, her dad was *supposed* to be dead. Like my dad. Only thing is, they *weren't,* not really."

Lottie got up, walked behind the boy, caught my eye, shook her head sadly.

"Her father was in prison. He probably could of gotten out by now, but he wouldn't rat on his partners. Vonni, she wouldn't care. But her mother," he said vehemently, his pale-blue eyes challenging, "*she* didn't want anyone to know, so they had to tell everybody he was dead, see?"

"How do you know that?" I asked, keeping my voice soft and reasonable.

"Well . . . maybe I don't *know*. Not for sure. About Vonni's dad. But I know *mine* isn't dead." He turned his head, looked at Lottie. "Is he, Mom?"

"They say he is, honey. You know that."

"But they don't know for *sure,* right?"

"Sweetheart, if your father was alive, he would have made contact. . . ."

"Nah. He can't do that. He knows they're watching. He's too smart for them, that's all."

I put it together in my head, asked, "Your father, he escaped from prison?"

"Yeah!" the kid said triumphantly. "See, Mom? Burke knows the score."

Later that night, alone in the rented house, I thought about the only score I really knew. Scores I'd made, scores I'd settled.

Fathers and daughters.

A long time ago, when I was just getting started, I had a father get word to me he'd pay serious cash if I turned up his daughter. He was a referral, from a guy I'd known Inside. Told me he didn't just want me to find his kid; he wanted me to make sure nobody else ever did. He never actually said the words, but his meaning was clear enough.

I took his money, a lot more than a simple locate job would ever be worth. Found the girl, too. It was easy enough—she was still doing what Daddy taught her, only now she was getting paid for it. By the time I showed up, she knew The Life was a lot uglier than the pimp's pretty pictures, and she came along with me willingly enough, once I convinced her that I wouldn't bring her home.

The pimp was even easier to convince. Gunshot wounds are real conversation-stoppers.

It should have ended there, except that the father got stupid. He found me in this Master Race bar where I was trolling for chumps, told me he wanted his money back—I hadn't done what he'd paid me for. I played dumb, said I'd done the job, found her, like he'd wanted. Didn't know what he was talking about. My voice was soft, and that gave him a bully's courage. He got right in my face, loud.

Too loud—that dive had more white rats in it than a cancer lab. A couple of days later, the rollers had me.

The way they broke it down, I had two choices—I could testify the father hired me to hit his daughter, or I could take a fall myself, for the unregistered piece they'd found when they'd snatched me.

Neither of the detectives said a word about running the ballistics on the slug the ER had dug out of a known pimp a little while back, but it hung in the stale air of the interrogation cell. A heavy hammer, waiting to drop.

Two very bad choices. Ex-felon, carrying, loaded-operable-concealed, I was looking at another trip Upstate. But testifying? That'd be worse. A snitch jacket would make it impossible to do time—that's the way it was back then. Besides, in my business, a rep for helping out the cops was the same as a vow of poverty.

When a man sets things up so the only way you survive is if he gets dead, he's just written a suicide note.

The whisper-stream tells a lot of stories. Ones like that are what got me this job.

"**H**is father . . . my husband, he's a hero to the boy," Lottie told me, later. "In Hugh's mind, Shane was a big-time gangster, some kind of Jimmy Cagney or Humphrey Bogart. The fact is, Shane was just a wild young man. Him and those friends of his. I was pregnant with Hugh, and we were broke. It was just that simple.

Shane was just that simple. My fool of a husband listened to his bigger fool of a friend, Davey Boy. I've no idea what they tried to rob. All I know is it was down in Florida. Nobody was killed. Or even shot. It was the first offense for both of them. But they still got so much time. . . .

"It wasn't even a year later when they just took off, running. Five of them. No plan, naturally—Shane never planned anything in his life. They made it to the edge of some damn swamp, him and Davey Boy, still together, when the posse caught up with them. They didn't have any weapons, but they wouldn't surrender—that's what the police said, anyway, later—so they opened fire. Davey Boy died right there. They said Shane was hit, too— he had to have been—but they never found his body.

"That was a long time ago. Nobody's ever heard a word since. In that swamp, there's a million things that could . . . dispose of a body. But Hugh, he is Shane's son, no doubt about that. Hugh is mortally certain his father's alive. Out there, somewhere. That's why poor Lewis never had a chance with him. How can you compete with a little boy's dreams?"

"You don't think there's any chance he's—?"

"No. Because Hugh's wrong about one thing, Burke. If my fool Shane was alive, he'd have come for me by now, even if a squad car was parked in the driveway."

We sat out on the back step, next to the ramp Flo's long-suffering husband had built, Lottie smoking, me pretending to, watching Hugh and The Brains of the Outfit deep in consultation under the scrawny tree.

"Did you know about Vonni saying her father was alive?" I asked her.

"*She* never said that, Burke. What she did, she went along with Hugh. My son wanted Vonni for a big sister. He's not old enough to say those words, not yet, but he can feel the feelings. So he gave them a kinship. It was his gift to her.

"He's the kind of kid, he thinks if you're true-faithful, if you wish hard enough, long enough, you can change things. So, little by little, this story of Vonni's father being alive came out of *his* mouth.

"And Vonni, may the Lord always love her, she was such a treasure, she never broke his dream. Their secret, it was supposed to be. But you saw for yourself: my Hugh, he can't keep a secret. Just like his father, the fool," she said, eyes wet.

"Maybe it's only his own secrets he can't keep."

"What are you getting at?"

"If Vonni confided in him . . ."

"Sure! He'd *never* tell. You're right, Burke. Hugh would consider that ratting her out."

"But if he thought he was talking to Vonni's father . . ."

Lottie took a long, deep drag on her smoke, closed her eyes as she exhaled. "This business about Shane being alive? I took him to a counselor. She told me that Hugh couldn't grieve for his dad until he acknowledged that he was dead. It wasn't good for him to keep believing Shane is alive, is what she told me."

"And if I *was* Vonni's father, that would . . ."

"Yeah. That would absolutely convince him that he's right."

"And you don't want that?"

"I don't. I'm not going to force my son to say his father's dead, no matter what some counselor says. But I'm not going to encourage him, either. He'll face it, someday. Not for a while, maybe. But he will, I know." She took another drag, ground out her cigarette. "And he'll have pain enough then," she said.

"Y̶ou and me, we've got to talk," I said to the boy that night. He was pretty well exhausted—dinner at Adventureland over in Melville, with a couple of hours in their endless arcade for dessert; a stop at Dairy Queen for a supplement, followed by three rounds of miniature golf in Deer Park. All with The Brains of the Outfit waiting patiently in the back seat of my Plymouth, sustained by what he apparently believed was his rightful share of every score in the food department.

The miniature golf had surprised me. After the arcade, I'd asked the kid what he wanted to do, expecting a crime movie or maybe even one of those paintball parlors, but he never hesitated.

And he was really good at it, too. Clearly disdaining any competition from me or his mother, the kid attacked par like it was his mortal enemy.

"Has he ever played real golf?" I asked Lottie, as the kid walked the course toward some through-the-windmill hole.

"No, he's not. Well, a man I was dating once took us to the driving range, but all he wanted to do was show off. Hugh never actually got a chance."

And neither did that moron, I thought. "Does he like it, though?" I asked her.

"How would I know, then?"

"Well, I . . . Does he watch it on television?"

"Golf?" she said incredulously.

"Okay. Uh . . . does he know anything about the game? The various clubs and stuff?"

"I . . . never asked him, to be honest. It's not like I'm going to take him to the country club."

"You can call him Boo," the kid told me a couple of days later. "Just not in front of people."

"Short for 'Brains of the Outfit,' right?"

"Right," he said out of the side of his mouth, giving me a wink.

"I'm with you," I told the kid, holding out an open palm.

He gave me a grave look, nodded, put his little fist in my hand. I squeezed it to seal our deal.

"I've got a budget for this one," I told Lottie, after the kid was asleep.

"What does that mean?"

"It means I'm expected to spend money. Spread it around. That's what you do when you're looking for information."

"I don't know anyone who could—"

"Me, either," I told her. "But if I don't spend the money, the people who hired me will think I'm not working."

"You could just lie to them."

"I'm not a liar," I lied, putting five hundred dollars in fifties on the kitchen table.

"You know what I'm up to, right?"

"Right," the kid said.

"And you're with me, right?"

"All the way, pal."

"Here's the deal, then, Ace. If Vonni told you secrets, it's not ratting for you to tell me. We're on the same team."

"Why'd you call me that?"

"What?"

"Ace."

"Oh. Well, it just fit, somehow. I mean, we've all got citizen names, like 'Hugh,' okay? But we also got *insider* names. Like 'Boo,' see? And if we're going to be working together, you need an insider name."

He was thoughtful for a minute. "Boo likes it," he said, finally. "I do, too."

"That's it, then."

"What's yours?"

"My . . . ?"

"Burke is your citizen name, right?"

"That's right," I said. "Actually, it's my middle name. My insider name, that's B.B."

"My mom has a friend. Bernice. They call her BeeBee."

"This is different," I assured him. "B.B. is initials."

"What's it stand for?"

"Big Boy," I told him, winking to make sure he kept *that* one between us.

"What kind of secrets?" the kid asked.

"It doesn't matter," I told him. "Anything about Vonni that the cops don't *know,* that's one place they didn't *look,* see?"

"Yeah . . ."

"So, if she had a boyfriend the cops didn't know about . . . ?"

"Nah. I mean, she had plenty of guys like her," he said, instantly loyal. "She was real pretty. But none of them was a secret."

"Any of them ever come around when she was ba . . . staying with you?"

"Nope."

"You sure?"

"Sure I'm sure."

"But if you were asleep . . . ?"

"Nobody'd ever get past Boo," the kid said confidently.

"I'm breaking every rule in the book," Lottie said.

"I know."

"You know? How could you know? You have any kids?"

"No."

"Never?" she asked, leaning forward, elbows on knees. "Never been married, either?"

"No."

"You're not gay. So you must have had girlfriends. And you're not exactly a teenager, so that's a lot of years for you to have been—"

"How do you know?"

"How old you are? I don't. But either you'll never see forty again, or you've had a *real* hard life."

"Not that. How do you know I'm not gay?"

"Don't be silly," she said. "Anyway, you think *that's* what I'd be worried about, you taking Hugh off to God-knows-where in the middle of the night? That's a load of crap."

"I'm not following—"

"That gay men are dangerous to little boys, *that* crap. The ones who . . . do things to children, what do you call them, pedophiles? They're not gay, they're . . ."

"Freaks," I finished for her.

"Yes! That's exactly what they are. They should be—"

"It sounds like you had to deal with . . . something about that."

"Oh, I *dealt* with it, all right," she said, snorting. "Some prissy-minded, so-called 'Christians' decided one of the teachers at Hugh's school was gay. And they drew up this petition to get him fired."

"Because he was a danger to the children?"

"See, that's what *I* thought, at first. I mean, I didn't know anything about it. But if it has to do with my son, you can bet I was going to find out. What it turned out to be was that these people just don't like homosexuals. They claim the Bible says they should all be killed. It wasn't about gay schoolteachers; they hate them *all*. This was just a convenient excuse."

"What happened?"

"Well . . . nothing, I guess. They picketed a little bit, and they sent some nasty letters, but Mr. Strethlend kept his job. In the end, all they did was, they took their own kids out of school."

"Freaks."

"They are. I was just telling—"

"No. I mean, that's the word you were looking for, before. 'Pedophile' is a fancy word, but it means how people feel, not what they do. People who go after kids, they're freaks. Understand?"

"Okay . . ."

"What's wrong, Lottie?"

"You just looked . . . scary, for a minute."

"Sorry."

"That's all right. Probably just a trick of the light."

"I don't know how to do it," the kid said.

"Neither do I, Ace."

"Then how am I going to—?"

"Well, I think you're supposed to walk around it a little bit, kind of get an idea of how it's laid out. Like you did before."

"Okay . . ." the kid said. He put the putter the pro in the golf shop had assured me was the right size for a kid his age and height over his shoulder and walked all around the perfectly manicured green with only the light from my flash to guide him. The Brains of the Outfit sat on his haunches, observing quietly.

"It kind of . . . slopes," the kid said. "Right here . . . See it?"

"Not me. It just looks like a little uphill, that's all."

"No, it's off to the left. You see how it sort of . . . rolls, I guess."

"If you say so."

The boy kept pacing, checking the terrain. Once he sighted down the length of his club.

"Ready to take a shot?" I finally asked him.

"Sure," he said, taking a stance over one of the three regulation balls I'd bought in that same shop. "Does this look right?"

"Ace, let me tell you, partner; I wouldn't have a clue. How does it feel?"

"Okay, I guess. It's hard to see with that flashlight."

"Just look at the pole."

The kid nodded, took a breath, let it out, and stroked the ball. It climbed the hill, banked to the left, and disappeared. The dog's ears perked up at a faint sound.

"What was that?" the kid asked.

"Let's go see."

The white ball sat at the bottom of the cup, like a pearl in an oyster.

"**A**h, was it really worth it, all that?" Lottie asked me, late that night.

"It wasn't so much. The club only cost—"

"Not the money, Burke. Breaking into the golf course in the middle of the night just so you could see if Hugh—"

"There's nothing to break into. It's just like a big field, with no fence."

"But it's still against the law."

"Probably. But it'd only be trespassing, not a burglary. And they never would have charged Hugh with anything."

"Yes, I understand that. But why couldn't you have taken him in the daytime?"

"Well, first of all, I'm not a member," I told her. Then I gave her a wink, switched to talking out of the side of my mouth, said, "Besides, this way it was a caper, see?"

The next time I came back, The Brains of the Outfit was wearing a red ribbon tied in a bow around his thick neck, thoughtfully chomping on a thick slab of what looked like raw steak.

"It's Boo's birthday," the kid informed me.

I piled them both in the Plymouth, and we hit the pet store. Found a truly outrageous leather collar with chrome studs, and half a dozen chew-toys.

The next morning, I found the two of them under the tree. The Brains of the Outfit was stretched out, nose to the ground, a mournful look on his face.

"He's sad," Hugh told me solemnly.

"Why?"

"Because of his birthday. He loves his birthdays. But that was yesterday, and it's over."

"Oh . . ."

"That's all right," the kid said, confidently. "I know what to do." He knelt next to his pal, scratched behind one ear. The way I used to do with my Pansy. "Don't be sad, Boo," he said softly. "It's *still* your birthday. Okay?"

The dog picked his head up and grinned.

T hat night, while I was talking to Lottie, the kid came into the living room, The Brains of the Outfit at his side.

"I want to tell you something," he said to me.

"Shoot."

The kid's face made it clear he wasn't going to talk in front of his mother. "Go back in your room, Hugh," she said. "Burke will be there in a minute."

When I went back, he and The Brains of the Outfit were in bed. I sat down on the edge.

"I don't know where Vonni was going, the day she . . . the day she didn't come back," he whispered. "But she told me it was going to be her big day."

"Her big day?"

"Yes. Vonni told me, when it was over, she was going to start being famous."

"W e're not going to see you again, are we?" Lottie asked, late that same night.

"I . . . I honestly don't know. It depends on . . . things I have no control over."

"Hugh really likes you."

"We're partners," I said.

"Don't partners see each other once in a while?"

"Some do. Some can't. He'll understand."

"Yeah," she said, with the first bitterness I'd ever heard in her voice. "Hugh's gotten real good at understanding."

"Lottie, could I . . . say something to you?"

"What?"

"Is Lewis really the guy?"

"He could be. But, with the way Hugh—"

"If Lewis wants it bad enough, there's one thing he could do."

"What are you talking about? He'd do *anything,* I know he would," she said. The "He'd fucking *better!*" subtext came across like a fire ax through old drywall.

"He needs to learn to play golf. He doesn't have to be any good, just good enough to take Hugh."

"You mean *real* golf? But how is Hugh going to learn himself? All he knows how to play is that—"

"He can take lessons. Lewis would have to bring him there. Maybe after school. Or on weekends. I guarantee Hugh would pick it up *fast*. The kid's a natural."

"Sure, and who's going to pay for—?"

"Maybe partners can't always be around," I told her, "but they can always back each other up."

"More of your 'budget,' I suppose?"

"No, Lottie," I said, "this is from me," reaching into my jacket. "I checked with the pro, where I bought the putter. It's enough for lessons for a year."

She got off the couch, faced me. "What happens after that?" she asked, hands on hips.

"By that time, they're going to be offering to teach him for nothing. And if they're not, here's a number you can call," I said, handing her a blank business card with the number of the pay phone at Mama's written on the back.

She just stared at it, shaking her head. "Christ."

"Yeah. Lottie, do me one more favor?"

"What's that?"

"Tell Lewis, when he's studying golf, be sure to find out what they call a hole-in-one."

When you're tracking, you always start the same way—with all the information you can put together stacked up like chips in front of you. That never changes. Even if the guy you're looking for suddenly calls you up, tells you to come right on over, you'd *still* want some information before you anted up. Because he could be anything from a macho moron to a pro holding a full house.

Information is a product. You can buy it, trick someone out of it, extort it. Muscle it over to your side of the table . . . even dig for it yourself. But there's no *Consumer Reports* for the product. You *don't* always get what you pay for. You have to put it together, piece by piece, always testing the next chunk against what you've got so far. One little flaw in the logic chain, and the gun doesn't fire. Or it blows up in your hand.

If Vonni didn't know her own killer, that meant he was either a roving freak or a professional. The fact that it didn't *look* like a pro hit didn't convince me. Sometimes, disguising the look is part of what the buyer pays for. You hire someone to kill your wife, you don't want a double-tap with a small-caliber piece at close range. You want what looks like she surprised a junkie burglar in her bedroom. Or ran into a rapist who didn't want to leave a witness.

But it didn't *feel* pro to me. The trick with murder-for-money is not to get too cute. That many stab wounds; wrapping the body they way they'd done; dumping it where they did—everything made it look *too* unplanned.

I know the sex-killers. A festering blob of poison inside them, pulsing against a fragile sac. When the membrane pops, the poison turns tsunami—wave after wave, crashing and crushing everything in its path. They go out into the night then, wrapping themselves in the darkness for power. Prowling relentlessly. Driving in figure-eight loops, driven. A jagged dissonance in their fevered brains, synapses misfiring on sex-hate cues. Building and screaming and calling until they spot her. The right one.

They know what to do then.

When they're close, when they're about to strike, their heartbeat slows, their pulse drops. They breathe light and smooth.

Their hands stop trembling. Even the sheen of sweat whisks off their skin. Coming home.

That's why dope fiends call it a "fix." It fixes things. Until the next time. When you need a little more. Or need it a little more often . . .

There's something else about them, too. All of them. The second they finish, a new wave hits. Run-hide terror floods in, driving them, again. Ted Bundy littered the ground with the bodies he made. John Wayne Gacy kept his in the basement. They all have the same fears, the freaks. Not of their "demons." Of getting caught.

Different directors . . . but always the same script.

But what had been done with Vonni's corpse was a kind of *controlled* panic—somewhere between fleeing the scene and taking the body someplace to bury it. The way I saw it, only a person connected to her in some way would have gone to that much risk *after* the murder.

Or Giovanni was right.

Once in a while, everyone in town knows who committed a murder, but they all look the other way. Especially when the consensus is that the dead guy just plain needed killing. That wouldn't fly here—Vonni hadn't been the town bully.

Still, if it was personal, why hadn't the cops come up with anything? My first thought was that maybe it was one of their own, but I tossed that out quick. The blue wall crumpled a long time ago. Coast to coast, from Abner Louima to Rampart Division. Too many cops had worked Vonni's case, from too many jurisdictions, for it to have stood a coverup.

What I really needed was to do my own interviews. Not just with Vonni's friends; with her whole culture. I was about thirty years too old to go undercover. I had to make them to come to me.

"Look, let me try it this way," I said to them. Tired but not impatient. Never impatient. "Michelle, you've lived in the City all your life, right?"

"Not *all* my life," she said, edgy.

"Sure," I replied, wadding up my jailhouse blanket and tossing it over the barbed wire before I tried the fence again. "What I meant was, you make your life here. You know the place."

"Do I not?"

"You do. So—where's Main Street?"

"Little Korea," she said, promptly.

"Not in Flushing, girl. In the City."

"*Main* Street? In Manhattan?"

"Yep."

"There's no . . . Wait a minute; up in Inglewood somewhere?" she guessed.

"No. Prof?"

The little man rubbed his temple, as if to prod his mind into action. "Fuck if I know, bro," he finally said.

"Anybody?"

I let the silence hold for a second, then said, "It's on Roosevelt Island. The only way I found out, I had a job out there once. But you ask a thousand people in this city, cab drivers to panhandlers, they'll never have heard of it."

"Where you going, son?" the Prof asked.

"To the truth, Prof. Just because a man knows something, that doesn't make him smart. Watch a quiz show on TV sometime. One guy'll know the first seven kings of Egypt, how many years each one ruled, and where they're buried. But ask him who Tommy Hearns beat for his first welterweight title, and he'll draw a total blank."

"I understand," Clarence said. "Burke, you are saying it isn't that these kids would be so smart, smarter than us, even. Just that they know different things. I mean, things we don't."

"That's it. And it would take us a dozen years to learn what they take for granted. Our problem is to get them to tell us. And tell us quick."

"The Mole will know," Michelle insisted, after the others had left the restaurant.

"Mole? This isn't science, girl. It's . . . it's not the kind of thing the Mole does. What's he going to do, give me some truth serum?"

"Come on, baby," she said. "What do you have to lose? A couple of hours. Come on. I'll go with you."

"You just want a ride."

"And if I do?"

"So your theory is that they have some sort of . . . collective knowledge?"

"I don't think they all know—"

"Collective, not shared," the Mole said. "Not the same thing. Each molecule is complete by itself, but the interaction between them is what produces energy."

"I . . . So you're saying they may have the information but they don't know what they know?"

"I think that is what *you* are saying."

"Fine. But that doesn't get me any closer. I need to tap into them, somehow. It's not enough to be *around* them, I have to get them talking. Maybe about stuff they wouldn't usually talk about."

"If you want to stimulate a reaction from a disparate sampling, you need to isolate common ground."

"With kids? How in hell would we ever—?"

"I think I know," Terry said.

We all looked at him. Nobody spoke. He flushed, not used to the spotlight. But he squared up, said, "I'm in science, right?" nodding at the Mole. "But I'm not on another planet. On campus, I know maybe two or three kids who want to write books. And a half-dozen who write poetry, okay?

"But I must know a *hundred* who've already written screenplays. I was talking with a girl at school . . ." He caught Michelle's look, reddened even more deeply, but soldiered on. ". . . and you know what she said? 'Movies are *amazing*.' You see where I'm going?"

I shook my head "No." Michelle widened her eyes and clasped her hands, the universal girl-signal for "Keep talking." The Mole's face was a mask, as if he feared any expression would divert his son.

"*Movies* are amazing," Terry said. "Not any *particular* movie, just 'movies.' That such a thing could even exist. To this girl, whoever invented movies made a greater contribution to civilization than movable type."

"So what does one airhead have to do with—?"

"She's no airhead, Mom," Terry said. "I mean, well, maybe *she* is, but that . . . attitude, it's like, everyone has it. Religious. Movies, they're something . . . different from anything else. Some guys, they're fans of *bad* movies, and people think *that's* way cool.

"Kids blow off some kinds of movies. It's not, like, edgy to go for those Tom Hanks–Meg Ryan flicks. Extreme uncool. But it'd be like . . . heresy to put down movies themselves.

"And you know what else?" he said, sure of his ground now. "Everybody wants to be involved with them. It's not just the performing-arts crowd. Even the suit-and-tie kids, they want to *produce* movies . . . or own a studio, or whatever. The techie kids just love them. The stoners. The jocks. *Everyone*."

"See?" Michelle said, glowing at her son.

"**I**s it really you?" the tall, slim blonde asked, cocking her head like a dubious bird. Even that slight movement sent her improbably huge breasts quivering.

"It's him or his ghost," the shorter, muscular brunette said, through a mouth that looked like a soft bruise. "Who else would know about what happened to Gresh—?"

"Shut up, Rejji," the blonde snapped. "You want to tell the world, why don't you just take out an ad in the papers?"

"Oh, chill," the brunette replied. And "Come on in," to me.

I sat down on a canted-back couch, glanced over at the side table, located an ashtray, and lit a smoke. The Burke they knew smoked, and, where they came from, nobody ever broke a habit.

"You've got to give us more," the blonde said.

"Where've I heard *that* before?" the brunette mock-giggled.

"Rejji . . ."

"All *right*. Fine. I'll go gag myself."

"Bitch."

The brunette grinned, stuck out her tongue, and runway-walked out of the room.

"What do you want me to show you, Cyn?" I asked the blonde.

"I'm not . . . sure, exactly. Scars all look alike to me. But I know you . . . Burke . . . didn't have that tattoo on his hand."

"It's new," I said quietly. "Like my face. But I'm still me."

"Prove it," the blonde said, vainly trying to cross her arms over her chest. "I don't mean to sound . . . ungrateful, or anything. We both . . . Ah, never mind. Just prove you're who you say you are, and we'll do what you want."

"How do you know what I—?"

"What*ever* it is," she cut me off. "Maybe I don't know your face—the face you have—but I remember what you . . . what Burke did. So . . . ?"

"You and Rejji are in the—"

"Don't tell us about *us*. We already know about us."

"And you don't really know anything about me," I said. "So how am I supposed to . . . ?"

The blonde didn't say anything. The brunette came back into the living room, fastening a ball gag behind her head the way another woman might adjust a piece of jewelry. She dropped to her knees, pulled the red ball portion away from her mouth, looked up at me, said, "You like me in this shade?"

That's when the key to their lock dropped into my hand.

"Thanks, Rej," I said. I turned to the blonde. "The last time I was here, you told me I was so vanilla that, if I walked into a room and saw a woman all bound and gagged, the first thing I'd do would be to start looking around for the villain with the black hat and mustache."

"It's you," the blonde laughed, coming over to the couch. She bent down, kissed the side of my mouth.

"You're the closest thing to movie people I know," I said, after I told them how I wanted to go in.

"We don't do mainstream," Rejji said. "But . . . well, two things: One, we do what we do for money. So, if anyone paid us, we would; it's not some artistic thing. Two, movies are movies, I think. They make them all the same way. The budgets are different, maybe. The scripts are for damn *sure* different. But the process, I think it's close enough."

"So you think we could fake it?"

"Fake what?" Rejji asked. "Fake making an adult video? Why would anybody *fake* that? I mean, how could you tell? Maybe somebody watching it later, maybe *they* could tell. But when you're *making* the movie, you don't know how it's going to look. Only how it feels. Sometimes, if it's no good, not even that."

"These are *kids,* you stupid slut," Cyn said. "We put word out that we're shooting even softcore, that'd be the end."

"I don't want to look at . . . what did you call them, head shots?" I told them. "I need to *talk* with the . . . actors, I guess they'd be. Each one. Separately."

"Cyn gets asked all the time," Rej volunteered, "to do videos."

"Asked isn't the same as doing, bitch!" Cyn snapped at her.

"Uh, you think we could get back to *my* problem?" I asked them both.

"How about a joint?" Rejji said. "I always think better when I'm mellow."

"None for me," I told her.

"That's my Burke," Cyn said, giggling. She walked over and plopped herself in my lap. "Too bad Rej and I aren't black girls. At least we could make an Oreo out of you."

"Not me," Rejji said quickly.

"Oh, lighten up," Cyn said. "You're as bad as he is."

"You can't be a director," Cyn said, later. "I mean, sure, anyone with a camera can *say* he's one, but somebody could just look you up."

"They can't *all* be registered."

"I'll bet the big ones are, someplace. Anyway, you said you had to talk to the kids, right? Directors, they might talk to the *stars,* but not to whole mobs."

"Could I be a screenwriter?"

"When's the last time you went to a movie?" Rej sneered. "*Anybody* could be a screenwriter. They might hang around, trying to soak up 'ambience' or whatever—remember, Cyn, when that pathetic little dweeb spent all that time on our set 'cause he was writing some movie about *making* porno movies?—but it wouldn't work. You want these kids to give it up, right? Listen, they'll do anything—to anybody—if you whisper 'movies' at them. We saw that when we were out on the coast, virgins blowing Great Danes because some greaseball tells them that's the way Monroe got started. But they'd have to believe you could make it happen. And a screenwriter can't make *anything* happen."

"What if I was a—?"

"Casting director!" Cyn blurted out. "That is just awesomely perfect. Right, Rej? Nobody knows their names, and they may not get the final say, but they thin the herd. If you don't get past them, the director never gets to see your tape."

"You're a genius, Cyn," Rej said. "Makes me want to crawl over there and kiss your ass."

"Don't pay any attention to her, Burke," the blonde said. "This one's our ticket, I know it."

"**H**ow you going to know what a . . . what was that again, Schoolboy . . . a goddamn 'casting director' wears to work?"

"This isn't the post office, Prof," Michelle said tartly. "Everyone doesn't wear the same uniform."

"But I have to look like—"

"You don't have to look *like* anything, baby. Trust the Mistress of the Wardrobe. What you have to look is cool. Hip, edgy, with it—understand?"

"I . . . guess."

"Well, I can do it. All I need is—"

"I know," I said, reaching into my jacket.

"**A**m I right?" Giovanni asked me.

"Nothing I found so far makes it seem so," I said. "And I never thought you were, going in."

He looked through the windshield of the midnight-blue BMW sedan, as if the answer were somewhere offshore. Even at three in the morning, the Brooklyn waterfront is never completely deserted, but Giovanni was calm and relaxed. Maybe because Felix was sitting behind me, where I couldn't see him. Or maybe because of the two cars backed into acute angles from us, facing out. A burgundy Cadillac and a white Range Rover—one from each of their crews.

"But you haven't found anything that would make me wrong?"

"No."

"Even the cops didn't?"

"Not in anything I saw. And I saw pretty much everything there was."

"They think it was just some sex fiend?"

"It's hard to tell what they think, from only looking at paper. But they've got no candidate, so that's where they'd go, eventually."

"Why would they be incorrect?" Felix asked.

"I didn't say they would be," I answered him mildly, not turning around.

"But if they were?" he insisted, his voice sable-silky. I guessed it wasn't his mother who'd named him Felix.

"If it was someone the . . . If it was someone Vonni knew, that would make them wrong."

"Yes," he said patiently. "But *how* would they be wrong? *Where* would they be wrong?"

"They would be . . . if there was a relationship they didn't know about. Or one they misread."

"Such as . . . ?"

"Such as someone she was . . . involved with outside the law."

"What does that mean?" Giovanni, edgy.

"A married man, for example," I said. "I don't mean outside the law like adultery, nobody goes to jail for that. I mean outside the law because of Vonni's age."

"This happens," Felix said, neutral.

"Happens with schoolteachers," I said. "And coaches. And priests. And freaks who troll the Internet. And—"

"We get it," Giovanni said. "But, something like that going on, what's the chances of the cops missing it?"

"Dismal," I said, holding back the card the boy Hugh had given me. Vonni's "big day." When it was over, she'd start being famous. Her last meeting hadn't been a chance encounter. Couldn't have been. Because whoever it had been with had never come forward. "But always possible."

"Sherlock Holmes is dead," Giovanni said.

"I'm not saying it couldn't happen," I told them, "but the odds are way against it, especially in a homicide like this one. Front-page stuff, all kinds of personnel assigned—that's a bright, *hot* light to be under. They'd pull out all the stops. I was looking for an Exceptional Clearance note, but—"

"What is that?" Felix asked, still soft-voiced. He was either naturally calm or a natural killer. Or both.

"When the cops know who did it but they can't touch them," I told him. "Just not enough evidence to act."

"How could that be? The police do not seem to need . . . overwhelming evidence to make many of their arrests."

"Not for some of them," I agreed. "But Exceptional Clearance is just what it sounds like. It's no run-of-the-mill thing. The cops can 'clear' a case without making an arrest if they can show their superiors a certain person did the crime, and also that they don't have enough on him to make it stick in court. Sometimes they've got plenty of evidence but they can't *use* it. Something they found during a bad search, maybe. Or off an illegal wiretap.

"The thing is, with a homicide, they could feel it's better to wait. If they move too soon, force it to trial with shaky evidence, the killer beats the case, and they don't get a second chance. There's no statute of limitations on murder, so they don't lose anything by holding back. If the guy had accomplices, or even if he had partners on *other* jobs, if he's a gang member . . . You see where I'm going. They'll figure like you said before, everyone says they can take the weight, until they step on the scales."

"Loyalty is . . . unusual now," Felix agreed.

"You said you looked for this Clearance thing?" Giovanni said.

"I looked for it. And it's not there."

"You're sure?"

"I'm sure I didn't overlook it. And I'm sure that the paperwork I got was righteous. Stuff like that's got to be double-documented, everybody playing CYA all the way up the command chain. If it was there, it would have been on paper. And—you know what?—if they *had* a candidate, they'd have leaked it to the press by now, if only to get some of the heat off themselves. You know, the old 'umbrella of suspicion' routine."

"So either they missed one of these . . . relationships, or it was someone she didn't know—that sums it up?" Giovanni said.

"Yeah."

"And if it was someone she *didn't* know, the way the cops would have doped it out, they'd make it for a sex fiend, like we said before."

"Exactly. And that seems like it's where they ended up. There's no local suspect."

"You're sure?"

"I'm sure of this: They called in the FBI, looking for a profile of the killer. And they asked the feds for pattern work, too, to see if there were any similarities between the way this was done and other . . . ones. All around the country, going back a number of years. It could be that they were just going through the motions, covering themselves with paper. But I don't think so."

"Why?" Felix asked.

"The locals wouldn't go that far unless they were serious. And empty. This wasn't a ransom kidnapping. No evidence that she was taken across a state line. No reason for the *federales* to have jurisdiction. And that would be the way most local departments would want it. They *talk* cooperation, but they're always worried about credit-stealing, especially when the feds have better access to the national media. So, if the locals *asked* for help, that tells me they really wanted to crack it."

"The feds," Giovanni muttered, half to himself.

"Not *New York* feds," I reminded him. "And not DEA," I put in, for Felix.

"I know," Giovanni said. "But what do they have, for all this? Nothing. Not a single—candidate, you called him, right?—not a single candidate in Vonni's life. And no 'pattern' they can link to a serial killer or whatever. You said it was maybe more than one, don't forget. To me, it *still* looks like just what I said. A hit. A hit to send me a message."

"What do you want me to do?" I said.

"You got a plan, don't you, Burke?" he asked, more anxiety in his voice than he realized.

"It may not be much of one. . . ."

"Yeah. Me and Felix, we don't *know* you, know you, see what I'm saying? But we know *of* you. Of your 'brother,' anyway, okay? We asked around, people who know. You got a lot of rep. For different things. One of them is, you see a chance to open a money vein, you stick in a big damn needle. So, sure, you got a plan. Only it'll cost a lot of coin, try it out; am I right or wrong?"

"You're right. And all that means for sure is that the *plan* happens, not the result. I'm not making any promises."

"That's what a reputation is," Felix purred. "It makes the

promises for you. And you have more than one reputation, Burke. This kind of thing. A child. You have a reputation about such things."

"Oh, I want him, all right," I admitted.

"Whoever he is?" Giovanni asked.

I turned to hold his eyes. "If he was Christ on the fucking cross," I said.

When you're on the run, "safe sex" is the kind you pay for. When you go anywhere near women you know, what you *can't* know is if they're going to keep it to themselves. Maybe they grapevined into a reward-money rumor; maybe they've got a case on them—there's all kinds of reasons, and it never takes a good one.

But buying sex doesn't buy you loyalty, and hustlers are always hustling.

So the best bet is strangers.

I'm good at being a stranger. It comes naturally to me. I've got a drifter's mind, and I've been enough places so I can speak "not from around here" convincingly, even half a dozen blocks from wherever I live.

You have to pick middle-tier spots. Upscale joints attract ambitious women, and even the most self-absorbed of those ask enough questions to see if you're going to be a good investment. The other end of the road is landmined so deeply you'd have to step on one to know it's there. Roadhouse girls are some of the sweetest ever put on this earth, but you never know whose woman you just made a mistake with, until you hear the bottle break on the bar.

Turned out Long Island has a cottage industry in cheaters' bars, catering to the daytime trade, before husbands get home from work. They all seem within easy driving distance of a motel, too.

But, after the first three, I figured out it wasn't sex I'd been missing.

"Two G's for . . . this?"

"Quite a bargain, yes?" Michelle said, cat-grinning to show she was misunderstanding me deliberately. "Bally makes such beautiful things."

"It's just a leather jacket," I said.

"Oh, pul-leeze! *Feel* it."

"It's awful thin for so much—"

"That is how it's *supposed* to be, you dolt. This is *summer* leather. Soft as butter, isn't it?"

"I guess."

"Aren't the gussets behind the shoulder a perfect touch? And that color . . ."

"It's white."

"It is *not* white, you heathen; it's eggshell. White is the opposite of black."

"And this is all I need?"

"We're making a statement," Michelle said, total confidence. "You can wear any damn thing, a T-shirt and jeans for all I care, so long as you wear this jacket. And you wear it *casually,* please. Just toss it over the back of the nearest chair. Anybody who knows what to look for will know you're a man who's used to the best."

"These are going to be kids, Michelle. They'll be looking for Tommy Hilfiger or the Gap, right?"

"No, no, no, honey. If you were one of *them,* sure. But you're not. And not trying to be. You're a *movie* person. That's a deity to them. You don't take your cues from them; they take them from you. They may not recognize the brand but, trust me, girls know how to tell 'expensive' at a very young age."

"And the boys?"

"Boys never know anything," she said. "Now pay attention. We're not done. Just a couple of more touches. How do you like these boots?"

"They look okay, I guess," I said, holding a pair of plain black ankle-high lace-ups with a one-piece sole-and-heel.

"Those are Mephistos."

"What?"

"It's a brand name," she said, tolerating my ignorance with an effort. "This model is called the Naddo. Supposed to be the most comfortable shoes on earth."

"They look like upper-class Doc Martens."

"See? Even *you* can tell they're high-end."

"Yeah, all right," I surrendered. "What else?"

"You need some kind of jewelry. A ring or . . . a bracelet, maybe."

"I'm not buying any damn—"

"Oh, Mama will have something," Michelle said breezily.

T he Mistress of the Wardrobe marched up and down in front of us, inspecting her troops. Clarence was all in black, right down to the buttons on his silk shirt. Max's massive torso was draped in one of the most garish optical assaults ever to come out of Hawaii. Terry had a bleached dungaree jacket over a Dark Horse Comics T-shirt. The Mole wore his favorite dirt-colored jumpsuit, a thick tool belt around his waist.

The Prof had carried her deep into the late rounds, but Michelle had finally TKO'ed him. The little man reluctantly sported a royal-blue knee-length Nehru jacket with thick white vertical stripes. Me, I had my white leather jacket and black boots. A pigeon-blood ruby ring on the little finger of my right hand. And a heavy chain Mama said was platinum on my left wrist, right next to a chunky, beat-up Casio multi-screen watch on a wide black nylon band. "The contrast makes the look," Michelle had assured me.

"Everybody got their roles?" I asked them.

"I am an executive producer, mahn," Clarence said, as if daring anyone to dispute it.

"Right. Max is security. The Prof is part of the . . . What did you call it again, Michelle?"

"The creative team," she sighed.

"Uh-huh. Okay, the Mole is tech. You can work that whole video rig we got, right?" I asked him.

He gave me one of his particle-accelerator looks, didn't answer.

"Terry, you're a studio intern. You're sure you can talk the talk?"

"We're going all-digital," he said smoothly. "It's the only way to get the *immediacy* the director needs for this project."

"Beautiful," I told him.

"Ah, you'll see, Burke," he said, with his mother's trademark self-confidence. "*They're* going to be the ones doing all the talking."

"Good enough. Michelle, you'll be my girl Friday."

"I will not. I should be at least a—"

"You don't look old enough to be someone high up," I said quickly.

"Oh. Well . . . you may have a point."

"A very good point, that is the truth." Clarence took my back.

"And what do *you* think?" she asked, turning to the Mole.

"What?" he answered vaguely, eyes blinking rapidly behind the Coke-bottle lenses.

"Do you think I look too young to be someone important at a studio?"

"How old would someone important at a studio be?" he asked, proving you can be a genius in some areas and an imbecile in others.

"You look like you're, maybe, twenty-nine, Mom," Terry jumped in gamely. "No more than that."

The Mole caught the signal, went from blinking to nodding until Michelle finally turned her attention back to me.

"You need one more thing," she said.

"What now?"

"This!" she said, pulling a black eyepatch out of her purse.

"Why should I wear an—?"

"Honey, ever since the . . . ever since what happened, you can't see out of both of them, right?"

"Not at the same time."

"And when they . . . fixed you up, all that plastic surgery, they didn't put it in . . . the same."

"So?"

She came over, stood next to where I was sitting. "Before it hap—"

"Before I got shot in the head, Michelle. You can say it," I told her. They could say anything they wanted about that night. Anything except Pansy's name.

"All right, baby. Before you got shot, you had the perfect con man's face. It wasn't . . . It didn't make a real impression, and it didn't stay with you, either. But now you look . . . distinctive. The scar," she said, sad and sweet, touching the spot on my right cheek. "Your eyes don't line up. And they're two different colors, too. The skin on one side is a little . . . tighter than the other. Your hair has those long streaks of white in it. And the top of this ear . . ."

"I get it."

"But, honey, listen. You wear this eyepatch and that's all people will see. It draws attention to one thing, takes it away from the rest. Anyone asks for your description, they'll say 'the man with the patch.' Let them focus on that instead of . . ."

"It's a good idea," I told her, to take away some of her pain. "And when we're done, and I take it off, it'll be like a new face."

"I didn't mean . . ."

"I *like* it," I said. "It's a good play, girl. Let me try it on."

"**H**ow did you know where I live?" the pudgy-faced guy said, standing in the doorway of his Chelsea walk-up.

"I can explain better inside," I said.

"Maybe I don't want—"

I turned to go, rolling my right shoulder away from him as I brought my left hand off the door jamb to smack softly against the side of his exposed neck, shoving him to the side, letting my momentum back me into the space he vacated. "Thanks," I said.

He retreated a few steps. I didn't move. He brought his hands up in front of his face, then dropped them immediately so I wouldn't think he wanted to fight.

"Stop it," I told him. "If I wanted to hurt you, you'd already be hurt."

"What do you want here?"

"I don't want anything *here*. I want something from you. And here is where you are."

"I didn't tell anyone—"

"What? That I came to you, asked you for a friendly favor? Who'd care?"

"Then why are you mad?"

"I'm not mad, Jerry. I'm just in a hurry."

"You didn't have to threaten me," he said indignantly. He walked over and dropped himself into a canvas beanbag chair.

"What are you talking about?" I said.

"That man who called me. Your 'reference.' He said if I didn't 'help you out'—that's the words he used, 'help you out'— then I'd better find a good morphine connection. Because the hospitals, they never really give you enough for internal injuries."

"You probably misunderstood him," I said, as I walked over to a blue Naugahyde recliner and sat down. I lit a cigarette, looked around for an ashtray.

"There's one on the shelf behind you," he said.

"Thanks," I said, now that I'd been upgraded from invader to guest. "Anyway, Jerry, here's the thing. I don't think I'm going to make it as a journalist, but I do keep my ear to the ground. I hear things, you know?"

"So?" he said, still resentful.

"So I need to ask your advice. About how to use this . . . thing I heard."

"We only publish material that we can—"

"I wouldn't want *your* magazine to publish this one," I said, sniffing out the ego issue and running with it. Violence or con job, it always comes down to the same thing—reading the other guy. "It's just a rumor, and I know you don't trade in rumors. Only facts. But the way I figure things, just because you wouldn't go near something doesn't mean you don't know how it works, right?"

"I don't think I under—"

"Okay. There's going to be a movie shot out on Long Island. Sort of a horror flick, but with a love story, too. The whole thing takes place at a high school. An independent production company has this dynamite script, and they're looking for actors. Only thing is, they have to be pretty much unknown, and they have to be local . . . for the accents and the look and all. And to stay within budget."

"So?"

"So the casting director is going to be looking for talent, but their team doesn't want word to get out. You know how they'd be swamped with all kinds of stage mothers and agents. They want to keep it low-key until they get the film mostly cast."

"What's this got to do with—?"

"You know the Internet, right? How it works?"

"I'm not a geek, I'm a journalist. The Internet is just the *forum* we use," he said self-righteously.

"Sure, I understand. But I'm not talking techno here. I'm talking about the *medium*. What I want is to get the word out about—"

"You said they *didn't* want—"

"That's them, Jerry. That's not us."

"Us?"

"You and me. And my partners. You know . . . you spoke to one of them. And what *we* want, we want the word to sort of *dribble* out there. Just a little. So it has to be planted in places where only kids from the local area would pick it up. We're not looking for national, see?"

"Sure," he said. Confidence returning. "And there's ways to do that *somewhat*. But the Internet is like a forest fire, especially when it comes to rumors. And when you add fucking *movies* to the mix, it'll spread, no matter what you do."

"How would you do it?"

"Me? One thing I *wouldn't* do is have a Web site. That would be fatal. What you want is a couple of little posts, maybe in one of the local newsgroups or on a message board. Not saying it *is* happening, just that they *heard* it might be, and could anybody help? You know, give info and stuff."

"Sounds good. Can you do it?"

"Me? Why me?"

"That would be your choice, why you. It could be for money, or it could be for a favor."

"A favor?"

"Yeah. A favor you do us means someday we could do a favor for *you,* see?"

"I . . . guess."

"But it's worth a thousand, if you just want the cash."

He fumbled around, found one of his cigars. Lighting it up seemed to return him to his role, tranq him down. After a few puffs, he peered at me through the blue smoke, said, "'Cash' means not a check, right?"

"I s this going to be a permanent thing, that patch?" Wolfe asked me.

"It's just for a job," I said.

"A job for . . . ?"

"Those same people."

"It's not exactly a disguise. I'd know you in a second."

"You would," I admitted. "But for people who've never met me, it might be all they remember."

"And you want a driver's license . . . *another* driver's license? Same name, same everything, only the photo has you wearing the patch?"

"Yeah. I checked. You only need vision in one eye to get a license. I've got the photos right here. . . ."

"Why did you come to me?" she asked. "Even with all the anti-terrorist squads on the job now, there's still a hundred places in the city you could get something like this done."

"I figured, it's your paper I'm carrying, you'd want it to all be perfect."

"Sure," she said.

"And I wanted to ask you something else?"

"*Buy* something else."

"Yeah. That's what I meant. I just . . . I just didn't know if you maybe already had what I wanted to know about, or if you'd have to ask around. So I didn't know how much it would—"

"I set my own prices," she said, blowing a perfect smoke ring into the night air. "And I always give them in front. You know that."

"Right. Okay, look, here's what I need to know: how dead am I?"

"To who?"

"I'm not following you."

"There's a lot of wires. They don't all route through the same terminals, understand? Which do you want me to check?"

"All you can."

"That's going to cost."

"Everybody pays," I said.

Her stare measured me for a few long seconds before she nodded an okay.

"**W**hat would we have to do?" Cyn asked, more than a trace of suspicion in her tone.

"You'd mostly be window-dressing," I told her. "Atmosphere."

"I've got citizen dresses," Rejji said helpfully.

"What's this 'atmosphere,' Burke?"

"It's something to draw the eye," I answered, thinking of the eyepatch. "These are going to be kids, mostly. No way a teenage boy is going to be watching me when he could be watching you two."

"We don't *like* boys," Rejji said, licking her lips.

"So let the *girls* look, then. Just don't touch."

"Don't be an idiot," Cyn said. "We only touch for money."

"And you pose for money, too, right?"

"*Yessss,*" Rejji hissed. "And we are very, very good at it."

"So think of this as posing, okay?"

"What *exactly* would we be doing?" Cyn wanted to know, still not mollified.

"Just dress up, prance around, act like you're part of the whole deal. When I need you to do something specific, I'll tell you."

"See, Cyn?" Rejji crowed. "He's not fooling anyone with that vanilla routine—Burke's a closet dom."

"Shut your silly mouth, slut," Cyn told her.

Rejji stuck her thumb in her mouth, made loud sucking sounds.

Cyn turned to me. Made a little twitch at the corner of her mouth, said, "So. How much money are we talking about here, boss?"

"Michelle can bless any dress, but you can't hide a ride," the Prof said. "That rust bucket you been driving around, it's not going to fly, Sly."

"My father is right," Clarence seconded the Prof's notion.

"This doesn't call for limo cover," I said. "We want . . . Never mind, I think I know where we can get what we need."

"You want . . . what?"

"Cars," I told Giovanni. "Three, four of them. Not flashy. Classy. Like this one."

"My BMW? Get out of town, Burke. What would I drive while you're doing this, that junker of yours?"

"That junker could surprise you."

"How? By *not* falling apart on the BQE?"

"It'd put this one on the trailer, easy."

"I hope you know more about investigating than you do about

cars, my friend," he said, laughing. "This is an M5; you know what that means?"

"Yeah, sure. A factory–hot-rodded version."

"Hot-rodded? This thing is put together like a Rolex."

"Some Rolexes run slow."

"So you're saying you got a big motor. What's that? I'm not talking about drag racing. There's more to a car than quarter-miles."

"Want to see for yourself?"

"Right now?" he asked, matador's eyes glittering.

"Sure."

"You know the Navy Yard?"

"Yeah."

"Meet me over there, at the—"

"That's not what I'm talking about, a race. I said see for your-self, that's what I meant." I pointed toward where the Plymouth lurked. "Key's in the ignition," I told him. "In the dash, not on the steering column."

Giovanni strutted over to the Plymouth, Felix a dark, feline shape next to him. I watched Giovanni get behind the wheel, heard the big-cube Mopar's muted throb when they fired it up. Giovanni gave it the gun. The Plymouth's rear end kicked out slightly, but he got it under control and roared out of the parking lot.

I t was about forty minutes before I saw the Plymouth's head-lights cut the corner and come my way. Giovanni backed it in slowly, exhausts gurgling like a powerboat's. He and Felix climbed out, Giovanni pausing to pat the Plymouth's fender like it was a racehorse who'd just given its best.

I was standing next to the BMW as they approached.

"*Dios mio,* that is a *stallion,*" Felix said. "A Ferrari would never defeat it."

"Want to trade?" Giovanni asked me. "Right now? Even up?"

"No thanks," I said. Lymon had promised me the Plymouth could pull an honest twelve-second quarter and top out at 150. I hadn't seen for myself yet, but I suspected Giovanni had.

"I don't blame you," he said.

"For what I do, the Plymouth is better. But for what I'm doing *now* . . ."

"I get it," Giovanni said. "And *you* got it. Make a list."

"I t's out there," Jerry the Journalist said.

"Any idea of whether it's being picked up?" I said into the phone.

"It's *always* picked up," he answered. "True or false, smart or stupid, it's all the same. For an extra touch, I even slipped it into the Internet Movie Database."

"What's that?"

"An online thing. Pretty helpful for something like what you're doing. What people do, when they hear a rumor, they 'check it out on the Internet,' see?"

"But how do they know if—?"

"They don't. And it doesn't matter. To them, if it's on the Internet, it's God's own truth. 'Cyber-chumps,' that's what I call them."

"That's pretty slick, 'cyber-chumps.' You make it up?"

"You ever go on the Internet?"

"Me? No."

"Yeah, I 'coined the phrase,' as they say."

"Cool. Thanks for the TCB."

"That's it?"

"If you really got it done, it is."

"Y ou're dead by NYPD," Wolfe said.

"*Dead* dead? Or just missing-and-presumed?"

"*Mondo morto*. They probably cleared a hundred cases behind your death. The last thing they'd want is for you to show up."

That's another way to get a case an Exceptional Clearance, I thought, *when the perp's not alive to bring to trial.* "What kind of cases?" I asked.

"Hijackings, assaults, armed robberies. Like that."

"They didn't put me in any . . . ?"

"What? Sex cases?"

"Yeah. Or . . . ?"

"No. In some strange way, they were almost . . . respectful. Or maybe they were playing it straight, staying with cases in which you were actually a suspect in some way."

"There's enough of those," I acknowledged.

"Apparently," she said dryly. "Everything else is whispers. People say they've seen you. Or heard you were back in town. Nothing specific."

"Sure. That kind of talk . . . There's some saying Wesley's still walking around, too."

Wolfe shuddered. Gave me a long, cold look.

I took it, let it come into me. Stayed soft-eyed.

"Remember Colto?" she finally said, heavy on the Italian inflection.

"That blowhard? Sure."

"He's running around making noises about settling with you."

"That *proves* the street thinks I'm dead."

"He says you stole eight keys of pure from him a few years ago, and you've been running from him ever since."

"He's lying to his bosses the same way he lied to me. It was five keys. And it was stepped on, heavy."

"They must have believed him; he's still walking."

"I never thought they bought it, myself. But Colto's a decent earner. They probably figured he puffed up the amount to cover his own ass, sure, but he could make it back up to them, they gave him enough time. He's just huffing now, behind some rumor that I'm back. That's the kind of guy he is."

"Yes," she said patiently, "I know. But gangsters gossip worse than housewives. And you *are* working for . . ."

"How much do I still owe you?" I said.

"It's on," Michelle said. "Clarence and I hit six, eight different houses between ten and three o'clock."

"They all bought it?" I asked her.

"Sure. Like it was an everyday thing, some production company asking about renting out their house for a movie. They don't know anyone this actually happened to, but they know it happens. Besides, who's more charming than me?"

"Nobody. You let Clarence do any talking?"

"I was the driver, mahn," Clarence said. "A nice sleek Mercedes. Not so fine a ride as mine, but it made the impression."

I'd vetoed Clarence bringing his prize '67 Rover TC into the game. In some neighborhoods, a black Mercedes was as generic as a yellow cab in Manhattan, but the immaculate-as-new British Racing Green sedan would stick in the memory.

I didn't mind him just playing the driver, either. We couldn't know the racial attitudes of any of the households we'd picked at random. And if anyone caught a glimpse of the nine-millimeter under his arm, well, a lot of chauffeurs are armed these days.

"It worked just like you said, honey," Michelle said. "More than half of the houses, it was kids who answered the door. And even when we found an adult at home, it's like teenagers have a radar for the word 'movies.' They'd be in the living room in a heartbeat, soon as it came out."

"We've got to hope their grapevine cuts across class lines," I said. "The only way to make this scouting-for-locations scam sing is to pick either real big houses or those with great views . . . or plenty of land. That always means money. So the kids in those houses, they'll tell *their* friends, but I don't know how far it's going to travel."

"All high-school kids clique up," Michelle said. "But they read the same magazines. Watch the same TV. Listen to the same music. It'll go across, baby."

"And we've got that Internet thing, too," I added, hopefully.

"What is next, mahn?" Clarence.

"The mall," I said. "Tomorrow afternoon. Then we'll know."

"I don't care *what* you heard," I told the mob of teenagers Michelle had herded over. I was sitting in a corner of the food court, with Cyn on one side and Rejji on the other. Max stood behind me, facing out. Better than a wall. "These are *not* auditions. What the company wants, *first,* is the right *look.* And the right *sound.* So you won't get any sides—"

"What's that?" a girl asked.

I exchanged knowing looks with Cyn, then went on talking as another teen snidely hissed that "sides" were pages of a script.

". . . because we need to get you on tape, being your*selves,* before anything else. The director is going to look at a *lot* of people. This phase is only about collecting *images,* so he can see who makes the cut. After that comes the readings."

"Who's the director?" a kid with horn-rimmed glasses asked.

This time, my look was exchanged with Rejji, who raised an eyebrow, dismissing the kid harder than a slap.

"We are *not* looking for extras," I went on, pointedly ignoring the uncool question, sending an etiquette message. "Not at this time. The film isn't cast yet. We're starting from scratch. But since it's going to be shot around here, and the script is written for teenagers, the director thought we might spend a few days surveying."

"Surveying?" a late-teens girl in a butterscotch blouse said.

"Shut up!" a younger girl in denim overalls hissed at her. "Let him talk."

I went on doing just that for a few minutes, verging just close enough on condescending arrogance to convince them I was the real thing.

"Anyone can try out?" a chunky girl with a round, shiny face and frizzy brown hair asked me.

"These aren't tryouts," I told her. "In the trade, we call this 'looking for the look.' It's our job to bring the director all kinds of different images. Like a list of ingredients, so he can decide what he wants to cook."

The chunky girl thought she heard a coded message in all that. Her face fell.

"I hope you can come," Michelle told her, voice carrying deep into the crowd. "You have *fantastic* eyes."

"**P**olice girl call." Mama's voice, on the cell phone.

"Wolfe?"

"What I say?"

"Okay, Mama. What did *she* say?"

"Say call."

"**Y**ou were looking for me?"

"Not me," Wolfe said. "That person we talked about."

"Does he know where to look?"

"You mean your . . . place?"

"Yeah."

"Not unless you've been a lot more careless than you usually are." Meaning: "Not from me."

"So where's he doing all this looking?"

"Remember Julian's?"

"Sure," I said, mourning the passing of one of the City's greatest poolrooms. Fourteenth Street wasn't the same since it had disappeared.

"A place in the same business. Only in a basement."

"I haven't been there in—"

"But you *used* to go there. People left messages for you with the old man who runs it. That's what he did; he left a message."

"What does the mope think he's doing, playing *High Noon*?"

"It does seem . . . outlandish. So it's probably not what it seems. But he *is* trying to make an impression. And I thought he might come to . . . that restaurant of yours."

"Even he's not that stupid," I said.

"Does anybody—*any*body—know I'm on your payroll?"

"Only Felix."

"The first couple of times we met, you had people . . . you *both* had people around."

"That was so they'd think—"

"Sure. I'm not criticizing your strategy. Only thing is, how sure are you of all the men who were there?"

"Dead sure," Giovanni said.

"Yes," Felix echoed. "Why do you ask all this?"

"You know a guy named Colto? Works Queens, out of the old airport crew?"

"I know who he is," Giovanni said, waiting to see my next card.

"A few years ago, he said Burke took him off for some powder."

"I heard about that. Heard the story, anyway. I don't think his boss bought it."

"That's how I got it, too. Thing is, this Colto, he's been making the rounds, telling people Burke's been on the run . . . from him. And now that Burke's back, he's going to settle up."

"Why do you tell us?" Felix said.

"I tell you because, one, if he got the idea Burke's back from one of your crews, it means things aren't as tight as you think they are. And, two, he's in the way. Of what I'm doing. About Vonni. You know what happens, a guy mouths off about something that sounds like business, sooner or later people pay attention. The last thing we want now is anybody paying attention to me."

"Colto's a fucking pig," Giovanni said. "If he was lying in the gutter bleeding to death, the whole neighborhood would send 911 a postcard. But, you know, he's got a little button."

"I understand," I told him.

"No, you don't," Felix said. "And you don't *do* anything, either. A balloon, it's only the air that holds it up."

"But if he comes around . . . ?"

"You said enough already," Giovanni told me.

"**W**here's your slips?" Rejji demanded of the two girls in matching red halter tops and jeans.

"Slip?" one of them asked. "I didn't hear anything about wearing a—"

"One of these," Rejji said, showing her a playing card. It had a joker on the face; the back was blank. "You have to have one of these, with a time and date on it. You know how many people we have to see? If they all came at once, this would be a mob scene."

"Oh," the other girl said, crestfallen. "Nobody said anything to us."

"Come over here," Rejji said, motioning them into a corner.

"**I**'m seventeen, but I can play any age from—"

"This isn't an audition," I said. "Not yet." I went into my "looking for a look" spiel, as Clarence tapped a zebrawood pen on the blank page of an open calfskin notebook. "We're just going to have a conversation. Like an interview, okay?"

"Ask me anything!"

"This is not about you," I said, putting a thin edge on my voice. "It's about how you come across. Do you understand the difference?"

"Sure! Absolutely."

"Okay, let's see. Talk to me about school. Are there a lot of cliques there?"

"**I**'m going to have to go back into the City, shop around, if you want me to pick up all this stuff, Pop," Terry said to the Mole, looking over a few pages ripped from a yellow legal pad covered with his father's hieroglyphics. "It could take a couple of days. . . ."

"Karp's Hardware," the Mole said, not looking up from his bench.

"What?"

"In East Northport. Karp's Hardware. It will be in the book. They will have everything."

"A hardware store?" the kid said, jaw dropping. "How could it possibly . . . ?"

"Everything," the Mole assured him, still intent on his instruments.

Hours and hours, one kid after another. Michelle was working one of the rooms, Cyn another. Clarence moved between the suites, taking notes. The Prof sat in a tufted easy chair, chain-smoking, being creative.

The Mole fiddled with equipment I couldn't begin to recognize. Occasionally, he pretended to listen to advice from the Prof. Rejji covered the door. Terry pulled kids aside for whispered conversations while they were waiting. Despite my telling him we wanted a representative sampling, his personal preferences seemed to dictate his conversational targets.

At night, we sat around and talked over what we'd pulled out of the day. Between us, we'd heard about a dozen different kinds of drugs—chronic to crystal, E to H—and SATs, booze, football, shoplifting, AOL chat rooms, vandalism, cars, a "master race" graffiti gang, hip-hop, the NBA draft, love affairs, Jell-O shots, steroids, Amy Fisher—opinion seemed divided between Guido victim and skanky slut—chick fights, clothes, MP3s, asshole teachers, fucked-up DSL service, the tragedy of Napster, music I never heard of, tank parties, comic books, huffing, movies, drive-bys, computer gaming. . . .

The next day, two boys in blue varsity jackets with white leather sleeves got into some kind of argument with one of the girls waiting to be interviewed. "Say you didn't! Say you didn't!" the girl dared them. One of the boys stepped to her, shoulders hunched. Max cat-footed over to where they were standing, put his finger to his lips.

"Who the fuck are *you* supposed to be?" the taller of the two demanded.

Max wrist-locked the kid to his knees, held him there effortlessly as he looked without expression at the other one.

"What's the worst thing that's ever happened around here?" I asked some of the teenagers, randomly.

Vonni's murder came up in less than half the answers. Three different kids claimed her for a close friend, one girl getting teary-eyed when she said the name.

But a year-old homicide generally didn't have much of a chance against who was crushing who, what guy was pure butter, which girl was total ghetto, who always acted like a real crackhead at school, what BMX move was totally sick, which new computer game was ultra-mega, where the next rave was supposed to be.

A few kids were focused elsewhere. Some talked about Columbine. Not about the slaughter scene, about poor Dylan and Eric.

A teen with a military haircut and camo pants told me McVeigh had been framed. "Where's John Doe Number Two?" he demanded, angry.

Some were very deeply depressed about the new run of *Buffy*. "Now even The Slayer sucks!" one cracked. A girl with lithium eyes was upset at how much child support they were making poor Eminem pay.

One kid had a "Death Before Dishonor" tattoo on his forearm. He told everyone who would listen that his brother was in the Marines, and he was going, too, as soon as he graduated.

Two girls got into an argument about whatever. "Bring it, B!" one yelled at the other. The crowd of kids snarled at them collectively to take it outside. The girls headed for the door. Nobody followed. The two girls stopped in their tracks. Stared at each other, sharing disappointment.

The ones we came to call the "movie kids" were surface-scarred by their marrow-deep smugness. So completely, condescendingly in the know that they felt comfortable pontificating about "gross points" and "final cut." They breezily corrected each other about who was "A-list at Miramax," and dropped names like "Denzel" as if he had been over for dinner the night before. But when it came to asking for credentials, they were all parties to a mutual nonaggression pact.

No problem, until a girl in a Joan Baez outfit started ragging on some studio for putting out a horror movie directed by a convicted child molester. "They're disgusting!" she said. "After what he did . . ."

A twenty-something with one of those lower-lip goatees and Buddy Holly glasses looked down his long nose at the girl, intoned, "Judge the art, not the artist," and looked to Terry for approval. Terry gave the kid a bright-white smile . . . a red flag to Max, who stepped between them, put his arm around Terry's shoulders, and muscled the kid over to where his mother was sitting. Quick, before life could imitate art.

A kid sporting double wallet chains and a "WWMD" medallion said college was "grayed out." Later, Terry translated. "WWMD" stood for "What Would Manson Do?" and "grayed out" meant "not an option."

A girl with a matchstick body and beta-carotene skin told us that we didn't understand—before anyone asked her a question.

One Goth boy, who looked like he'd played vampire prince so often that he'd ended up hematologically challenged, drove a black PT Cruiser, customized to look like a hearse, with "aR$_x$thur R$_x$ules" in neat white lettering on the fender.

A good quarter of them started every sentence with "Basically," as if it were some kind of verbal tic.

Boarders and bladers stood apart from cyber-geeks. Poseurs, players, and self-proclaimed pimps got along—punks of a feather. Cheerleaders didn't mix with cholas. But even whiggers and skinheads shared pieces of the same room without so much as an eye-fuck. "Reminds me how guys act in full minimum," I told the Prof later. "Walking on eggs, right? They know one wrong move gets them sent back to the Walls."

They all talked different, but they all talked. And none of them said anything we needed.

"We still have a ton more of them," Michelle said. "How many of those cards did we spread out there? Thousands?"

"Not that many," Rej said. "But a lot. A real lot."

"Cyn?"

"The girls talked about it more than the boys. But that's natural, I think."

"They doing any speculating?" I asked.

"The ones I talked to, they all seemed satisfied. Scared and satisfied," Michelle offered.

"Satisfied that some monster was just passing through?"

"Yes. And scared that he could come again. But not *truly* scared. More like . . . fascinated, maybe. A few even made *Friday the Thirteenth* jokes. *Très chic.*"

"You've got their pedigrees?" I asked Clarence.

"Mahn, this is a job for a clerk, that is all. Rejji gives them this form to fill out, and they do. Every single line. They *want* us to be able to find them, do they not?"

"Yeah. And you all put check marks on the ones who said anything about Vonni?"

Michelle and Cyn nodded.

"Terry?"

"I high-signed Clarence every time one of them said anything, too."

"You do any better than we did?"

"No . . . but I didn't push, either. Like you said."

"I've got three for you to try up-close-and-personal, tomorrow," I told him. "For now, let's call it a night."

"You like that mom-and-pop food, huh?" Rejji said, smiling at my blue-plate special of meat loaf, mashed potatoes, and chopped spinach.

"I like just about anything I can pronounce," I told her.

"Bet he tops off with vanilla ice cream," Cyn cracked.

"Why can't we just stay at the hotel?" Cyn asked me on the drive back. "You already paid for all those rooms, didn't you? I mean, we're going right back there tomorrow. . . ."

"If we tried to sleep there, we'd be bombarded by kids sneaking past security. I'll rent a couple on another floor starting tomorrow, okay?"

"They really *are* insane about being in a movie, huh?"

"You talked to them, Cyn. What do *you* think?"

"Fetish is fetish," she said, nodding agreement.

"Did anybody hear the name Vision?" Terry asked, the next night.

Clarence shrugged a "No."

"Not me, honey," Michelle said.

"I'm drawing a blank, too, kid," I said. "Why do you ask?"

"I was just hanging out with some of the ones who were waiting, you know? One of them says to another, 'I bet this is killing Vision—a real movie being made right here.' And the other says he was in one of Vision's movies. The first guy says, 'For real?' And the other guy says, yeah, the whole fraternity was, kind of.

"But when the first guy presses, the other guy says he's not allowed to talk about the initiations. Then I had to go. One of the girls was saying—"

"Anyone else hear that name? Vision?"

"I did," Cyn said. "Remember when you had that idea, do two or three of them at a time, get them talking to each other? Well, this Asian girl, Mei-Mei, she said she'd been in a movie before, and the other two gave her a 'Shut the fuck up!' look. I let it slide like I wasn't paying attention.

"But then I got her alone later, like I wanted to see how she did with some other material, blah-blah, and I walked her around to this movie she was in. She says, 'Oh, it was just one of Vision's. A video, not a movie.' I moved on, right over what she was saying, so she couldn't even be sure I heard her."

"You played it perfect, Cyn."

She and Rejji mid-fived with their hips.

"So there is a young man making videos," Clarence said. "What good could this be to us? Half of these children said they had made some kind of video."

"Two people mention this 'Vision' guy," I told him. "And, both times, someone asks a question, they dummy up quick. That gets my attention."

"Probably makes porno," Michelle said sourly.

"Can you come and see me, please?" Hazel Greene.

"Anytime. Just say the—"

"Right now. I know it's late but—"

"I'll be there in under an hour," I told her.

"I found something," she said.

"Something about—?"

"I don't know *what* it's about. I don't know if it . . . means anything. But Vonni had it . . . hidden."

"And you just found it, is that what you're saying?"

"Does it matter?"

"Not to me."

"Then why did you ask me?"

"Because, if you had it all this time, then you had your own reasons for not turning it over to the cops."

"You . . . you *would* think like that, wouldn't you?"

"I don't want to fight with you, Mrs. Greene."

"What happened to 'Ms.'?"

"I don't . . ."

"*Ms.* Greene is what you called me before."

"My apologies. Just tell me which you prefer and I'll—"

"I don't care," she said.

Not about that, I thought. Said, "All right. Do you want me to—?"

"Vonni was a good girl. I don't mean a virgin—although she was, I would have known—I mean good in her heart and good in her ways. She was honest and kind and sweet. Everybody loved her."

"I know Hugh sure did."

"Yes. Lottie told me how you . . . That's why I'm showing you this now. Of course, when your child di . . . is taken from you, people never want to say anything bad about her. But this was all *before*. The good things, I mean. Nobody killed my Vonni because they hated her; I know this."

"People don't have to have a good reason to hate, Ms. Greene. You should know that, too."

"My . . . color, you mean? Yes. Yes, I know that. This isn't what I wanted to tell you. I'm not making myself clear. I would trade it all. How good she was. How proud she made me. Everything. If I could have my daughter back as a prostitute or a drug addict or brain-damaged or . . . It wouldn't matter; I would take her and love her and be grateful forever."

"I know."

"Do you? How could you? How could you know a mother's feeling for her only child? Were you one?"

"A . . . ?"

"An only child? Were you one?"

"I don't know," I told her. Thinking, *She nailed it. That's me. Only a child, once. And, now, even being back home, back with*

*my family, an only child, forever. Hazel Greene will never have
another child. Neither will Giovanni.*

"How could you not . . . ?" she asked.

I just looked at her, waiting for the message to arrive.

"Oh," she said, when it did.

"I don't know anything about them," I told her. "Either of
them," I said, so she'd know I was talking about my mother and
father. "If I have biological brothers and sisters, I'll never know
that, either."

"That's terrible."

"Compared to what? It doesn't matter."

"It *must* matter. I'm so sorry."

All of us down here, only children.

"I believe you are, Ms. Greene. And I believe Vonni had more
love in sixteen years than most people get in a lifetime."

She nodded her head slowly. Said, "I'll get them," and walked
out of the room.

"**V**ideotapes?"

"Yes. This is all of them. I found them in Vonni's room. In the
bottom of an old army footlocker we got at a flea market. We used
to go to them all the time. Vonni said she . . ."

Her voice trailed off. I stayed silent, afraid to blunder around
in the spun-glass forest of her memories.

"I'd never gone in there," she finally said. "Vonni had a padlock on it—I always thought that was where she'd kept her diary.
When the police said they were going to . . . search everything,
I couldn't bear for them to be the ones to read her private
thoughts. So I took the hasp off with a screwdriver.

"You know what's funny, Mr. Burke?" she said, rage somewhere in her quiet, throbbing voice. "Vonni *did* have a diary.
But it was sitting on her desk, right out in the open. I never
knew. She trusted me so much. . . . The police told me about
it. After they were . . . done with it. They're keeping it . . . for
evidence."

I never considered trying to comfort her. Just stayed in my silence.

"All those years, I guess I could have sneaked a look anytime," she said. "Only I never did. I never saw it until after . . . it happened." She went quiet for a long minute. "I always thought her diary was in her footlocker. But it wasn't. I was looking . . . and that's where I found these."

I looked at the stack of videocassettes. "What's on them, Ms. Greene?"

"How do you know I looked at them?"

"Because you still have them. And the cops don't."

"Could I have one of your cigarettes, please? I don't smoke, actually. I used to, when I was a kid. We all did. But I stopped when I got pregnant. Then I started again, but I stopped years later. When Vonni got upset with me for it. Now there's no reason. . . ."

I shook one out of my pack, held it out to her. She took it. I fired a wooden match. She lit up without touching my hand.

"The police never asked me to . . . help them understand what was in Vonni's diary," she said, her voice chilly and controlled. "They just read it themselves, and asked me questions. 'Who's Jermaine?' Questions like that."

"I understand."

"Do you? Were you a police officer once?"

"No, Ms. Greene. I understand how angry you are at what they did. It wasn't just disrespectful; it was stupid. Who knows Vonni better than you?" I said. Not proud of myself for strumming those strings.

"Yes," she said. "And . . . I thought maybe I would . . . see something on the tapes, I don't know."

I didn't say anything.

"What's on them?" she said, tight-voiced. "Craziness. Stupid . . . craziness. *That's* what's on there. Nothing else. I can't imagine why Vonni would have—"

"What kind of craziness, Ms. Greene?"

"A . . . dogfight. A vicious fight, with people watching and . . . Their faces! Some kind of . . . gauntlet a boy had to run, between other boys with fists, hitting him. A bunch of girls paddling another girl, like for some sorority initiation. Some people spray-painting a swastika on the side of a Jewish temple. What looks like a . . . mugging, I guess you'd call it. Some insane young boy on a skateboard jumping right through a plate-glass window. All kinds of things like that."

"Vonni's not in any of them? Not even her voice?"

"Just one. By herself. There's no sound. She's running. Jogging, like. In the woods. She hears something. Or someone. And she gets scared. Starts to run really fast . . ."

"Did you see who—?"

"The tape just trailed off," she said. "It trailed off with Vonni running. Still running."

"I don't have the equipment to do that," the Mole said. "Not here."

"But you could get it?"

"Sure he could!" Terry said, jumping up. "Come on, Pop. Let's take a ride."

"You think people around here notice all this coming and going?" Michelle asked.

"This neighborhood? Sure. They probably think we're running a tweek lab."

"I wish we'd picked a nicer place, baby. I mean, if I am going to be spending all this time here . . ."

"You want to stay at the hotel tonight, girl? I can fix that easy enough."

"And not see what's on those tapes? Don't be demented."

The dogfight was made more hideous by the lack of sound, especially the expressions on the faces of the spectators. Looked like a single-camera setup, but it wasn't static. The lens picked up all kinds of strange angles—one from what had to be damn near inside the pit itself. No matter how many times I asked the Mole to stop on a particular frame, isolate pieces of it, and blow them up, I couldn't make out any real details—the quality was about as good as an ATM surveillance camera.

"Isn't this against the law?" Michelle asked me, her voice vibrating just below breakage.

"In New York it is," I said. "Not in all states."

"Do you think it was filmed here, though?"

"I can't tell. There's nothing that would ID a location."

"What's the penalty?" she demanded. "I mean, if they were caught, what would happen to them?"

"A fine, probably; not more."

"For having the dogs do . . . that?"

"Yeah."

Max watched the next tape intently, holding up his index finger for the Mole to stop the action, twirling the same finger for him to resume. The Mongolian nodded a few times, as if working out a problem in his head. At his signal, the Mole started the tape from the beginning.

The tape had shown us a teenage boy, Latin, with a West Coast cholo's haircut. He faced a group of young men, and yelled something. Then he made a "Come on!" gesture with his hands, waving them in. The gang circled slowly until the boy was surrounded. Then they rushed him, fists and feet. When it was over, the boy was on the ground, not moving.

Nobody knows the mechanics of physical combat better than Max. The dogfighting couldn't have been faked, but . . .

I made a "Well?" gesture. Max gave me the sign for "Yes." This one had been the real thing, too.

But it nagged at me. So I ran it again a few hours later.

"It's a jump-in tape, all right," the Prof said.

"No doubt?"

"That was the Max man's verdict, too, Schoolboy," he reminded me. "And who knows a bone-breaker better than the widow-maker?"

"Yeah," I agreed. "But . . . there's something about it. I just don't . . ."

"What, bro?"

"I . . . can't tell you. It has to come to the surface by itself. But there's something *off* about it, Prof."

The little man closed his eyes, concentrating. Then he looked over at Clarence, said, "Let's glide, Clyde."

The drag races were easier. The cameraman made sure you couldn't see the license numbers, but to anyone who knows cars, some of the rides were as distinctive as fingerprints.

"I think I may have seen the shoebox," I told Clarence.

"What's a shoebox?" Rejji asked.

"The '55 Chevy," Clarence said. "You sure, mahn?"

"Not a hundred percent. But there's something about the stance . . ."

"I've seen a million of these," Cyn said, pointing at the screen, where a slender girl was bent over, palms against the wall, her shorts and panties around her ankles, being paddled by a taller girl in a sorority sweater and pleated skirt, while a bunch of other girls watched. "It used to be a big deal, to do the real thing, no acting. Years ago, some of the product even came with warranties. You know, 'All the girls in this session were *really* spanked.' But now there's so many subs going into the business that there's no market for fakes. This one doesn't even look professional."

"Because of the single camera?"

"No. Most of the digital stuff—you know, for the Net—is that way. But the camera doesn't come in on her ass, to show you it really is red from the punishment. And the paddling doesn't last very long. It doesn't even *look* like a good hard one."

"So you couldn't sell this?"

"Oh, you could sell it, all right. There's one thing about it that's different from the commercial stuff."

"The look?"

"No," Cyn said. "It's that they're *all* so young. I can't tell their ages . . . and you can't really see their faces, but those are high-school girls. Or maybe college. Anyway, it looks like whoever shot this was hidden. As if the girls didn't know they were on camera. For that, there's a *real* market."

"Yeah. Remember when that guy paid us to shill?" Rejji said.

"How's that work?" I asked her.

"Well, this one time, all we had to do was go to a club where a lot of girls hang out. Act real drunk. Then get up on the bar and take our tops off, dance around."

"So the guy could film it?"

"Not film *us*. I mean, he *found* us because we were *in* films, already. No, see, our job was to get the *other* girls to take it off. What he said was, it's completely legal. Because he was right out in the open with the camera. So they were *consenting* if they did it with him there; that's what he said."

"And there's all that 'upskirt' squick, too," Cyn said. "You know, little perverts walking around with minicams in their briefcases. They put them on the ground, film right up a girl's skirt without her knowing. Then it goes straight to the Internet. You wouldn't think anybody would want stuff like that, not when there's a million girls who'll let you film anything—*anything*—if you just pay them. But it's a different head."

"So you think this one . . . ?"

"Who knows?" Rejji said. "In New York, it's legal to videotape a person without them knowing, so long as there's no sound track, can you believe it? There's got to be some freaky politicians behind *that* law.

"Anyway, BDSM by itself isn't illegal, even if you take money for it. And, this one here, there's no sex in it. Like Cyn said, on the Net there's a market for anything. There's even sites for scumbags who beat their own kids and sell the pictures of it."

"But you're sure this one's not faked? Not acting?"

"No," Cyn said, certain-sure. "That was real. It happened."

T he people who spray-painted the synagogue were wearing ski masks.

The camera was in so tight on the nipple-piercing that we couldn't tell anything about the girl.

The only way we knew the sex of the person carried into a darkened room was from her body—her head was hooded with a pillowcase. The girl was either drunk or drugged. That didn't seem to bother the three males who took turns with her. The camera never went near their faces.

Michelle stood up suddenly, pointed at the VCR screen. "Whoever made these tapes, we know them," she said. "We know who they are. We just don't know their names."

"T his is the last one," I told them.

We watched Vonni run a dozen times. The look on her face was pure terror.

"I cannot tell," Clarence said.

"I say no, bro." The Prof.

"I'm with the Prof." Michelle.

Max shook his head "No," agreeing.

"So this one's the wild card," Cyn said, speaking for us all. "This one's a fake?"

"Maybe," is all I could say.

"**T**hat has to be it," I said to Max, pointing at a ramshackle house at the end of a long, straight block. In a better neighborhood, this would be a cul-de-sac. Here, it was as if the street had just surrendered to a prairie-sized vacant lot.

Abandoned cars lined both sides of the street, each one flying some kind of gang sign. Drugstores.

The summer sun that kissed the beach a few miles away was hostile here, bleaching everything into a single bleak tone. Heat waves trembled off the asphalt. The early-morning air was already sodden. Nothing moved.

For this run, I'd lost the eyepatch, the jewelry, and the fancy leather jacket, and switched back to the Plymouth. Max stayed with one of the sumo-sized Hawaiian shirts—I think he'd started to like the look.

As I pulled into the driveway, a brindle-colored blur shot around the side of the house and charged the car. The pit bull leaped onto the hood, slipped slightly, clawed its way toward the windshield, growling death threats. I could see a heavy leather collar around its neck, attached to a length of chain that could anchor a tugboat. I jammed the lever into reverse and hit the gas. The pit bull slid off the hood and hit the ground, then immediately pogo'ed up like it was on springs. Its huge head filled my window, enraged.

I backed off until the Plymouth was beyond the end of the pit bull's chain. Looked a question at Max. He shrugged.

A tall, slope-shouldered black man wearing white painter's coveralls and a matching cap strolled up to us. He'd come around the same side of the house the pit bull had materialized from. He walked down the driveway toward the car, ignoring the frenzied animal, making a motion for me to roll down my window. As soon as I did, the pit quieted down, as if this was a routine he knew well.

"What you want?" the man asked. His skin was light, covered with freckles, his eyes an unsettling stormy blue. I'd have given five-to-two the hair under his cap was red.

"Ozell," I said.

"What you want with him?"

"I want to make some money with him."

"Yeah? And how you going to do that?"

"Where I am right now, it's the wrong address to discuss it."

"What address you talking about, mister? You said you looking for Ozell, right?"

"Right man, wrong address," I told him. "Where I'm sitting right now, like this, all this noise, people maybe watching, the address is Front Street, you with me?"

"You got the stones to get out that ride?"

"You tell me you'll handle your bulldog, I'll take your word."

"Give me a couple of minutes," he said. "Then walk around back. Walk slow."

We gave him five and change. Then we moved out, Max going first. The man was in a backyard that stretched into the vacant lot, with no visible border between them. He was seated on an old couch that the pit must have used for a chew-toy. The dog was chained to a stake a little smaller than a cut-down telephone pole. A long cable ran from its collar to the man's hand.

"Have a seat," he said, indicating a couple of aluminum-and-webbing beach chairs.

We did.

"This thing I got here," he said, holding up the cable, "all I got to do is push on it, that chain comes right off Azumah's collar. You with me?"

"All the way," I assured him.

"When I see Ozell, what you want I should tell him about the money you going to make with him?"

"I heard Ozell was the man to see if you wanted to give your dog a roll."

"Not one word of that sounds like money to me, friend."

"Anyone can make *sounds*," I said. "When it comes to cash, what you want is *sight*, am I telling the truth?" Before he could answer, I pulled a thick roll out of my jacket pocket.

"I been to Chicago," he said suspiciously. "Been to Kansas City, too."

I tossed him the roll. He caught it with his off-hand, never letting go of the cable. He thumbed the rubber band off the roll.

"There's all twenties here, look like."

"Your money. If you can help us out."

"Help you out how?"

"I want to show you a tape of a pit contest. And I want you to tell me—"

"Nah, man. I don't eat no cheese."

"Not what I want. Just look at the tape, let me ask my questions. You don't want to answer them, so you wasted a few minutes. You do, we leave, and the cash stays."

He bounced the roll on his palm, thoughtfully. "I let Azumah loose and you going to be leaving *anyway*."

"You want us to leave, just say so. Toss the money back and we'll be gone."

"I'm thinking, maybe that's right. You *should* leave. And maybe I should keep something for my trouble, too."

"You don't want to be like that," I said. "We came here respectful. Don't go all Bogart on us. It'd be a mistake."

"Is that right?"

"Yeah," I said, sliding the pistol out of the same pocket I'd taken the money from.

"Bullet wouldn't stop Azumah," he said calmly, "even if you *could* hit him on the run."

"I got a full clip," I told him. "And that knife you're holding somewhere won't stop my partner."

The man tunnel-visioned in on Max, his pit-trained eyes measuring, adding up the score.

"I ain't going nowhere with you," he said warningly. "Money or not."

"You won't even have to get off that couch," I promised him.

"You want me to run it again?" I asked Ozell.

"No need," he said. "What you want to know? For your money," he added, quickly.

"You know where this was shot?"

"Could be."

"Yes or no, friend."

"Is that enough? For the money, I mean?"

"No. Look, I don't need to know the exact location where it was shot. Just if you recognize it, so you remember if you were there for this particular bout."

"Why?"

"Because, if you were, you saw somebody with a camera. The one who made this tape."

"*That's* what you want, man?"

"For the money," I reminded him.

"It was a white boy," he said. "I don't mean a white boy like you is a white boy. I mean a for-real boy. Punk-ass kid, couldn't be more than, I dunno, twenty, twenty-two?"

"He have a dog going that night?"

"No, man," he said, dismissing the thought. "He was just this weaselly guy. Comes up to me, asks can he shoot with that fancy camera? I tell him, he don't get the fuck outta there, I throw his puny ass in the pit, too. He says there's five yards in it for me. Says I can watch him close as I want—he's only gonna shoot the dogs, not the people. I *know* he's not The Man. So, I figure, why not?"

"How long was he there?"

"Maybe two, three bouts. Paid me up front. I didn't even see him go. Be lucky if the pussy made it back through the parking lot, that place."

"Describe him."

"I told you, man. A gray boy. Nothing special about him. About your height, maybe a inch or two taller. He wasn't fat and he wasn't skinny."

"Hair?"

"He had a cap on, man. Some kind of baseball one, I don't remember. . . ."

"What about his face?"

"Wasn't like yours, man. No offense, but I'd know *you,* I ever saw you again. This kid was just . . . plain, like. He had, I *think* he had, an earring," Ozell said, touching his own left ear, "but I couldn't swear to it."

I didn't trust his ghetto-game accent any more than I did those bad blue eyes. But I went at him another few minutes, and the vacuum bag didn't get any fuller.

"Thanks," I told Ozell, holding out my hand to shake. "This guy ever contacts you again, you call that number I left you, there's five in it for you, all right?" I said, leaving it ambiguous, five hundred or five thousand.

"All right," he said, not going for the bait. He'd negotiate when he had something to trade, not before.

"Yeah," I said, moving very close to him. "And one more thing. You don't want to be calling anybody else, Ozell. I wouldn't forget *your* face, either."

"Y̶ou like her in those?" Cyn asked me.

Rejji pranced around the room in a pair of side-laced black boots that went to her knees.

"I don't go for those cloven heels," I said. "Or those built-up soles, either."

"You're old-fashioned. Miss the stilettos, huh?"

"Maybe just old, period."

"No man's so old that Rejji can't make him sit up and pay attention," Cyn said, smiling knowingly. "That bitch's got a tongue so educated, she can lick up a bowl of fudge ripple and never touch the ripple."

"I'll take your word for it."

"Oh, I wouldn't want you to do that," she said. "Just sit there, smoke your cigarette, and pay attention."

"Nothing," Terry said, his tone somewhere between disgusted and offended. "Two of them, I don't think they even knew her."

"It was odds-against," I told him.

"Worth a shot," the Prof said.

"The one girl, Heidi, I think she was a friend for real," Terry said. "She was crying when we talked about it. But she said the cops had talked to her—talked to everybody in the whole school, she said. She didn't know anything."

"That wasn't our last chance," I assured him.

He didn't look comforted.

The girl in the pink T-shirt with a black "NHB" curling over her small, high breasts looked vaguely Hispanic. Maybe it was her long, dark hair, or the gold hoop earrings. But her voice was pure Ozone Park Italian.

"You look like you've been in some," she said, "but you're, like, too old now."

"I'm the manager," I told her.

"Manager? You must have us confused with the UFC or Pride, mister. The purses here are five hundred dollars, for the *top* of the card."

"That's all right."

"You mean him?" she said, tilting her head in Max's direction.

"Yep."

"You look like a grappler," she said to Max.

He bowed his head, very slightly.

"Doesn't he speak English?" she asked me.

"No," I told her, truthfully.

"He ever go No Holds Barred before? This isn't karate, you understand. People get hurt. . . ."

"We understand."

"Well, you bring him around, I can make him a match." She looked at Max appraisingly. "He's what, two twenty?"

"About that," I agreed. "But we'll go against whatever you've got."

"All right. Bring him down on Friday. Not this Friday, a week from."

"Uh, is anyone going to be taping?"

"Taping? You mean like for TV?"

"No. Just . . . You allow cameras?"

"No. No, we don't. The only video in there is what we shoot. If you want a copy, it costs—"

"But, sometimes, you let other people tape, don't you?"

"Where did you hear that?"

"Let me show you. I've got a machine in my car."

"Sixto!" she yelled.

The sound of feet pounding on boards. The door in the back of the dojo opened, and three men walked in. Triangle formation. The guy at the point was half a foot taller than Max and a hundred pounds heavier, with a shaved head and keloid eyebrows. His arms were so densely covered in apolitical ink—crosses, daggers, skulls—that they looked black.

"This guy's asking questions about taping. He says he's got something in his car . . ." the woman told him.

"What is this?" the big man asked, moving closer.

"I want to get my guy into a match," I said. "So I brought him around, find out what the deal is. See, I heard about this from a tape. . . ."

"*What* fucking tape, man?"

"That's what I was trying to explain to this young lady. I watched a piece of tape. Looked pretty good. In fact, unless I miss my guess, you were in it."

"Me?"

"Sixto, that must have been when—"

"Shut up, Vicki," he cut her off. Turned to me. "You trying to sell me something?"

"The opposite. I'm buying, not selling."

"Buying what, man?"

"Look at the tape first," I said.

"I never saw this before," Sixto said, fascinated as he watched himself on the portable playback screen. "I took that mother-fucker *down*!"

One of the men with him slapped Sixto's extended palm. Hard, signifying total agreement.

"So you said you were buying something . . . ?"

"What I'm buying is, who shot that tape?"

"This one here?"

"Yes."

"What's it worth?"

"Couple a hundred."

"Yeah? Give me the money."

"When you're done."

"I'm nobody to fuck with, pal. You just seen that for yourself."

"Right. And I'm *not* fucking with you. Who made that tape?"

He stared at me, letting his eyes glaze and his breathing go short and sharp. Prison-yard stuff. I looked between his small, close-together eyes, waited.

"I don't know his name," he finally said.

"What do you know?"

"I don't . . . Vicki, you know?"

"Yeah," the woman said. "He paid us; remember, Sixto? To tape just one match. Only we had to let him right in the ring. Remember . . . ?"

"Yeah! Now I do. Sure. That little guy was in-fucking-sane! We warned him he could get himself crippled, doing that. But he said that was okay, it was his risk."

"What did he look like?" I asked.

"He didn't look like nothing, man. About like you."

"White man?"

"Yeah, white."

"Anything else?"

"Vicki?" he asked, his tone respectful, not role-playing anymore.

"He had real nice teeth," she said. "All white and perfect. I remember those teeth."

"Good," I complimented her. "You have a fine eye. His face, did he have any scars?"

"He didn't look like *you,* if that's what you mean," she said, smiling.

"What size was he?"

"Next to Sixto, all men look small to me," she said proudly.

"Was he sporting gold?"

"No. Not that I could see."

I stroked her for a couple of minutes more, but she was dry.

"Appreciate it," I told her, handing over the money.

"What you said . . . when you came in, that was all bullshit, right?"

"Sure."

"What'd he say, V?" Sixto asked.

"He said this guy here," pointing at Max, "wanted to get into one of our events. He doesn't speak English."

"He's got the look," Sixto said. "You want to try me? Right here. We got a ring set up in back. Just for fun?"

"No thanks," I said. "We were looking for something a little more his speed."

"I spent a lot of your money," Cyn said, pointing at a couple of cartons of videotapes. "I went as downscale as I could, but you can't tell from the labels—a lot of stuff they call 'amateur' isn't. *True* amateur stuff is actually more expensive, believe it or not."

"Did you look through it yet?"

"I figured you'd rather do it yourself," she said, grinning.

"Wouldn't you and Rejji recognize most of the . . . performers? If they were pros, I mean?"

"If it's our kind of stuff, we should," Cyn agreed.

"Then just save me the ones you don't," I told her.

"You got a good guinea suit?"

"Guido, or top-shelf?"

"Either one," Giovanni said on the phone. "Just don't get all Seventies on me, okay? I'm picking you up. One o'clock. Northwest corner of Hester and Broadway."

"One in the morning?"

"The afternoon," he said, sounding annoyed.

"You look fine," Giovanni said, taking in my loose-draped charcoal sharkskin suit and teal silk shirt, buttoned to the neck. "This hour, we take the West Side Highway to the Henry Hudson, we're there in an hour, tops."

"Where?"

"It's not the place," he said, "it's the person. How you doing?"

I knew he wasn't social-dancing. "I don't know," I said honestly. "There's things that might lead us in, but I can't tell. Not yet."

"You want to run anything past me?"

"No."

"I'm not asking for anything in writing, Burke. What's your problem?"

"The problem is, I have to ask *you* some questions. And the more you know about what I'm doing, the better the chance your answers won't be as good to me."

"Asshole!" Giovanni muttered, stabbing at the brakes as a

white Corvette shot across our bow, heading for the Ninety-sixth Street exit.

"Good," I said.

"Good? What's good?"

"You're good," I told him. "A lot of guys would've lost it over something like that. Chased the jerk in the 'Vette down and—"

"—and what, grabbed a fucking bat out of the trunk and crunched him? I'm a businessman, not some stupid *cafone,* throw my life away over shit like that."

"That's what I mean; good. Something like . . . something like what we're doing, a short fuse could knock it off the rails."

"What do you want to ask me?" he said, finally getting it.

"You know *anything* about Vonni besides what her mother told you?"

"I . . . No, I guess I don't. You're not asking me if I ever saw her alone, or anything?"

"I'm asking you what I asked you, Giovanni. This isn't some grand-jury perjury trap."

"I know she was—"

"You know if she was gay?"

"What?!"

"Did her mother ever tell you Vonni was—?"

"No," he cut me off, face so tight I could see the skull beneath the skin. "Her mother never fucking told me Vonni *was* anything. Just what she was . . . doing, like. Sometimes. Where'd that come from?"

"The stab wounds," I said. "So many of them. The . . . you know, the way she was . . . mutilated. You're convinced that proves it was a message to you. But nothing I've come up with makes that work."

"That doesn't mean—"

"It doesn't mean anything," I conceded. "There's a bunch of other stuff, stuff I can't make anything out of yet. Or, maybe, there's nothing *to* make out of it. But when the cops find a guy hacked to pieces in his apartment, the first thing comes to their minds is, did he have a boyfriend? That kind of rage . . ."

"Yeah, sure. And so? How's a sixteen-year-old girl going to have that kind of . . . thing in her life, and nobody knows about it?"

"I think that's true, what you just said. And I also think, if she was . . . anything, it wouldn't matter—her mother would have told me. She'd love that girl if she was a mass murderer."

He stared at me, as if his eyes could decode my words. Said, "So why'd you ask me?"

"Sometimes, a kid will tell a stran— someone she's not close with, things they wouldn't tell their own mother, right?"

"I told you, I never spoke to her in my whole life. Not even on the phone," he said. A vein throbbed in his temple.

"Hi, Gio," said the dark-eyed girl with a Bronx accent, a lot of lipstick, even more mascara, and still more hair. She looked up at him from behind the receptionist's desk.

"Hey, Angel. How's my girl?"

"I don't know," she said. "How *is* she?"

"Don't be like that, baby," Giovanni said, taking her hand and kissing it.

"Oh, don't play with me," she said, pouting her lips. "You've got so many women, I'm surprised you can remember my name."

"I'm going to surprise you *good,* one of these days," he said, smiling.

"I wish!" the girl said. "I know he's waiting for you. Wait, I'll go back and tell them."

I guess she could have used the phone on her desk. But then Giovanni wouldn't have gotten such a good look at what he'd been passing up.

"Uncle T!" Giovanni crossed the room to where the remnants of a man sat in a wheelchair, his wasted frame propped into position with carefully wedged pillows. Giovanni bent to kiss the old man. "You look a hundred percent better than the last time."

"Who's your friend?" the man said, his voice sandpapery but clear.

"Uncle T, this is Nick. Nick, my Uncle T."

"I'm honored," I said, offering my hand.

"You Irish?" the man asked.

"Me? No. Why?"

"The Irish, they got that bullshit thing down perfect. Or maybe you seen too many movies, huh? You so 'honored.'"

"I didn't mean to insult you," I said tightly. "Giovanni told me you were a very important, very special man. I didn't think he brings just anyone here to see you; that's all I meant."

"Yeah?" he said, making no secret of studying my face. "But I don't know you, right?"

"No. You don't know me. And I don't know anybody you know, either." I looked over at Giovanni, said, "You want me to wait outside?"

"Stay right here," he said. "Uncle T, he's just looking out for me. Like he always does."

"Sit down, sit down," the man said, gesturing to a pair of pink-ish side chairs. "Don't pay no attention to my bad temper; it's the fucking chemo—takes all of the sugar out of your blood."

"But it's working," Giovanni said. "That's the important thing."

"It's not working, Little G," the man said, sad and loving, the way you tell a kid Christmas is going to be lean that year. "What it's doing, it's keeping the *lupi* back in the hills, that's all. They're just waiting for the right night. That's when they come, you know. In the night."

"Hey! You don't know—"

"I know," the old man said. He turned to me. "You think I care about who *you* know? Like your bloodlines? Where you come from? You know how I get my name? Little G, he give it to me. When he was a baby, he couldn't say my name, 'Carmine.' What he says, he says 'Tarmine.' What kind of name is that? So we made it into 'T,' just for him."

The old man shifted his head slightly, making sure he had my eyes.

"Little G called me 'Uncle,'" he said, "because he couldn't call me 'Pop,' the way he always wanted to. You getting this?"

"I got it," I promised.

He read my face for a full minute. Then he nodded.

I looked over to where Giovanni was sitting. His thumb was pressed against the wall, making a screw-driving motion.

"Anyplace you can smoke around here?" I asked.

"Outside," the old man said. "They got a little patio thing. Ask the girl out front."

I gave them a half-hour, most of it spent with Angel pumping me about whether Giovanni was married. Or, even if he was, did he ever . . . ?

When I came back into the room, Giovanni was next to the wheelchair, whispering in the man's ear. He saw me standing there, gave his uncle another kiss, got up to leave.

"Be careful," the old man told him.

"Uncle T's not what you think," Giovanni said, on the drive back.

"How do you know what I think?"

Giovanni made a bent-nose gesture. "Right?"

"How would I know if a guy's made?"

"Made? For*get* that. Uncle T, he was never in our thing. He was a craftsman, you know what that means? A shoemaker. Not some fucking flunky, puts on soles and heels, like in Grand Central. I mean, he could *make* shoes, starting from scratch. Custom. He had a little shop on Broome Street. Everybody with coin went there."

I didn't say anything; sometimes, that's the only way to keep the tap open.

"He's old now. And his mind . . . from the chemo, it's not like what it was. Sometimes, he's sharp. Like today. Other times . . .

"But what he said. To you, I mean. That was the truth. My father, he was nothing. Nothing to me, nothing to nobody. He went Upstate when I was just a little kid. You believe the movies, you think—what?—the 'boys' come around, make sure my mother's got everything she needs? That's not the way it happens. My father, he was what they call an around-guy. Only he was never around, you staying with me?"

"Yeah."

"Anyway, my mother never takes me up to see him. What's the point? I'm just a little kid; I don't even know him. And my mother, she's got to earn a living now.

"Uncle T, I got to know him 'cause he hired my mother to work the front of his store. The neighborhood, this I find out later, they always thought he had something going with her. But that was never it, no matter what they said."

Giovanni took a deep breath. Let it out, said, "Finally, my old man catches a shank in Greenhaven, so he never comes home."

"How old were you then?"

"Four, five, I don't remember. See, I never thought he *was* coming home. He wasn't like a real person to me." He zipped down his window, lit a cigarette. "My mother, all she ever really told me was, A nigger killed your father. Like it was worse than if a white guy had done him. She said it over and over. Like so I'd never forget."

"Your mother and T got together?"

"Never! It wasn't her he wanted, it was me," Giovanni said. He looked over at me, then flushed scarlet at what he thought I was thinking. "Not for . . . Uncle T, he couldn't have kids. I didn't know why. Something happened, back home. Roma, I mean, not here.

"He was real up-front with me. From the very beginning, soon as I could understand. He always wanted a son, he said. A fine son, like I was. He couldn't be my father. He didn't feel that way about my mother, and it would be . . . dirty, like, to take up with a woman he didn't care about just to have a son."

"That's stand-up," I said, bowing my head slightly to show respect.

"Oh, let me tell you, Burke. Uncle T, he was a hell of a lot harder than those goombahs sitting around in the sun on Mulberry Street, smoking their Parodis and sipping their anisette.

"One time, the summer when I turned thirteen, I never forget it, I slugged it out with Fat Vinny," he said, nodding to himself, as if to confirm the memory. "It was right around the corner from Uncle T's shop. He heard the yelling. It wasn't just the other kids, the old guys always gathered around when there was a fight; they fucking *loved* it. And he ran out. Fat Vinny was the biggest of all the kids in our grade, but he was a stone punk weasel coward motherfucker. What happened was, he pulled up Marcella's skirt. She was the same age as me, but she went to Catholic school. You know those stupid uniforms they had to wear? He pulled up her skirt, right in the street. Big joke, letting everyone see her underpants.

"Marcella was crying like she had a stake in her heart. I ran up and clocked him a beaut, right in the eye. Fat Vinny knows he can't throw with me, so he keeps rushing, trying to get me on the ground. I know what he'll do then, so I keep slashing at him. But I'm getting tired.

"All of a sudden, there's a guy holding me. Holding me back, I mean. And the same with Vinny. A man comes across the street. Slow, like he's a fucking king, you know? Who's this? Fat Vinny's father! *And* he's a goddamned capo! I didn't know any of that before. . . .

"He asks, What happened? And Vinny tells him I sucker-punched him with a brick in my hand!" Giovanni said, as outraged at the injustice as if it were yesterday. "I wanted to tell my side, but Marcella had run home. I didn't blame her, she was so humiliated by what that fat fuck did. I don't know what to do. I don't want to tell this guy, Go ask Marcella, she'll tell you. So I just say, Yeah, I clocked Vinny. I hate the fat piece of shit, I say, but it was a fair one—I didn't hit him with nothing but my hands.

"That's when Uncle T runs up, all out of breath. I remember

he was wearing his apron, still had an awl in his hand—from working on the shoes. He says to Fat Vinny's father, 'I'm Giovanni's uncle, what is all this?' And that fat fuck Vinny tells his lies again. But *this* time, I know someone's going to listen to *me,* so I tell Uncle T what really happened.

"We're all standing there, like frozen. The capo looks at T. He says, 'You know who I am?' And I remember, I swear, I can see it as clear as through this windshield right now, Uncle T, he says, 'I know who you are.' But the *way* he says it, Burke. Like, I know it's Wednesday. A fact, that's all it was.

"The capo says, 'He needs a good beating.' Meaning me. Uncle T grabs me by the neck—his hands, they were like the leather he worked with—tells me to come with him.

"And that was it. I never got that beating. Uncle T makes me tell the *whole* story. When I finish, you know what he says, my uncle? He says, 'Giovanni, you were a real man, protecting that girl. I'm proud of you.'"

Tears came down Giovanni's cheeks, but his voice stayed steely, and his hands on the wheel never moved.

"*That's* the kind of man he was, Burke. You understand?"

"I wish he'd been *my* uncle," I said, every word a separate truth.

G iovanni pulled into the side-street lot where I'd left my car. He turned off the ignition, looked at me.

"You're wondering why I brought you up there, right?"

"He's your polygraph," I said. "And you wanted his read on me." When he didn't say anything, I went on: "I don't care why you did it, Giovanni. I meant what I told him. It *was* an honor to meet him. I just didn't know how much of an honor it was when I said it."

"After that, Fat Vinny went away," Giovanni said, as if I hadn't spoken. "He never came back to school in the neighborhood. I don't know where his father put him, but the next time anyone saw him, you wouldn't recognize him. He was, I don't know, seventeen, eighteen years old. Not an ounce of fat on him; he was buffed out like Schwarzenegger."

"Did he make a move on you?"

"No. He pretended like he didn't even know me. He was already working for his father then. Going places. But he was still a punk in his heart. He changed his body. He even changed his name. But he was still the same fuck who did that to Marcella. That's what I wanted to tell T."

"I don't—"

"Fat Vinny," Giovanni said, dropping his voice so I'd listen close, "when he changed his name, he told everyone to call him Colto."

I got into the Plymouth, started it up. Just as I was ready to pull away, I saw Giovanni walking toward me. I rolled down the window, waited.

Giovanni leaned in, close. "My Uncle T, he loves me," he said. "I'm his son. His only child. Anything I ever did, it would be all right with him."

"I know."

"No, listen to me. This isn't about Colto. Things like that, I tell my Uncle T all the time. But . . . the other thing, I never could have told him, Burke. Not when it first happened. Not now.

"I trust my Uncle T with my life. He'd never say anything, no matter what anybody did to him. It's not for me I don't tell him; it's for him. It would . . . it would hurt him to know. Hurt him deep in his heart. I could never do that to him."

On the drive back, I wondered which of Giovanni's two secrets he believed would have hurt the old man the most. And if he wasn't disrespecting his uncle's love, by believing that proud old man would have given a damn about either one.

"You think there's a key, don't you, honey?"

"I know there's one," I told Michelle. "And I know I'm right next to it. But when I reach out . . ."

"You know how to do it, baby. You have to let it come to you."

"Sure," I said, not hopefully.

Michelle walked across the room, perched herself on the broad, padded arm of an easy chair, crossed her spectacular legs.

"Tell Little Sister," she said. "Just tell me until you get stuck."

"The tapes, the ones Vonni had . . ."

"Yes . . . ?"

"They were real. I mean, as far as we can tell, those things happened. I spoke to those people—not an actor in the bunch. The pit-bull guy, that's what he does, I saw it for myself. The underground fights, same thing. And Max says the jump-in was real, too, remember?"

"I remember."

"That sorority stuff, Cyn didn't recognize any of the players. And she even said it looked like someone stuck a camera through a keyhole, but . . ."

"But what, honey? It *was* only the one camera, like you said before. Maybe whoever made the tapes was a fly on the wall."

"No, girl. He *paid* to be around at least a couple of the others, remember?"

"You're thinking he didn't pay *everybody,* right? Not all the people on those tapes? And that's the way in?"

"I don't know. But that's not the . . . Damn! Michelle, you remember that Puerto Rican Day Parade riot a few years ago? When all those girls were getting grabbed and groped? Assholes ripping their tops off, spraying them with those water cannons?"

"I remember that *very* well. Probably no one would ever even have been arrested for it except . . . Oh, Burke! That's right! The cops made the cases from the *videotapes.*"

"Yeah. Amazing how many good citizens bothered to *tape* it, instead of trying to *stop* it, huh? What a shock. And how often every station in town ran some footage of it. But the thing is . . . remember what Cyn and Rejji told us? About shilling?"

"You don't think it was a setup, that whole thing? Just so someone could *tape* it?"

"The parade? No. But I think I know what the difference is now."

"The difference between what and what?" she asked, impatient despite herself.

"That thing at the parade, it just . . . happened, I think. A few punks get out of hand, and the mob goes right with it. Even sheep can kick you to death when they stampede."

"Okay, now take the dogfights. That was no accident. If you were tipped, you knew it would be at a certain time and a certain place. It was a planned event."

"And the thing at the parade wasn't. So . . . ?"

"So what about the jump-in tape? And when they sprayed those swastikas?"

"Those had to be planned, too. You don't just suddenly—"

"Planned, sure. But not *announced*. You had to be a . . . member, I guess, to even know when it was going down, much less be right there on the scene."

"Freaks film themselves," Michelle said, her voice a cold reminder of our childhoods. "You know that as well as me. They take trophies, so they have what they . . . do, captured forever. And for Nazi graffiti, it's perfect. No matter how quick someone repaints the church, on the tape the crap they sprayed is always there. You think the scumbags who knocked down the World Trade Center and killed all those people don't get their rocks off watching the videotapes, over and over?"

"That's right. They tape everything, right up to rape and murder. One of those tapes *was* a rape, it looked like—that girl with the hood over her head, she must have been drugged or drunk. But people tape themselves for fun, too, right? Just for their own private use."

"Like Pamela and Tommy Lee?"

"I don't know *why* they made those tapes, girl. Do you?"

"There's that," she conceded.

"Anyway, just because we found them all in one place doesn't mean the same person made them, I know. But that tape of Vonni? Where she was running? It's not right."

"I don't get you. Because it's a fake, like Cyn said?"

"Not only that. It's just a snip. Like a sample, or something. All the rest are . . . stories. Not that they have a beginning and an end, but you can always tell what's going on. What you're supposed to be seeing. Except for Vonni's. It's a mystery, what she's running from. And it's the only mystery in the whole stack."

"What are we going to do?" Michelle said, standing up. The way she always does.

"Not what's *on* the tapes, Mole. The tapes *themselves*. The whole package."

"There are no good tests for that," he said. "Not precise enough ones. I won't be able to tell you much from—"

"Just take them apart," I said. "And tell me what you can."

"I got yearbooks," Terry said, bursting into the suite. "Look!"

"You did not steal them?" the Mole asked.

"No, Pop. I just borrowed them. I'll bring them back."

"That is too much risk," the Mole said. "Once you have—"

"No, I really borrowed them! From a couple of girls I met. I've got this year's, and . . . a few others, too."

"They know you have them?"

"Yes," Terry said, patient with his father.

"Oh," the Mole said. And went back to his work.

Every working professional keeps some sort of Rolodex. Mine's in my head. That "expectation of privacy" crap is fine for attacking a search warrant, but by then the cops already have the info. And that smoke never goes back into the cigarette.

I've got a list of experts. In all kinds of things. Carefully culled over the years. Because one thing I've learned: just knowing things doesn't make a person useful.

When I was on my first bit, a group of researchers came into the prison, looking for volunteers. By then, I already knew enough to pay attention when certain people had something to say. Tucker was an old veteran con who'd jailed down south when he was a young man. He was always telling us that New York joints were country clubs compared to The Farm at Angola. There, Tucker said, they used to give you time off your sentence if you let them experiment on you—a new yellow-fever vaccine, stuff like that. But the courts made them stop doing it. I guess they figured, when you spend your life as a work animal in the fields, whipped by freaks who love *their* work, you spell "volunteer" a little differently.

But some stuff was still okay, like the psych "studies" they were always doing on us. They told us that we wouldn't get anything if we participated. So, naturally, every con in the house figured the parole board would mark you lousy if you didn't, and there was never a shortage of "subjects."

I remember one time, especially. All the visitors wanted was a blood sample and an interview. Big deal. Anyway, everyone said the nurse drawing the blood was a real piece.

That part turned out to be true. She was a Puerto Rican woman, slender, with big brown eyes and wicked thighs. And she smelled like flowers I'd never know the name of. That needle sliding into my vein was the gentlest touch I'd felt since they'd locked me down.

The interviewer was a young guy, only a few years older than me. Bushy-haired, with wire-rim glasses. He was wearing a blue work shirt under a putty-colored corduroy jacket with leather patches on the elbows. He told me I had an XYY chromosome. I didn't know what that was, but I could see it made him very excited.

"We can't be sure," he said. "The data aren't all in yet. But this is some of the most important work that's ever been done in the field."

"What field?" I asked him.

"Biocriminology," he said. "Let's finish your interview, and then I'll answer any questions *you* have; fair enough?"

I lied my way through the rest of his questions, practicing my survival skills. When it was over, he gave me one of those "This is going to be *profound*" looks, said, "Haven't you ever wondered why you're . . . the way you are?"

"The way I am?"

"A violent offender," he said, looking around quickly, as if he'd just discovered we were alone in the room. "A habitual criminal since early childhood. Haven't you ever wondered what *made* you like you are?"

"That XYY thing?"

"It could very well be," he said solemnly.

So it's true, what they've been saying since I was a kid, I thought to myself. *I was born bad.*

After I got out, I studied everything I could find about XYY. The library had a ton of stuff on it, but it was just a bunch of people arguing with each other. That's when I read about this famous professor. The article said, when it came to genetics, he was out on the edge. Supposedly, they kicked him out of some big university because he was too far ahead of the rest of them to fit in.

The article said he lived in New York. I asked around. Picked up that he lived somewhere over on the Lower East Side. In a big loft that he'd turned into some kind of mad-scientist laboratory. No phone.

I didn't know anything about genetics, but I knew how to find people.

I just showed up one day and knocked on his door. It was opened by a powerfully built black woman with a big afro and startlingly green eyes. I told her I wanted to ask the professor a question about genetics, and she brought me right to him, as if he got visitors like me every day.

He didn't look like my movie idea of a mad scientist. Didn't even have a white coat, just a pair of chinos and a flannel shirt. Cleanshaven, with a neat haircut.

I asked him about the XYY.

"Someone told you that was you, yes?" the woman said.

"Yeah."

"And you think this 'explains' something? About your behavior?"

"Maybe," I said, wondering if the professor was ever going to say anything himself.

"It doesn't," she said flatly. "There are those with the extra Y who are pillars of the community. And plenty of vicious psychopaths with the standard XY."

"Oh."

"'Oh'? What's wrong? You want Dr. Drummund to tell you himself, is that it?"

"No. I mean . . . I thought . . ."

"You think I'm his, what, secretary?"

"I thought you were his wife," I said.

"I'm a whole lot more than that," she said, suddenly grinning.

"D o you know any Japanese?" the professor asked me.

"Not a word."

"No, no. I mean, do you know any Japanese *people*?"

"Sure."

"Businesspeople?"

"Absolutely," I assured him. Remembering what Mama had told me about the market for powdered rhino horn and tiger testicles. I knew about markets for other things, too.

"You asked for it," the black woman said, winking at me.

And then the professor was off. It was a good fifteen minutes before I understood his life's ambition was to find a way to breed male calico cats. He rattled on about the orange color being sex-linked to the X, and the only way to get a male calico was from an error in chromosome separation, so they're very rare. And almost always sterile, too.

"But what's the big deal about—?"

"They're worth a fortune," he said, dead serious. "To collectors. In Japan, if you know the right people, you could get maybe twenty thousand dollars for a single cat."

"Nelson," the black woman said gently, "let's have tea."

By the time I left, I knew that all I had gotten from my bio-parents was my hair and eye color, maybe some physical and mental capacities. "But even those are far more environmentally determined, as they eventually manifest themselves," the professor told me. His woman looked on, smiling . . . at me, once she was satisfied I got it.

And the professor had my word, the minute he broke the code to producing male calico cats, I'd get him a pipeline to the Japanese collector market. I'm still good for it.

I dialed up the Rolodex in my mind, did my search. Then I pointed the Plymouth toward a quiet building in Greenpoint.

"Of *course* there's a market for keyhole stuff," the generic-looking man told me. We were in his top-floor apartment, sitting at a kitchen table. He was drinking Zima. I passed.

"There's only two things that count in this game," he said. "Rarity and matchmaking."

"Matchmaking?"

"Let's say you had a tape of some famous actor taking it in the ass from another famous actor, okay?"

"Okay."

"All kinds of buyers for product like *that,* right?"

"Sure. Especially the actors themselves."

"Exactly. But let's say they're *not* famous, okay?"

"Okay."

"*Now* who wants to buy it?"

"Someone interested in that kind of porn, maybe?"

"Uh-huh. But only *that* kind. To you, I couldn't *give* it away, because that stuff doesn't turn your crank. So, sure, it's got *some* value. To *some* people. But it's no hot product. Nothing you could sell to the *Globe* or the *Star;* you've got to go out and *find* a buyer. See what I'm saying? That's the art to it. Match-making."

"So no matter what I had . . . ?"

"If it was rare enough, I could move it," he said, his voice utterly devoid of doubt. "There's people, they'll buy dirt from a serial killer's grave, you convince them it's authentic. That's the no-starter, authentic. You don't have that, you've got nothing.

"There's girls making a living selling their smelly panties on the Internet. This one chick I know, she told me she goes through twenty pairs a day, sometimes. Authentic, see?"

"Same for rape tapes?"

"If it was real, and you could prove it, *hell,* yes. There's been rumors for years about the Homolka tapes."

"Homolka?" I asked, faking a blank.

"Bernardo and Homolka, you heard of them, right? Husband-wife team, up in Canada. They snatched young girls, sex-tortured them in their basement. *Very* heavy stuff. Then they killed them. Anyway, the cops *found* the tapes. The actual tapes. But the government closed the courtroom when they showed them during the trial. Anyone had one of those, he'd be rich."

"Why do you call them the Homolka tapes?"

"Homolka was the broad. Blonde chick. Young. She got some nothing sentence. For testifying against the husband. The prose-cutor made that deal before they got hold of the tapes. Anyway, *she's* the one everyone's interested in. Even has fan clubs on the

Internet. She's going to be out soon, I think. Word is, she may have a couple of the tapes hidden away. . . ."

"And people say there's no such thing as snuff films."

"There's such a thing as *anything*. That's where the match-making comes in."

I nodded at the wisdom. "I want you to look at a couple of tapes," I told him. "I brought them with me. Tell me what you think."

"It's your money," the man said.

"I could move those," he said later.

"Every one of them?"

"Not all of them so quick. And not *any* of them for a lot of coin. The paddling one, that was pretty hot; I could unload that in a few hours. But you're talking maybe a couple of hundred for it, max. And only if you convince the buyer that it wasn't faked."

"You mean, that the girl really got paddled?"

"Nah. Sure she did. So what?" he said, unknowingly echoing Cyn and Rejji. "You'd have to convince the buyer that it wasn't a *scene*, understand? That they weren't working from a script. Buyers are always on the watch for the mass-produced stuff. They'd never trust anything on DVD—video's the only way to go. If it was a sneak tape, it'd be worth a lot more. Even the toilet freaks, all they want to buy is the spy-cam stuff. You'd think shit is shit, right? Not to those sickos."

"What about the girl who got the knockout drops?"

"Like I said, I could move it. But you're talking a real cheap sale, there. The people who buy that stuff, they want to see . . . a struggle, like. Of course, with that bag over her head, you could say she was a celebrity, maybe. . . ."

"Mole found something!" Michelle greeted me as soon as I walked in.

"What?"

"Come on," she said, tugging at my hand.

The Mole was hunched over the coffee table, a rectangular magnifying glass in one hand, a videocassette in the other. Terry was sitting next to him, a notebook to his right.

"CV," the Mole called out, softly.

"Got it," Terry said. He looked up, saw me, said, "We've only got two more to do."

I sat down on the couch, holding Michelle's hand so she wouldn't run over there and disrupt everything in her excitement. "I told you, I told you, I told you," she whispered at me.

Finally, the Mole stood up. And walked out.

"He's just going to the bathroom," Terry said. "Come over here, I'll show you what we figured out."

He handed me the magnifying glass, then used what looked like a dentist's pick to point toward the corner of one of the cassettes. "It's real small," he said. "And reverse-embossed. Kind of sunk right into the plastic. So it's the same color; hard to pick out. Pop said he had some stuff that would bring it up, make it stand out, but he didn't want to mess with it until you looked for yourself."

It took me a minute or so before I saw what Terry was talking about. A pair of tiny block letters: FV.

"What does that mean, 'FV'?" I asked Terry.

"It's a code of some kind. There's three of them: CV, FV, and NV. We thought it might be something they did at the factory, so Mom sent me out to buy some blanks, from the same manufacturer. I went to four different stores. And you know what? Not one of the other tapes had anything like this on them."

"Is there any pattern to them? The letters, I mean?"

"I don't know," the kid said. "Pop said that part isn't science. He said you'd figure it out."

I turned the cassette over in my hands, as if its weight could tell me something. Shook my head.

"Let me see." Cyn.

Terry picked up another cassette, waved her over to the table. Cyn bent forward, her barely restrained breasts in the kid's face, said, "Hold it for me, honey," as she winked at me over her shoulder.

The kid handed her the magnifying glass and held the cassette in both hands, steady as a dead man's EKG. "It's on the bottom," he said. "Right near the erase-protect piece."

Cyn stopped playing around. "Tilt it a little toward . . . Yes!" A few seconds later: "Rej, get over here! Take a look at this."

The women switched places around Terry like he was a piece of furniture.

"You thinking what I'm thinking?" Cyn asked her.

"Uh-huh. Let me just . . . Sure, that's it, Cyn."

"What?" I asked them.

"It helps when you've seen one before," Cyn said.

"Seen what?"

"A branding iron," she said. "This little 'NV' thing here? That's what made it."

11

Habla español?"

"*Poquito. Muy poquito.*"

"*¿Y que?*"

"*Bodega, botanica, bruja, plata, jefe . . .*"

"*¿Y que mas? . . .*"

"*Pistelola, gusano, violencia, puerco, ropa, compadre, mordida . . .*"

"*¿Maricón?*"

"I've heard the word."

"What does it mean?" Felix asked me. His voice was still sable-soft, but his eyes were freezer burns.

"It's a word for—"

"No, *hombre*. Not what it *is,* what it *means, comprende?*"

"I'm not follo—"

"Somebody calls you *un maricón,* that means you have to *do* something, yes?"

"Oh. Yeah, maybe. Depending on who's saying it. Or where."

"A man calls you '*maricón*' in prison, he is saying—what?"

"Inside? Depends who's doing the calling. Some cliques, that's the conversation. Play the dozens all day, every day. But that's only between them*selves,* see? If you mean to someone you don't know—like for an insult?—never happen. Nobody *challenges* you to a fight in there. If you're really after a guy, you don't warn him. There's none of this 'I'll see you after school' stuff," I said, wondering if he was asking, or testing.

He nodded. Not like he was agreeing, like he wanted me to keep talking.

"Not much fistfighting in there, either," I told him. "Except for when a guy just loses his temper—it's mostly the young ones who do that. Now, in the bing, solitary, guys call each other out all the time. You see a lot of cell gangsters, mouth-artists who get real brave when everybody's locked down. It's 'You're dead, nigger!' this, and 'My homeboys are going over to your house and fuck your daughter in her white ass!' that. Around the clock. Never stops. But it's just background noise.

"The only reason you might call names in there would be an intimidation thing. A test. You wouldn't hear '*maricón,*' though. You'd hear 'pussy' or 'punk.'"

"And what must you do then?"

"Stick 'em or slice 'em," I said, as no-option flat as when I'd first heard the rules explained to me a million years ago. "Maybe not right that minute, but you have to do it. And pretty soon. A man calls you something like that, he's trying to break you with words. But behind the words, if you don't give it up, there's always a knife. His or yours."

"But outside of prison? Then, for an insult . . . ?"

"Sure. That's right. Then it *is* a challenge. Or something you yell out your window at a guy who just cut you off."

"A *great* insult," he said. "It is calling someone a coward, yes?

To most people, means the same thing. *Maricón,* it means you have no courage?"

"Like another word for 'punk'?" I said. "Yeah, that's right. I guess it all comes around in a circle, words like that. When I was a little kid, I thought 'punk' meant someone who wouldn't fight—like when you 'punk out,' okay? But as soon as I got Inside, I found out 'punk' is what you are if some jocker owns your ass."

Felix leaned forward, lit a cigarette. "In my . . . culture, in my world, you understand what it would mean, to be thought of . . . that way?"

"Yeah. I did enough time with Latinos to—"

"I don't think so. I don't think an Anglo *could* know. It's different from prison. When you were there, did you know of *maricónazo* who could fight?"

"Sure. Hell, I knew some that *loved* to. I mean flat-out gay guys who were way too bad to fuck with. One guy, Sidney, he was a sensational boxer. Lightheavy. Take you out with either hand, and look pretty doing it. I knew some who were blade men, too. Everybody walked soft around them."

"So they are not all alike?"

"Nobody's all alike."

"That is the difference between our worlds, Burke. In mine, *un maricón* could be accepted. He could do work—there is a contract killer, *muy famoso,* everybody knows what he is—but he could never *lead,* you understand?"

"If you say so."

"I read once, in World War I, some white men died because they would not take a blood transfusion from black men. I do not know if this is true. But I know this. For those who play '*mas macho,*' they would never follow a leader who was not, in their eyes, a 'man.' And that will never, ever change."

"Maybe not."

"You give nothing away, do you?"

"You called this meet, Felix. I thought Giovanni would be here, too. So I drive all the way uptown, find this place, and . . . it's just you."

"You are very trusting," he said, sarcasm dusting his voice.

"You had plenty of chances, if that's where you were going," I told him. "From the very first meeting. Way before you spent any money."

"So? I brought you here because I wanted you to understand that this thing you are doing, it is a very delicate matter."

"I always knew that."

"And you also knew . . . about me and Gio, didn't you?"

"Not before I met you."

"But then, yes?"

"Yes."

"You think it is so apparent?"

"No. Not at all. You *let* me see, didn't you? A test?"

"Of a sort. If it was, how do you know if you passed?"

"Because I'm not dead," I said.

"You think I am a killer?"

"I think you just told me you were."

"Gio thinks it is a *federale*." Felix tilted his head, as if Giovanni were in the room with us. "He already told you why. But there is another possibility. One I believe you have not considered."

"What's that?"

"That the message was not for Gio; it was for me."

I watched his eyes, asked, "A message that whoever did it knows things?"

"Yes."

"What would be the point?"

"For me to step away. Gio would not be a problem for . . . for the people in my organization. He is not one of us. Who you do *business* with, that is just business. If I moved aside, whoever took over for me, that man could continue with Gio, as before."

"That doesn't add up for me," I told him.

"Why not?"

"If somebody knows something, something that would make you move over, if they had proof, why wouldn't they just mail you a sample of *that*? What's the point of a homicide?"

"Because they would need me to move away," Felix said. "But they would need Gio to stay."

"So what are you telling me? That Giovanni *would* stay?"

"*Sí*, he would stay. This they would expect. Business is business. And Gio doesn't know any other business. In their minds, he would not be . . . emotional about it."

I didn't say anything.

"They don't know him," Felix said, very softly. "Gio would defend me. But, if he had to fight on two fronts, he could not win."

"Why tell me all this?"

"Because I am trapped," he said calmly, a man who'd been there before and recognized the landmarks. "I cannot tell Gio. I cannot tell him that maybe his daughter was killed because of someone who wants something from *me*. That would mean it is one of my people, not some 'fed.' But I know information is a weapon. And I want you to have it all, for what you must do."

"What happens if I can't find out, not for sure?"

"Then it could end as if each of our bosses called me and Gio 'maricón,'" he said, almost in a whisper. "What choice would we have?"

"I've got something for you." The note was under my door in the hotel. Signed "C."

I walked through two sets of connecting doors to the last suite. Cyn was sitting in an armchair. Rejji was kneeling in a far corner, her back to me. She was nude except for a pair of red stiletto heels. Her hands were bound behind her back with a red silk scarf.

"I got your message," I said to Cyn.

"She's so pretty when she's been bad," Cyn said.

"You said you had something for me?"

"Don't you like her?"

"I like you both."

"Ooo!"

"Cyn . . ." I said, shortly, in no mood to play.

"We found her."

"Who?"

"The sorority girl."

"From the tape?"

"Yep. The one using the paddle."

"Are you sure?"

"We looked at that tape a hundred times, Burke. We bothered the Mole so much that . . . Michelle—is that his wife, for real?—Michelle went off on us.

"So he showed us how to stop the frames and do everything ourselves. Then we took the yearbooks, that the kid got us? It was a long shot, but we had to do *something* to kill time out here, so . . ."

"Let me see."

"Look," she said, pointing to a blown-up photocopy of a picture of a teenage girl whose most striking features were long straight hair and a prominent nose. "And here's a still from the tape. The Mole hooked it up with some cables so we could just—"

"Sssh," I said.

"Do you know what calipers are?" I asked Cyn.

"Sure. To measure. In school, we had to—"

"In the room where we keep the equipment, on the long table, there's a whole set of them. Little ones, with metal points at both ends. They're in a leather case, blue plush lining. Could you get them for me?"

"What do you need them for?"

"I'll show you when you get back."

"Okay." She walked over to where Rejji was kneeling and lifted her thick dark hair with one hand, revealing a red collar and a short length of chain. Cyn grabbed the chain and pulled it sharply, forcing the brunette's head all the way down until her nose was in the corner. "Stay!" she said.

"Was she a good bitch while I was gone?" Cyn.

"Perfect."

"I doubt it," Cyn said, taking a leather riding crop from a dresser drawer and walking purposefully over to the corner.

"What are you *doing*?" Cyn demanded, a few minutes later.

"It's a very good match," I told her. "And whoever thought to make the two blowups the same scale knew what they were doing—"

She leaned over, very close. "That was Rejji," she whispered. "But she's still being punished, so I'll tell her later."

I nodded, went on: "But we're comparing a relatively sharp photo, from the yearbook, with one that has a lot more grain, from the videotape. And they weren't taken at exactly the same angle, so I'm trying to narrow things down."

"With those?" she asked, meaning the calipers I was holding.

"Yeah. There's things about your appearance you can change—hairstyles, gum in your cheeks, a mustache—but there's some things that always stay the same. A guy named Bertillon discovered this a long time ago. Way before fingerprints. The distance between the pupils of the eyes, that's one of them."

"*Your* eyes, they . . ."

"Yeah, I know. But that's one in a million, Cyn. For most people, even with plastic surgery on other parts of their face, like, say, a nose job, that distance would stay the same. Nobody's going to get their eye muscles severed just to change their appearance. You lose your—"

"I didn't mean . . ."

"It's okay. Here, look: this thing is measured in tiny units. Every time you move the points, there's a little click. . . . See?"

"Oh!"

"So we lock it in like this . . . one tip in the center of each of her eyes, okay? Now we move it to . . . here, and . . ."

"It's the same!"

"I think it is, girl," I said cautiously. "I think it is."

"Y̶ou hauling the load, you get to pick the road, Schoolboy," the Prof said.

He had just finished telling me how he and Clarence had run down a couple of members of the crew that had beaten the Latin kid. "Our boy, he don't just pop up on the set, bro. This video guy, he pulls one of the gang aside. Says he knows they jump in new members; maybe they want a tape of the next time they do one? The guy he speaks to, *he* goes back to the whole crew. Or maybe just to the boss, I don't know. Anyhow, he gets permission. I asked the ones we spoke to, why didn't they just kick the video guy's ass and take his tape when he was finished? One of the boys, he says, yeah, that's exactly what *he* would have done. But the leader, he put the kibosh on it."

"Sure," I said. "The boss wanted to be in a fucking movie."

"That's what I say, too, mahn." Clarence. "It is true what you tell us from the start. These young ones, they are insane for this."

"You get anything on the video man?"

"Same as you, Schoolboy. White man, nothing special."

"They didn't know him? From around?"

"Nope. They said he was a little older than what *your* guy said, but I figure that's just in the way people see things, right? Your man Ozell, probably Mr. Video looks like a punk kid to him, so he comes up younger in his eyes. The kids we talked to, they were—what?—nineteen, tops. So a guy twenty-five, he's old, to them."

"Not even his car?"

"Zero, bro. Never saw it."

"Out here, if he's driving some generic, nobody in that age group *would* see it. Unless he's *trying* to make his wheels stand out, they'd be invisible."

"That's why it's your play to say, son. You want to use those obey-for-pay broads, it's your call, that's all."

"There's only so many ways to get people to talk," I told them. "We've got a lot of cards in our hand. And we can put most of them on the table. But we can't make people tell us what they don't know. And if Cyn and Rejji are right, and it *is* the same girl, she knows more than anything we've got so far."

"Y ou're incredible," I said.

"That's the consensus." Michelle smiled. "Besides, we already had her name, from the yearbook. The rest was as easy as a crack whore."

"Where's this camp, exactly?"

"Up in Dutchess County," Terry said. "We could pick up Ninety-five North at—"

"We can't take a whole convoy up there, Terry."

"But . . ."

"Anyway, I need you here. You're our best bet at getting some of these kids to talk. If it wasn't for you, we wouldn't even *have* the yearbook."

"He's right, honey." Michelle.

"Pop?" the kid appealed.

The Mole caught Michelle's eye, quickly ducked his head and concentrated on his equipment.

"S he was a senior in that yearbook, and that was over three years ago. So she's at least twenty now."

"Michelle said she's a junior in college. That sounds right," Cyn said.

"This camp, it's just a summer job. Supposedly, she's done it every year since she was fifteen. Pretty fancy place."

"We're not just going to walk up to Administration and ask for her, are we?" Rejji said.

"Last resort," I told them. "The map says there's a town about ten, twelve miles from the camp. I don't know what's in it, or even if the counselors get weekends off, but it's worth a shot first."

"You're going to pass yourself off as a college boy?" Cyn laughed.

I reached over to where she was sitting, pinched the top of one smooth thigh, hard. "I'm a casting director, you stupid bitch," I said.

Cyn squealed . . . a lot more than the pinch merited.

Rejji giggled from the back seat.

"I'll see *you* later, miss," Cyn mock-hissed at her.

"**T**he bar is called The LSAT," Rejji said, the minute she walked into the motel room. "That's for 'Law School Admission Test.' The story is, the owners were planning on going to law school, but they got such a low score on this test—I guess you need to get a certain number to get into *any* law school—that they decided to open up this bar instead."

"And it's the right crowd?" I asked her.

"I think so," she said. "There's a little college not far from here, but it's pretty much closed down for the summer. So there's only the trade from the camp, and how much could that be? This isn't the kind of town where a lot of the young people stick around after high school. It's got a few bars, but they're either gin mills or topless joints—either too rough or too expensive for college kids to hang out in. No, this is the only one it could be."

"All right," I told them both, "let's play it that way. Tonight's Friday. We'll give it two nights. If she doesn't show, we'll take a ride over to the camp on Sunday."

"That's probably the worst time," Rejji said.

"Why?"

"Visiting day. The parents will be up, they'll have all kinds of activities. . . . No way the counselors would get any time off."

"You know a lot about this stuff, Rej?" Cyn asked her, curious.

"Yeah," Rejji said. She got up, went into the bathroom, closed the door.

"Want to dance?" The guy was standing at our booth, arms crossed so he could puff out the biceps his neatly cut-off sweat-shirt displayed.

"I'm with him," Cyn said, pointing at me.

"What about you?" Muscles asked Rejji.

"Me, too."

"You're *both* with him?"

"Sure," Rejji said.

"You their father?" he asked me, leaning forward, locker-room aggressive.

I looked at his tanned-and-bland face, wondering if those big white teeth were caps. "Their manager," I said.

"Yeah? What do they do?"

"We're entertainers," Cyn told him, no smile.

"That means we get paid to entertain," Rejji said helpfully, her mouth as flat as Cyn's.

Muscles stood there for a minute, downloading. Then he went away.

Rejji's hand, under the table, on the inside of my thigh, squeezing. "That's her! That's her!" she whispered.

"You sure?"

"Let me go talk to her, I'll tell you in a minute."

"You know what to—?"

"*Yes!* Let me out, Burke. Quick, before she gets stuck in a booth."

"I don't know anything about a videotape," the girl said. Her long black hair and hawkish nose gave her a proud, near-exotic look, but her eyes were like tiny Japanese lanterns—bright light behind fragile paper.

"You brought me all the way up here for *this*?" I said to Cyn, sharp-voiced.

"You said yourself she'd be perfect," Cyn said, half-annoyed.

"But if she's not the same one who—"

"You don't *want* an audition?" Rejji asked the girl, brisk and businesslike.

"That was supposed to *be* an—" the girl said, then cut herself short as she realized what she had just admitted.

"I'm not responsible for amateurs," I said, clipped and impatient. "I have to look at *miles* of tape just to get a few winners, every time. That's the way it works. We've been casting for a few weeks now, and your loop turned up in a huge pile of stuff. Cyn over here, she spotted you first; got me to take a look. And I agreed, you *might* be perfect. But, you understand, those things are not my decision; it's the director's call."

She opened her mouth to say something. I held up a hand to cut her off, said, "Look, if it's not you on the tape, there's nothing to say. The camera loves some people. Others, it doesn't. I need the quality I saw on the tape. If that's not you, I'm sorry we bothered you. But if it *is* you, I hope you won't let whoever sold you a bill of goods spoil your chances in the business."

"What would you . . . ? I mean, if I was . . . ?"

"It's the same for everyone," I told her. "You know how it works. I'm the casting director. Myself and my crew interview the prospects. The best ones, the ones we think the director will *love*—those we put on tape. Free-form, no set lines. We're looking for a *quality*, not a specific performance. If you get through the interview, you go on tape. And if they pick you . . ."

"It was me," she said, biting her thin lower lip.

"**D**on't go too heavy on the makeup," Cyn said to the girl through the open bathroom door. "When you get on the set, they'll create a look for you right there."

She came out, a little self-conscious, but not nervous. Maybe it was that half-hour she'd spent on the phone, on our tab, in one of the other rooms we rented. Or maybe it was the minibar we'd left her the key to. Cyn pointed her toward a chair with a spiral back and a round, padded seat. Rejji tightened the locknut on the tripod, adjusting the minicam, while Cyn rheostatted the lights up and down until Rejji nodded agreement.

"Come in *tight*," I told Rejji. "Tight on her eyes, tight on her lips."

"She's not miked," Cyn reminded me.

"We need some tape of just pure expression," I said. "Eyes and mouth, that's what talks. It doesn't matter what they say. . . . What we're looking for is *expressive*, got it?"

I turned to the girl. "Tell me about your audition," I said. "Tell me with your *eyes* as you talk."

She arched her back, widened her eyes, said, "Well . . . it's a little complicated. It was a play-within-a-play, like *Hamlet*. Only it was a different form. Unique. We didn't really have lines."

"Like improv?" Cyn asked her.

"No. Not like improv at all. Because there *was* a script. Only I was the only one who knew what it was."

"How did that work?" I asked, making a "Give me more!" gesture toward my face.

"It's a new form of *vérité*," she said, darting her tongue quickly over her upper lip. "Very complicated. They . . . the other girls . . . they were supposed to be auditioning *for* parts in a movie. I mean, the movie *was* that they were supposed to be auditioning. Like, that was the plot. Only, there were *two* plots. The *real* plot was that Adrienne had humiliated me at school, and I planned the whole thing to get even. The movie, I mean. It was all a fake. Am I telling this all right?"

"It doesn't matter," I assured her. "Just keep talking, so we get enough tape. And bring your hands into it a little. Just touch your cheek once in a while. Like . . . that! Yes, exactly!"

"Perfect," Rejji pronounced.

"I had the only acting job, actually," the girl went on in a cat-with-cream voice. "But the others never knew it. I had to make it real. Like, I really *had* set the whole thing up myself, just so I could give it to Adrienne. See, they were acting *like* they were acting, that was the script. The plot, I mean. *One* of the plots. But I was acting like I *wasn't* acting, see?"

"Ummm . . ."

"Vision was right, about what he told me. He said people want to be in the movies so bad, they use their fantasies like a shoe-horn—they *make* things fit.

"I mean, Adrienne, nobody could see her face. What did she think she was auditioning for, ass model? So, if I *had* set the whole thing up, just so I could do that to her, it *would* have worked. In real life, I mean. The same exact thing. That's the *vérité.* I didn't *actually* set it up, but if I was a good enough actress, it would be just *like* I did."

The girl glanced over at Rejji, who gave her an encouraging nod. She darted her tongue again, went on:

"You know what I told him? Vision? I told him, if this was *really* real, like I had planned it all for revenge, you know what would happen? We'd have to do a lot of takes. So Adrienne's fat ass could get paddled over and over again."

"Was that what you did?"

"No," she said, pouty. "Vision said that the camera would know."

"What does that mean?" Cyn asked her, a reporter interviewing a star.

"Well," the girl said, tossing her hair slightly, "in real life, she wouldn't *start* with her ass all red, see? That would give the whole thing away. So we had to do it all in one take. And I did it, perfect," she said, chesty with self-satisfaction.

"What happened with your audition?" I asked.

"Well . . . nothing. Yet. Vision said, even if I didn't get picked for a part, my tape would make the rounds. He had more of me, too, in case they wanted to see other stuff. Like more of my face, like you're doing here. And I got paid, too," she said proudly.

"Is that right?"

"I made five hundred dollars," she said smugly. "Plus, I got to beat Adrienne's ass. And *she* didn't get paid a cent."

"**W**hat's the score?" I said into the cell phone.

"I'm not gonna lie; we been playing for the tie."

"That's not us. We need another move."

"Got one," the Prof said. "But Michelle finds out what we running, she's gonna come gunning, bro."

"You got Terry out there *alone*?"

"What you want us to do, Schoolboy? Play ofay? This here's the boy's turf, not ours."

"But you've got Clarence close?"

"He's right here with me," the little man said. "Just a coupla niggers in the parking lot of this monfucious mall, anybody looks."

"Does the Mole know?"

"Man wants to speak to you," the Prof said, answering my question.

"**Y**ou're a light sleeper," Rejji said.

"And you two would make lousy burglars," I told them, glancing at my watch—three-thirteen. "What've you been up to? This town can't have that much going for it."

"We were with Kori," Cyn said. "Playing sorority initiation."

"You're sure?" I asked Rejji, who was draped over the foot of the bed, on her belly, a pillow under her hips.

"She's an amateur," Rejji said. "But she knows what she likes."

"I appreciate you taking one for the team," I told her.

"Me? Please! We taught her a new game. It's called 'turning the tables.' Maybe you heard of it."

"Yeah. What did you get out of her?"

"You mean, *after* Cyn made her—"

"Rej, you can tell me all about it some other time, okay? But, for now, how about you go back to where you started?"

"She's not a rocket scientist, Burke. But she's smart enough to know when to be scared."

"Of this 'Vision' guy?"

"No. According to her, he's a real sweetheart. Butter wouldn't melt in his mouth. It's the twins."

"Who?"

"Stop teasing, bitch," Cyn said, walking over and giving Rejji a loud spank on the bottom. She sat down on the bed, facing toward where I was propped up against the headboard. "Twin brothers," she said to me. "Brett and Bryce Heltman. Used to be hot-stuff athletes, a few years ago. Big, *strong* boys. With really foul tempers. Kori says she heard they got away with murder when they were in school—they were seniors when she was still in junior high, so it's just rumors, but she sure believes every word."

"And they're with Vision?"

"Not 'with' him, like part of his crew or anything. But . . . And I want to tell you, Burke, this is *all* stuff she 'heard,' okay? So it could be one hundred percent bullshit. . . .

"There was this girl mad at Vision. Because of some video thing, Kori doesn't know for sure. The girl ended up gang-banged. They didn't just fuck her, they fucked her *up*. Broke her jaw and one of her arms. And they stuck a—"

"I get it. And word is that was these twins' work?"

"That's all it is, the 'word,'" she said. "The girl never . . . Well, it never went to court. The girl said she didn't know *who* did it. But, supposedly, she told one of her friends that it was the twins."

"Maybe it was. But that doesn't mean there was any—"

"Kori knows of at least two more."

"Girls who got raped?"

"No. People who got the crap pounded out of them right after they had some kind of beef with Vision. And here's what's *not* a rumor. Kori went to meet him, Vision, once. At the Tackapausha Preserve—that's, like, a big nature park, somewhere around where they live. She figured Vision wanted to tape her outdoors or something. When she got there, he walks her down this trail. At the end, sitting on a tree trunk, there's the twins. She said they didn't *do* anything, but they scared her to death—it was like being in a cave, back in those woods."

"What was Vision doing?"

"Taping."

"Taping what?"

"Taping her being scared, Kori said. And probably taping her when she ran away."

"Which one is the paddling tape?" I asked Michelle.

"They're all labeled, honey. With Post-its. I've got the master list here." She ran her finger down a column, said, "It's number four."

I carried it over to the workbench the Mole had put together. Flicked on the gooseneck halogen, picked up the magnifying glass, double-checking.

"NV," I said.

"What does that tell us?" Michelle asked.

"I don't know yet, girl. We need to sort them first."

It took longer than I'd have thought, rechecking the tiny little brands. When we were done, we had one high stack, and one short one. And one orphan.

CV: The dogfights, the NHB contest, the jump-in tapes . . .

NV: The swastika spray-painters, a girl trying on blue jeans in a booth, the sorority paddling . . .

FV: Just one. Vonni. Running.

"We tanked," Terry said, walking into the suite, disconsolate.

"Burke didn't," Michelle said brightly.

"What'd you crack, Jack?"

"I'm not sure," I told the Prof. "Where's Cyn and Rej?"

"I'll get them," Terry volunteered, ignoring his mother's look.

"Those codes must mean something," I told them. "And Cyn and Rej may have given us a roadmap."

Rejji ducked her head, modestly. Cyn crossed her long legs, displaying the pronounced flex-line on her thigh.

"The NV and the CV ones, they look alike, right?" I said. "Real. Like someone snuck a camera into whatever was going on. Only what this Kori told us, the NV one—the one she did, anyway—it was a scam. A production, all right, but not the one the players thought it was. And one of them, Kori, she was in on it from the beginning. An acting job. For *her,* not for the rest, no matter what they thought. If we assume all the NV ones are the same game, then one of the spray-painters was in on it with Vision, but the others thought they were making a movie. Acting."

"Or maybe they didn't know at all," Cyn said thoughtfully.

"But what would be in it for—?" Michelle asked.

"For Kori, it was doing something she wanted to do, anyway," I said, as Cyn nodded agreement. "*And* getting paid for it. *Plus* believing that she was the only one doing the *real* acting.

That's a big-hit trifecta. It could be the same for the play-Nazis, if one of them *wasn't* playing. Let's say he wants to be the leader of some 'white power' crew, but he doesn't have what it takes to pull that off. Vision tells them that they're *acting,* okay? Auditioning for the movies. But the guy, the one who's in on it, he gets to *be* what he wants, if only for a little while. Just like Kori did. And the tape is the proof."

"That young woman. The one trying on the dungarees. She was alone, mahn," Clarence pointed out.

"I think I have that one scoped, too," I said. "None of these loops have titles, or credits. I don't know whether we're seeing the whole thing, or just some snip out of the middle. But it *could* have been a deal where the script is supposed to be some girls playing a trick on their friend, sticking a little camera in their pocketbook, so they made a tape of her changing. Then they post it on the Internet or something."

"If that was the script, then which one would be the actor?"

"Not the one we saw," Cyn said. "Not the girl pulling her pants down, the one *taping* it. I'll bet there was more to it. The stripper *knows* it's a 'movie,' so she takes her pants off while 'acting' like she *doesn't* know she's being taped. But the one doing the taping, she's doing the *real* acting, because her job is to *get* those pants off. Same as with Kori, see?"

"Huh!" I said as it hit me.

Cyn put her arms over her head, stretched luxuriously. "I just *look* like this," she said. "It's not all I know."

"Tell him!" Michelle applauded.

"But what do they get from this, mahn?" Clarence asked me. "The tape would be the same if the girl was acting or not, yes? All the cameraman wants is to see her pants come down."

"No," I said, "he wants more than that. I'm just not sure what."

"**I** got it! I got it!" Terry said, running over to the VCR and hitting "Pause."

"What do you have?" the Mole asked.

"'CV.' I know what it stands for. All those tapes, they weren't acting, right? They were just real things, that the guy taped. *Cinéma vérité!*"

"What's that?" I asked him.

"Just what's on those tapes, Burke. Like Frederick Wiseman did in *Titicut Follies*."

"Terry, I got no idea who . . ."

"No, listen to me," the kid said, all worked up. "*Cinéma vérité* just means, like, super-realistic. You watch it, you don't know if it's a documentary or a story. That's what all that stuff was like, right? The pit bulls and the fighting and stuff?"

"Yeah . . ."

"And 'CV'? Come on!"

"I am certain he is correct," the Mole said.

"When's the last time *you* watched a movie?" Michelle said to him. "But he is *so* right," she said to us.

"Okay . . . But, if the CV stuff is real, and the NV stuff is acting, at least for *some* of the players, what's FV?" I asked the room. "Because that's the only one Vonni's in."

Nobody said anything.

"**I** never heard of them," Wolfe told me.

Rain slanted across the windshield of her battered old Audi. Bruiser was lying across the back seat, a thick blot of darkness in the shadow.

"I'm not looking for their reps," I told her. "What I need is their location."

"So you can . . . ?"

"Ask them some questions."

"I know who you're doing this work for, remember?"

"I'd never ask you to put someone on the spot."

"*Ask* me? No, you wouldn't do that. What you're offering to do here is *pay* me."

"If I was doing it so I could take them out, you're the last person I'd bring into it," I told her, truthfully.

"And why's that? Because you respect me so much?"

"You know that's true," I said, ignoring her tone. What I didn't say was the other truth—if I used Wolfe to bird-dog a hit, I knew exactly how she'd pay me back.

"Y ou think it's someone from our world?" Cyn asked me that night.

"Your *work* world?"

"Yes. Power power power."

"I don't see how, Cyn."

"There's those who say violent porn causes people to . . ."

"That's not your world."

"No, no; I didn't mean me and Rejji, the way we play. But . . . you know about our Internet business?"

"No."

"The deal is, we live together—which is the truth—and I own her—which is true—and if you're a subscriber—we take credit cards, checks, and money orders—you can dial up our daily channel and watch me discipline her. If you're a *premium* subscriber, you can tell me how you want her disciplined, and watch it on a private channel.

"It's simple enough. We seeded the ground with a few pictures. I have a special boudoir chair I punish Rej in. It kind of makes her lean way forward. . . ."

Rejji got up off the floor, walked over, and sat on a straight chair so she was facing backwards, her legs positioned outside the rungs. She turned her head to the side, arched her back deeply so her bottom protruded over the edge.

"See?" Cyn said. "That's a good example. And there's plenty of others. Always a market for *le vice anglais*. Me birching her, topless, that was our best seller."

"You making any money?"

"Look at her," Cyn said pridefully. "We're making a ton."

"Nothing illegal about it, either," I complimented her. "If you can skate under the IRS, you're golden."

"We're a small business," she said, smiling. "We even have a pension plan. And health insurance."

"Okay, but what does this have to do with . . . ?"

"Burke, if you saw some of the 'requests' we get, you'd lose your lunch."

"People have weird tastes."

"Some of them want me to *hurt* her. I don't mean make her cry, Burke. I mean—"

"Yeah, but . . ."

"But *what*? Do you understand what I'm really talking about?"

"Yeah. And I *don't* think whoever asks for stuff like that got the idea from you spanking your girlfriend."

"Come here!" Cyn said to Rejji. The dark-haired girl slid off the chair and crawled over to where we were sitting on the couch.

"Tell him," Cyn ordered her.

Rejji put her head in Cyn's lap. The blonde girl patted her. Gently, comforting.

"That's how it started. Before we were on the Net. With Gresham. She wanted to do it to me herself," Rejji said softly. "Hurt me for real. She . . . she terrified us. And when we wouldn't go along, that's when she—"

"I know," I said. "And it's all over now. But this thing . . . with Vonni, it doesn't scan for me like S&M gone ballistic."

"You know that woman, Lana something, the one up in the Northwest somewhere?" Cyn asked me, stroking Rejji's hair.

"Never heard of her."

"She was a branded slave in a power-exchange group. That's supposed to be an all-consent thing, right? *Exchange*. Like me and Rejji do, our pact. You know how it ended up there? The 'masters,' they finally couldn't get it up for consent. So they kidnapped and raped some college girls, visiting here from Japan. They figured Japanese girls, they'd be natural submissives. And this woman, she was right there with them. Helping out."

"So they were morons as well as freaks. What's your point?"

"It can spring back on itself," Cyn said. "If you can't control *being* in control, it can amp over. Master the master."

"That's not just for sex," I said.

Rejji looked up from Cyn's lap, turned her head toward me. "Power power power," she said, barely whispering the words.

Sleep sneered at me. My mind was so hard on Vonni that I felt a stabbing pain behind my eyes. I tried to drift—sometimes that worked.

I wondered if I was really looking at the same kind of overlap Cyn had been talking about. Where the truth was.

Power power power.

I'd walked Candy on a leash. Listened to her wet-whisper how she'd do whatever I told her to; whatever it took. Candy took a lot. Mostly people's lives. Candy would be whatever she thought you wanted her to be. She used the roles like a deranged Doberman I'd known once. He hated other dogs; I never knew why. His trademark was to pretend to be injured or crippled. So they'd come close.

Belle liked to be spanked. She also liked driving getaway cars, brawling, and revenge. She was about as submissive as a pit bull on angel dust. But she could take it, all right. The last thing she took was a hail of police bullets meant for me. I told her I loved her only that one time, just before she went over.

Fancy dished it out, in full costume. Her sister, Charm, took it. Fancy held the whip, but Charm held the handle. Tricks and games, but not fun ones—the roots were too twisted.

Strega would do anything for me. A lot of women say things like that. The way Strega meant it scared me as much as it drew me.

Gem would say, "Yes, master," slyly, expecting a smack on the bottom as a response. But she'd been her own boss since she was a baby. She'd had to be—her childhood had been the Khmer Rouge, hunting and haunting.

Belle and Candy were dead and gone. If there's anything to the Bible, they'd gone in opposite directions.

Fancy was just gone, leaving Charm just dead. I didn't know where Strega was, but that wouldn't stop her if she wanted to see me.

One way or another, women always left me. They didn't all die. Sometimes, when whatever brought us together was done, so were we.

Gem didn't end like that. I'd left her. In Portland. I told her I couldn't send for her until I knew how it would be for me back home. And now I wondered if I would ever know.

Or if she'd still be there when I did.

Who'd *want* one of those "true submissives" that inadequates are always trolling for, anyway? "Every man wants to spank a domme," Michelle had told me years ago, winking as if she knew something more than she was saying. And maybe there's some truth in that. At least it would be special. Just for you. A person, not a role.

I like spike heels and seamed stockings. On *some* women. If their legs are too thin, the seams don't look erotic; they look like huge varicose veins.

I like bratty, sometimes. Hate bitchy, all across the board.

I knew a girl, years ago. She'd spent years as a slave to some guy, wearing the collar, living the life. When he told her he was "moving on," she Swiss-cheesed him with his own custom-made shotgun. Stupid bastard died because he'd never learned the first rule of survival when your girlfriend's a borderline: abandonment is a capital offense.

If the only way you can make it work is with a woman who lets you tie her up, that's one thing. But if the only women you can get are those who'd let *anybody* tie them up, then who's the one in bondage?

No matter what any chump thought he was buying from their Internet business, Cyn and Rejji were true partners. And the bond between them didn't come in leather.

I found the house easily enough; it looked like it had been the first one in the neighborhood to surrender.

The woman was expecting me. Short and stocky, dressed in an orange jumpsuit that looked like it was on loan from the county jail. She opened the huge white floor-standing freezer and took out a plastic bag that was sealed crooked at the top. Not a Ziploc, one of those do-it-yourself jobs they sell on infomercials.

The woman laid the bag on a fake-wood chopping block, and sliced open the top with a Ginsu knife. She poured the contents onto a sheet of imitation Saran Wrap, folded it over lightly, then tossed it in a grungy gray microwave. When the oven beeped, she opened the door, unfolded the wrap, and rolled some of whatever was in there into a cigarette. She lit the confection with a Zippo lighter sporting the Harley-Davidson logo. "Very collectible," she assured me.

"My man? Rodney? Did you know he used to be with another woman? But when he lost his arm in that motorcycle accident, she up and left him."

"Because he had to go on disability?" I played along.

"Nah. Because he couldn't applaud with only one hand," the woman said, cracking herself up.

"That's a good one," I told her. "And that's the kind of material you did for Vision?"

"Yep! The way he explained it, we'd both get what we want. I'd get an audition tape I could send around to the clubs. And he'd get White Trash Wanda on tape before I get famous. You have any idea of what tapes of Roseanne before *she* made it would be worth?"

"A lot, no doubt about it," I said, paying the freight. "So how do you get in touch with Vision?"

"Oh, I don't," she said loftily. "As soon as he's finished with the editing, he's going to bring it by."

"Did you ever wonder how we knew where to find you that first time?" Cyn asked me that night.

"I do work," I said. "People—some people—know."

"There's plenty of men who . . . I mean, when that . . . happened to us, we could have gotten ourselves a—"

"You could have gotten yourselves in a worse jackpot, and you knew it," I said. "You wanted a man for hire, a professional. Someone who does his work, gets paid, and gets gone."

"That's why you did it, for the money?"

"Why else?"

"We're doing all . . . this, with you, now, aren't we? And we're getting paid, too, sure. But the money's not *that* great. And we're not making anything out of our business while we're helping you."

"What are you saying?"

"Just what we heard—that you take money, but certain kinds of stuff you *like* doing. Just like us."

"What difference? As long as I get it done."

"I . . . don't know," she said. "I'm not sure. Rejji and I, we love to play. And getting paid for it, that's perfect. I always thought, if we *didn't* love it, maybe we wouldn't do it so well on camera, understand?"

"Sure."

"Except that's not . . . Well, what I mean, I see now, it wouldn't matter. If Rejji *didn't* like it, there'd be a buyer for *that*. That was what Gresham . . ."

"You say that name too much," I told her. "Isn't that what you told Rejji when I first came to see you?"

"This is different," she said, brushing aside what was in her way. "You, you're doing this for that girl, no matter *what* you say. The *way* you're doing it, it's like the way you were when we . . ."

"She's right," Rejji said over her shoulder, from the corner where she was standing. "And that's part of the word on you, too."

"What are you talking about?" I asked them both.

"You got it bad for . . . certain kinds of people."

"Gresham was just a freak. Nothing personal. A job. I didn't feel anything for her."

"You felt something for *us*," Cyn said. "Tell the truth."

"That's me, all right, Cyn. A knight in shining armor."

"Oh, you've got plenty of armor, all right," Rejji said.

"Somehow, I never pictured you as a sports nut," Cyn said later.

"You ever watch this?" I asked her, pointed at the screen where Bryant Gumbel's *Real Sports* was running on HBO.

"No. We don't like—"

"Shut up and give it a chance."

"Ooo! You better do it, Cyn," Rejji teased. "You know what Burke'll do if you're a bad girl."

"You silly . . ." Cyn stopped herself, caught by the images on the screen. Children playing baseball together. Lots of children, with all kinds of disabilities. Blind, in wheelchairs, brittle-bone syndrome, muscular dystrophy. Something they called the "Miracle League," organized by a bunch of parents who just wanted to give the kids a chance to play. Each kid had a special buddy, another kid, an athlete who went every step of the way with the kid who needed it, from helping to hold a bat to pushing a wheelchair around the bases.

Rejji came over to see what we were looking at. She sat down, and watched, transfixed, until it was over.

"Some people," she said, choked up, "they . . . they *torture* their own kids. And these ones, they . . ."

"Makes you think there's two different species, huh?" I said.

"There are," Cyn said, holding Rejji's hand.

I spent the next day working the phones. Calling in favors. Hard to do secondhand, but Mama was an ace at relays.

The strip mall a few minutes away had a halfway-decent deli. I had them make me a rare roast beef on rye with a slice of red onion and Russian dressing. A side of potato salad, and a bottle of Dr. Brown's black cherry. Picked up a copy of the *Post,* took it all back to my room, and sat down to watch the news.

It was the usual mulch. My eyes drifted back to the paper. I was deep into a self-righteous article about "unprovoked" shark attacks when the TV suddenly blurted something about a "daring daylight assassination" of a "known mob figure." I dropped the paper, upped the volume. The victim had been sitting at the wheel of his white Cadillac SUV—in a no-standing zone in midtown, the announcer said, as if this confirmed some significant point—when someone walked by and put a single slug into his left ear. A police spokesman solemnly announced it "had all the trademarks of a professional killing."

It had gone down in broad daylight. Nobody had seen or heard a thing, not even the SUV's passenger. He had just stepped into a local store for a few minutes, asking the driver to wait. Found the body when he came back out.

The screen showed a close-up photo of the dead man. He had a round face that made his little eyes look even smaller. The announcer asked anyone with information to call a special number the cops had set up. The name of the victim was in bold black type beneath his photo. Vincente "Colto" Zandrazzi.

I was still watching television, thinking maybe the late news would have more on the killing, when the connecting door between our rooms opened and Rejji crawled in.

She came over to where I was sitting, said, "Cyn told me I had to—"

"You don't have to do anyth—"

"I need to tell you a secret," she said. "Please?"

"Rejji, I don't want—"

"I *know*. Please . . . ?"

"What?"

She crawled over to the TV set, poked around until she found the switch, turned it off. The room went into darkness, except for the light spilling from the connecting door.

She crawled back to where I was sitting. "I have to stand up to tell you, all right?"

"Sure."

She stood up, bent over so her lips were right against my ear. I thought of Colto.

"I want to do this," she whispered. "I want to see what it feels like. I want to know. But I can't just . . . Cyn has to *make* me. But not really. You know what I'm . . ."

"What about me?" I asked her.

"What?"

"What do I want to do, Rejji?"

"Do *me*," she whispered.

"Not with—"

"She won't come in," Rejji said. "And I won't look."

"**U**h! Uh! Uh!"

Rejji, on her hands and knees, blindfolded, making an explosive little noise, somewhere between a grunt and a squeal.

I was right behind her.

"Don't untie me," she whispered, dropping her shoulders to the bed. "Not yet, okay?"

"It was like . . . a string of little firecrackers, going off in me."

"Did you find out what you wanted to know?"

"Yes. Cyn was right."

"About what?"

"You know," she said. "Can she come in now?"

"You know what I *do* hate," I said to Cyn, much later that night. "Movies."

"Movies?" she said, propping herself on one elbow. "You mean *some* movies, right?"

"Remember what you always said is the answer to every question?"

"Power power power," Rejji whispered, from the foot of the bed.

"Yeah. You ever see a movie called *The Bad Seed*? An old one, from the Fifties, black and white . . . but they show it all the time on TV, still."

"I did!" Rej said. "It was the scariest movie I've ever seen in my life."

"I've seen it, too," Cyn said. She reached out one hand, pulled on Rejji's chain so that the dark-haired girl came closer to her.

"You think it was true?" I asked them both.

"You mean, like, based-on-a-true-story true?" Rejji asked.

"Yeah."

"I think it *probably* was," Cyn said guardedly. "Parts of it, anyway."

"So you think that little girl, the one who committed all those murders, she was born the way she was?"

"She *was*," Rejji said. "It . . . skipped a generation, like. Wasn't it her grandmother who was also—"

"I don't even remember," I said. "What I do remember is the whole idea of the movie. Some people are just born evil; it's in their genes. It doesn't matter how they're raised, or who raises them; they are what they are. Destiny. That little girl in the movie, she had *great* parents. They adored her. Even the neighbor, some woman, she was mad about the kid. They gave her everything."

"Why does that make you so furious?" Cyn asked, tuned in now.

"Because it's the dirtiest fucking lie ever told," I said, remembering the calico cats. "The worst one of all. No kid is born bad. Or born good, either. There's no genetic code for rapist, or serial killer."

"But there's been kids from good homes who—"

"This isn't about some abuse-excuse rap," I said. "Some people turn out to be no fucking good no matter how they're brought up. But they weren't *born* to it. There's nothing about their DNA that makes them that way."

"Why is that so important?" Cyn asked.

"Because that one miserable fucking movie probably did more to condemn kids than anything the government ever did. You think people on juries get their information from scientific studies? They get their 'knowledge' from movies. You just proved it, the both of you."

"Well, how are we supposed to—?"

"I'm not blaming you, Cyn. I guess I'm agreeing with you. It's all about power. And the movies have it, in spades."

"Well, there isn't a lot you could do about that, honey, is there?"

"We can find this Vision," I told her.

"**V**ision?" the Prof scoffed, the next morning. "Motherfucker's name should be 'Invisible,' hard as we've looked for him."

"We don't know the turf," I said. "It's not like any tracking we ever did."

Cyn and Rejji sat quietly, together, listening. Michelle was off somewhere with the Mole. Terry was out working the teens.

"You think the children know, mahn?" Clarence.

"You know what, brother? I *did* think so. But now I don't. Whoever he is, he rides the thermals, drops down whenever he sees something he wants, then skies away. I think the mistake we've been making is assuming he's like other freaks—the kind we're used to. You see what I'm saying?"

"Yeah, Schoolboy. You can always tell where they going by where they been. Not this boy."

"Not this boy," I agreed.

"Come on with it," the Prof encouraged me. Like he'd been doing since I'd hit the prison yard that first time.

"It's not a new thing, right?" I said. "Cameras. They've been used as everything from lures to kill-props since they were invented. When I was just a little kid, I remember hearing about this maggot. Glatman, I think his name was. He did it real simple. Just put an ad in the papers for photo models. He was smart. Worked L.A.—that's a refugee camp for pretty girls from everyplace else. When a woman would answer his ad, he'd tell them he was on assignment from one of those 'detective' magazines they had back then. Needed some damsel-in-distress stuff . . . no nudity, just a little cleavage. And some ropes.

"The ones who went for it, he just drove them to the 'location,' out in the desert, tied them up, did what he did, then left them there, dead."

"There's always been that," the Prof agreed. "Most of it's not about murder. Sometimes, it's just a scam to get a woman's clothes off. And some cockless motherfuckers, they need the prop, you know? Remember when the Times Square joints used to have those 'camera clubs,' son? You could rent a camera from them, pose the girl the way you wanted. Only thing they wouldn't let you in those rooms with was a roll of film."

"Yeah."

"But we don't know what this Vision guy wants," the Prof said, tapping one temple.

"Not yet we don't," I said. "But I'm sure of one thing. That camera of his, Prof, it's no prop. He's not faking. Whatever he wants, he wants it on tape."

"Burke! Wait till you hear this!"

"Calm down, Cyn. What's so—?"

"We went back to see Kori . . . the paddle girl . . . again," Rejji said.

"Why?"

"Because Cyn always knows," Rejji said. "And she was *right*."

"You found out where this Vision . . . ?"

"No," Cyn said. "She really doesn't know any more about that than she told us. But you know what she *does* know?"

"Cyn . . ."

"She knows about a guy who pays teenage girls to pose. Just like that Glatman freak you were telling us—"

"Bondage photos?" I asked her, listening hard now.

"No . . ." Cyn said reluctantly. "'Naughty schoolgirl' stuff."

"What's that mean?"

"Oh, you know, Burke. A cheerleader lifting up her skirt to show her panties, like that."

"So what makes you think—"

"Well, he only uses *actual* schoolgirls. He has to see a birth certificate, a photo ID from school, and even a report card! He's only into the real thing. . . ."

"That's a long ways from homicide."

"But, come on, he might *know* something, right?" Cyn said, almost pleading with me.

"Tomorrow afternoon," I promised her. "Now let me get some sleep."

I didn't even try.

One of the channels had a story about this guy who killed his girlfriend and stuffed her into a trunk in his apartment. He was a well-connected rich boy, so they gave him bail. He jumped bond and made it out of the country. Ended up living in France. Living *good,* too. For years, the French wouldn't extradite him, because he was facing the death penalty here, which went against their high moral principles. France is famous for protecting people from oppression. Ask Roman Polanski.

I heard the echo of Terry's school conversation in my head. *Movies are amazing.*

And Cyn. *Power power power.*

"**N**ot to be conceited, but I am, like, *so* cute, all my friends tell me I could be a model, except I'm not tall," Michelle girl-gushed into the phone. "Is it, like, for real that you have a studio and everything?"

. . .

"Oh, *wow*! I know where that is. That would be perfect. Only, it has to be after school, all right? Like right around this time? Not at—"

. . .

"Do you pay, like, by the hour?"

. . .

"Oooh! Really? How many hours could I—?"

. . .

"A gif? You want me to send you a . . . Oh, you mean, like, to see if I . . ."

. . .

"Couldn't I just . . . ?"

. . .

"Oh, okay. But I don't have any really *good* pictures of myself. I mean, that's what I wanted *you* to . . . ."

. . .

"I'll do it tonight! Just give me your addy. . . ."

. . .

"Thanks! Buh-bye!"

"You did it perfect, honey," I told Michelle.

"Swear to God, I closed my eyes, I thought you were seventeen," Rejji praised her.

"But it's no good, right?" Cyn said, catching my eye.

"I don't think so, Cyn. You see what he's doing, scamming girls into sending him pictures of themselves over the Internet, so they can 'audition' to be 'models' for him. He probably does have a little studio set up in his house. Maybe even actually pays a girl, every once in a while. It's sleazy, but probably not even a crime. He didn't ask you for nude shots, did he, Michelle?"

"No, baby. I gave it back to you, word-for-word. He wasn't even *suggesting* anything. But, you know, *some* of those stupid girls, they're going to go ahead and . . ."

"Sure," I agreed, guessing their real reason was closer to the need-greed border than it was to stupidity.

"Couldn't you at least go and talk to him?" Cyn said.

"There's one thing that would qualify him," I said to them all. "But I have to go back to the City and ask."

I looked a question at Gateman as I came through the door. He shook his head. As good as the white-dragon tapestry in Mama's window.

I went up to my place. My empty place.

It only took me a few minutes at the keyboard to get the answer. The Mole had scanned all of Wolfe's paper on Vonni's case into the hard drive of an IBM laptop, and Terry had shown me how to search the documents.

I cross-checked the info from Cyn—name, address, phone

number. Nothing. Then I tried some keywords for the kind of thing he liked to do. Blank.

The man who scammed teenage girls into cyber-sending him naughty-cheerleader pictures had never been interviewed by the cops.

Late that night, alone in my place, I wanted the comfort of the blues. I cued up some Roy Buchanan, drifted along with "Drowning on Dry Land." Rode all the way up to Chicago with Charlie Musselwhite, a bluesman who had made that same trip. Spent some time there with native son Paul Butterfield, then went back down to Texas for some of Delbert's honkytonk.

Finally, I put some Henske on, closed my eyes, got myself lost in Magic Judy's "Dark Angel." When I got to the end of that road, I picked up the cellular and dialed Gem's number.

It rang twice. Then came the series of tones that were a signal to leave a message.

I never could think of one to leave. But I let her hear the music for a few seconds, so she'd know it was me.

I looked out my window. Down into the dark. The deep dark. The Zero. But it didn't pull at me like it had once. The Zero is everywhere. Always waiting. If I had wanted to . . . just not be anymore, I wouldn't have come home to do it.

"What do you want?" He was a middle-aged white male, nothing remarkable, standing in the doorway of a modest Cape Cod. Nine-fifteen on a Thursday evening; just past dark.

"Allow me to introduce myself, sir," I said. "My name is Mr. White. And this," I said, nodding toward Clarence, "is my associate, Mr. Black."

"I'm not buying—"

"And we're not selling, sir. May we come in?"

"What is—?" he said. But by then we were all inside.

"Thank you, sir," I said. "This won't take a minute. Is there a place where we could sit down?"

"I . . ." A guy who'd made a career out of suggesting—hinting, implying, making sure you got the message, without actually saying anything himself. He'd read Clarence's shoulder holster like a billboard. His eyes never left us as he walked over to a living room dominated by a blank-faced projection TV set.

"All we want is for you to take a look at this photograph," I said, sitting down.

His mud-brown eyes came alive when I said "photograph," but I didn't know him well enough to guess whether it was fear or excitement.

I handed him Vonni's picture. He took it, tentatively at first, then visibly relaxed as he examined it.

"Have you ever seen her?" I asked him, already knowing the answer.

"No," he said—indignant, now that he was innocent. "What's this all about?"

"We're trying to locate anyone who might have been in contact with her," I said.

"Why? Is she a runaway or something?"

"She's dead, sir."

"Oh. I didn't . . . I mean, what happened?"

"It was in all the papers," I told him. "About a year ago. That's Vonni Greene."

"That's her? I mean, I know what you're talking about now. I think I did see a picture . . . in the papers, right . . . but this doesn't look like that one, I don't think. You guys, you're not cops, are you?"

"No, Mr. Trebin, we're not the police. That's what interested us. When the police were investigating the case, they talked to everyone who might have been involved in this girl's life. Anyone who might have come into contact with her in any way at all. And it seems like they never talked to you."

"That's because I never—"

"That's because they didn't have your name," I cut him off. "But we can fix that, if you'd like."

"I . . . I don't care," he said, falling way short of defiant. "I told you, I've never even seen—"

Clarence caught my eye, nodded. But we kept him talking for another few minutes, just to make sure.

"I don't like ghosting those country cribs," the Prof said, back at the house. "People out in the sticks, they don't mind their own business the way city folks do."

"How long did it take you?" I asked.

"To get in? It was a cheesebox, Schoolboy. Maybe ten seconds. We didn't have a floor plan, but I could hear you all talking, so I knew where I had to keep to."

"Where was it?"

"Basement, bro. Just like we'd figured."

"And he had a computer?"

"Yeah. I don't know nothing about the damn things, but he sure had him a big-ass screen for it. Like you said, I didn't touch it."

"Find anything else?"

"Pictures, bro. Motherfucker had *hundreds* of them, minimum. Tacked up all over the place."

"And they were all—"

"What Cyn said, honeyboy. Like a yearbook from a girls' school, only in color. Nothing he's ever gonna go to jail for. One thing, though . . ."

"What?" Rejji asked.

"No blacks, no Asians, no Latinas—hell, no fucking *Indians*. Not one. For this boy, all-white was all right."

"That clinches it," I said. "He's not the one."

"These two are a prize pair of dirtbags," Wolfe said, handing over a couple of mug shots.

They looked identical, right down to where their bullet heads just inched past the "74" on the vertical measuring bar. Nice specimens. Square-jawed, heavy cheekbones, not a lot of nose or forehead. Prominent trapezius ridges sloped from their thick necks to their wide shoulders. They even had the same expressions on their faces—barely blunted aggression, just a few hundred RPM short of redline.

"What did they go down for?" I asked her.

"They didn't," she said. "These are from the arrest. Never went to trial."

"What were they charged with?"

"This time? Rape. Before that, Assault Two, Assault Three. That's kind of their specialty."

"They *never* went to trial? On any of all that?"

"They pled out to YO on some of them."

"*Some* of them?" Youthful Offender status is usually a one-time present from the criminal-justice system.

"That's right. Probation. And sealing."

"No expungement?"

"They *did* get expungement, on the ones that were dismissed."

"And this one, for rape, it was dismissed?"

"That one, too."

"But don't the cops have to destroy the photos and prints when the court—?"

"Please!" she said scornfully.

"Sorry. You have anything else?"

"Oh, there's a *lot*. The boys were impressive athletes in high school. Brett was a wrestler; Bryce played lacrosse. Despite marginal transcripts, they each did *very* well on the SATs. They went to school upstate, on full scholarships."

"And . . . ?"

"On their records, it says they withdrew. Truth, they were kicked out."

"You know what for?"

"They're rapists," she said, cold and flat. "But even with all those muscles, they'd still rather use drugs."

"Date-rape drugs?"

"Oh yes. More than once, at that same school. Nothing ever proven. What they *could* prove was steroids. Using and selling."

"That was . . . back in '97. They get popped any since then?"

"Sure. They're hired muscle; it goes with the job description. But the victims not pressing charges, that's one of the job *bene-fits*. So getting busted, it's only a minor inconvenience. Never lasts long."

"Are they mobbed up?"

"Not that I could see. And they don't seem to have any ambition to go into business for themselves. They may be twins, but they're not exactly the Krays."

"You have an address?" I said, getting to it.

"All the paper we could find in New York directs to the same place, out on the Island. But that's their parents' house—they haven't lived there for years."

"Damn."

"They're in Jersey now, I'm pretty sure."

"How come?"

"Because I know where they work," Wolfe said, handing me a piece of paper.

"Is it a mob joint?"

"You mean, does a family own it?" Giovanni replied. "I don't know; I can find out. But that's territory, down there. I mean, it's *mapped* territory. So a family man may own it, or may have a piece of it. Or not. But no matter what, I promise you this much: to operate a strip joint anywhere within a hundred miles of Trenton, they're paying tolls."

"I don't want to step on anyone's toes."

"I can handle it."

"See, that's the thing," I told him. "It *can't* be handled in front. If I work this right, there's no reason for anyone to know I've even been there. It only has to be handled if the wheels come off. That happens, I just want to be sure these guys aren't able to call in any heavy artillery."

"Give me a couple of days," he said.

"They're not *with* this Vision guy," I said. "No reason why they wouldn't talk to me, especially for some cash."

"Why not ask boss?" Mama said.

"I'm not . . ."

"Ask *their* boss. For permission. Boss say, You talk," she said, pointing her finger at me, "they talk, right?"

"You're right, Mama. Only the person who'd have to ask their boss, Giovanni, he can't come into this."

"Ah."

"I don't feature those 'roid boys, bro," the Prof said. "Motherfuckers would have to *mainline* Valium to get calm enough to reason with."

"I'm still saying, why not?" I insisted. "They're not master criminals. Or even angle-players. Just muscle-for-hire. I'm not interested in anything *they* did. All I want is where to find the guy who makes the tapes."

"It sounds so reasonable, mahn," Clarence said. "But my father's wisdom is a good guide. If they do not . . . accept you, you must be prepared."

"Take Max," Mama said, settling it.

"Max, Giovanni. Giovanni, Max."

Giovanni extended his hand. Max shook it briefly, bowing his head a fraction of an inch.

"I heard about him," he said to me. "Max the Silent."

"He's in the room," I said.

"I'm sorry. I thought he . . . *you* couldn't hear," he said, turning to Max.

Max pointed to his lips, then folded his hands into a book, scanned it with his eyes.

"You read lips!" Giovanni said—delighted, like a kid who just got a present.

Max nodded.

"It's better to gesture while you speak," I said. "And you have to watch Max to hear what he's saying, okay?"

"Yeah, yeah," he said to me, impatient. To Max: "You're a karate expert, right?" stepping into a boxer's crouch.

Max held his thumb and forefinger close together.

"He says 'a little bit,'" I told Giovanni.

"I can *see* what's he saying, Burke." Giovanni took a coin from his pocket, held it out on his open palm. He made a gesture of snatching the coin away with his other hand, then extended the coin hand toward Max.

Max's lips twisted. He made a circle of his thumb and forefinger, held it to one eye, and mimed cranking a reel with the other.

"Only in the movies!" Giovanni laughed. "I love it. Your friend is some—"

The coin jumped off Giovanni's palm into the air. Max opened his fist. The coin was inside.

"Christ! How'd he—" Giovanni caught himself, turned to Max, said, "How'd you do it?"

Max handed the coin back to Giovanni. Opened his hand, tapped the palm. Giovanni nodded, replaced the coin in his own hand. Max moved his right hand, slow-motion, so we could see the middle two fingers welded together. He swept them beneath Giovanni's palm, touched the underside of that same hand. . . . The coin jumped up like his palm was a trampoline. Max's hand flashed, and the coin vanished again.

"Madonna mi!" Giovanni said. "I never saw it. Not *any* of it."

"You never would," I told him.

The joint was a free-standing one-story building in the middle of a partly paved lot. It looked like a warehouse wrapped in neon.

"He's inside," I said to Giovanni. I pointed toward the back, nodded a "Yes" so that Max could hear, too. "It's him. Or, I should say, one of them. They've got him working the curtain."

"Lowlife skell," Giovanni muttered.

"We don't care what he *is,*" I told him. "Just what he *knows,* remember?"

"I'm ice," Giovanni assured me.

I turned to Max. Made a gesture of driving a ridge hand to the neck, shook my head "No."

Max nodded, patiently. We'd been over it a dozen times. One thing I learned as a kid—even if you hit someone a good shot, especially with something like a tire iron, you never know the result. One guy gets a headache; another one gets dead.

"It's a little after two," I said to Giovanni. "I don't know how long they keep a place like this open, but I figure we're in for a wait."

"Yeah. Maybe some of those hillbillies like to stay up late, catch the Grand Slam at Denny's before work."

"We're not that far from Trenton here."

"Far enough," Giovanni said. "This is like something out of fucking Kansas, all those farms and crap."

"If he lives close by, we'd have a lot of trouble tailing him, especially if it's off one of those back roads we passed on the way in. I don't want to spook him. So we're going with the original plan."

"You know what he's driving?"

"No. But there won't be many left in the parking lot after closing time."

"I don't see why we don't just stick a *pistola* in his mouth. He's a sex freak, right? I never heard of one of them that was a hard guy."

"You watch too many movies," I told him.

"What's that mean?"

"I've known baby-rapers who were cold as winter marble, and twice as hard. Stereotypes can get you killed. We're trying cash first."

"You're the driver," Giovanni said, settling down in the back seat to wait.

I passed some of the time by taking a set of Velcro-backed New Mexico plates out of the trunk. They were handcrafted fakes—two different sets cut down the middle, with the mismatched halves epoxied back together. I slapped them over the New York ones that matched the Plymouth's registration, using a simple loop. I didn't expect anyone to be reading the numbers, but their sunburst-yellow color might stick in someone's memory bank, give us a little edge.

My watch said four-nineteen when the back door opened and he came out. By then, there were only three cars in the rear lot: a black Lincoln Navigator; a turquoise Thunderbird, one of the new ones; and a red Mustang drop-top resting on huge chromed rims.

"Three to one on the Mustang," I said to Giovanni.

"Go!" he whispered.

The target was wearing a waist-length white satin jacket, carrying what looked like a gym bag in one hand. I opened the door to the Plymouth. The dome light didn't go on. I slipped out, leaving the door slightly ajar.

I hadn't gone ten yards when I heard a sharp *chirp!* The Mustang sprang to life like something in a horror movie: the headlights snapped on, then the engine turned over. Was someone waiting for—? His arm was extended, holding something. Sure.

One of those remote starter devices they sell to people in real cold climates, so they can warm up their cars without leaving the house.

I moved sideways until I was coming from behind him, as if I'd been inside the club all along.

"Mr. Heltman . . . ?" I called out, in a respectful tone.

He whirled to face me, pulling the gym bag behind his hip like he was cocking a right hook.

"Who're you?"

"My name is Casey," I told him, closing the space between us. "I wonder if I could buy some of your time."

"For what?"

"Just to talk. About a business proposition," I said, still moving.

"I don't know you," he said.

I was close enough to see the thick veins in his neck. "Well, let me introduce myself," I said. "As I said, my name's—"

"Cocksucker!" he grunted, driving his left into my ribs.

I was already spinning away from him when the punch landed, but it still felt like an anvil on a chain. I went down, rolling. He charged, the gym bag held club-high in his right hand. I X-ed my forearms for protection, brought a knee up to shield my groin, just as he . . . made a strangled sound and staggered back. Max had him in a one-arm choke. But when he shifted his weight to lock it in, the twin screamed—and launched Max over his back like a catapult.

Max landed on one knee, pivoted and came up ready to . . . But Heltman was already sprinting in the opposite direction.

The Mustang roared out of the lot, leaving us both on the ground.

Max beat me to the Plymouth by a couple of seconds, dived into the back. The motor was idling quiet, Giovanni behind the wheel. I shoved him over, stomped the gas, and plowed sideways across the gravel, the Mustang's lights still in sight. I took the hint, hit the rocker switch on the dash, and our own taillights went dead.

He had maybe a quarter-mile on us as he wheeled onto a stretch of two-lane blacktop. The Plymouth swallowed the distance in a gulp.

"He's heading for home," I yelled. "We don't stop him first, we're done."

"He's the one who's done," Giovanni said, jerking a chrome semi-auto out of an ankle holster. "Get alongside of him."

The Mustang's taillights were huge in our windshield. They went bright red as it skidded almost to a full stop before suddenly lurching off to the left.

"He knows he can't take us on the straights, so he's going for the twisties," I said.

"He's ours," Giovanni said, patting the Plymouth's dash affectionately.

Heltman knew the roads, but it wasn't enough. I held the Plymouth in second gear, barnacled to his rear bumper.

The Mustang slashed back and forth, trying to shake us loose. I had to end it before the noise woke up the wrong people. As he leaned into a long right-hand sweeper, I hit the high beams and the landing lights at the same time, flooding his mirror with blue-and-white fire. I dropped the hammer. The Mustang seemed suspended in place as the Plymouth came on like a rock from a slingshot, dead-aimed at his exposed right rear quarter-panel. I rammed the soft spot, and he lost it. The Mustang went into a wild spin as we powered on past.

I decked the brakes, threw it into reverse, and ripped back to the scene, Giovanni watching out his opened window. The Mustang was against a tree, crushed all the way into the windshield. Its airbag had deployed, but the driver's face was buried under blood—he hadn't been wearing a seatbelt.

Max hauled him out and laid him out on the ground.

"His wallet," I said to Giovanni. "Quick! We need an address."

I ran back to the Mustang, wrenched open the glove compartment. A pair of black leather gloves, some condoms, and the owner's manual. The gym bag was on the floor in front of the passenger seat. I ran back to where the others were.

"He's out," Giovanni said. "This was in his back pocket"—holding up an alligator billfold.

"We've got to split," I told him. "Even way out here, someone might have heard the crash, called it in. Don't worry about him; he won't be able to identify any of us."

Giovanni looked down at the sprawled body, said, "Any chance he was one of the ones?"

"Giovanni . . ."

"One of the ones that killed my daughter?"

"I don't know. Come on!"

Giovanni dropped to one knee, pinched the twin's nose closed with one hand, blocked his mouth with the other.

"Giovanni, no! It'll take minutes for that to . . ."

Max grabbed Giovanni under his arms, lifted him off the ground, and tossed him to the side. He looked at me. I nodded. Max rolled the twin on his stomach, mounted him, one knee against the spine. He took the twin's head in both hands, pulled it all the way back, and gave it a short, vicious twist.

Maiden Lane," I said, my mini-Mag trained on the driver's license we'd found in the dead man's wallet. "That's right around here, close by; I remember seeing it on the map. This *must* be a good address. Only I can't see asking for directions at this hour. Even a gas-station attendant would . . ."

"Maiden Lane," Giovanni said into his cell phone.

He listened for a minute, then said, "Drive, Burke. We've got a street map on the screen. Just go where I tell you."

The Plymouth's right-side low beams still worked, but they threw light at the same angle as the Mustang driver's neck. I couldn't feel any difference in the steering; it tracked straight and true. When you build a car to bounce off the wall at Talladega, nerfing a Mustang isn't going to change its personality.

The wood-frame house stood well back from the road. My flash picked up a "30" on the mailbox.

"This is the one," I said. "Let Max out," I told Giovanni.

I counted to a hundred in my head, said, "Some of the lights are on. He's not going to spook at a car coming up the drive; he'll be expecting his brother. Max is going to come in from the back. Ready?"

"Yeah, yeah. Come on!"

I motored up the long driveway, not trying to be especially quiet, but not making a show of it, either. As soon as I saw the pristine red Mustang convertible at the far end, I knew the dead man's driver's license hadn't lied.

We walked up to the front door, Giovanni behind me and to my left. I pounded on the door with the side of my fist.

Nothing.

I did it again.

Heard sounds of someone moving, somewhere in the house.

I pounded harder.

"Who is it?" An angry, guarded voice, slurred with . . . sleep?

"Fucking *key*!" I grunted, hitting the door again.

The door opened a little. "You asshole . . . ," someone said. I hit the door with my shoulder, drove it open as Giovanni slip-streamed in behind me, his pistol up. The twin chopped at Giovanni's wrist, as panther-quick as his brother had been. The pistol hit the floor. I dived for it, took a sharp kick in the side of my neck. Giovanni was against the wall, his right arm dangling useless at his side. "Come on, pussy!" he offered the twin.

But Max had him by then. With both arms this time.

"**M**ove the car around the back," I told Giovanni, urgently. "Make sure it's in shadow. I don't know how fast they'll find the wreck, but if they run its plates, they could be coming here, and we'll need the edge. Pull the dummy plates off the Plymouth. And take that white square off the driver's-side door. It's not painted on—just a piece of vinyl—there's a couple of pull-tabs along the top."

In the back bedroom, I found a woman. Naked, lying on her belly, head twisted to one side. She was breathing raggedly through a wide-open mouth, a thin line of drool trailing down her chin to her neck. A large blue dildo was sticking out of her like a freakish flagpole, anchored in what looked like dried blood.

"Filthy fucking animals," Giovanni said, over my shoulder.

"An address book," I reminded him. "*Anything* that looks like names and phone numbers."

I was expecting a computer. Hoping for a laptop.

Nothing.

There was a big-screen TV and a VCR, but the tape collection was all commercial porn.

A sharp *crack!* Max snaps his fingers when he wants you to come and he's out of sight-line.

Even with handcuffs on his wrists, the twin looked dangerous. Giovanni held the pistol in his left hand. Max kept his forearm over the twin's Adam's apple.

"We came for the tapes," I told him, flat. His brother had taught me not to offer money, so I was groping, blind.

"I don't know nothing about no—"

"Then you're dead," I said, doing the math for him.

"Who sent—?"

"Vision, who else? Now guess how many times I'm going to ask you again."

"That little cocksucker. He said we could—"

"He changed his mind," I said, placing my bet. "This is simple enough even for you, wet-brain. Yes or no. Live or die."

"I . . . I got it hidden."

"It better be hidden *here*."

"You're gonna kill me anyway," he said, stalling. Thinking his brother would be home soon.

"We just want the tapes, you fucking moron," I told him, lying with my eyes.

"What for? I mean, all we got's a copy. He said we could—"

"He doesn't want it floating around no more," I said. "Come on. You give us what we came for, that's the end of it."

"You swear?"

"May my mother die," I said. The one statement I could always pass a polygraph on.

"Let me get up."

I nodded to Max, who changed grips.

T he kitchen counter was lined with gallon-sized plastic jars of bodybuilding supplements. A stainless steel blender stood next to several bottles of yohimbe and shark cartilage. The hiding place was a cut-out slot in the wall behind the double-wide refrigerator. Not bad, actually—if Max had to strain to wrench it away from the wall, it would take at least two normal men to do the job.

I unwrapped the package like it was a Bomb Squad assignment. "There's only one tape here, pal," I said to the twin, looking at the standard-size cassette. The label showed four naked women, on their hands and knees in rows of two. They were yoked together by some kind of harness. Standing behind them, another woman in porno-regulation black leather, brandishing a whip. The title said: *International Slut Racing Tournament!*

"That's the only one he let us keep," he said, annoyed. "It's *proof,* man. That we didn't do anything. It don't show no . . . Hey! What are you going to do?"

"We're going to watch the movie," I said.

The tape opened with a woman standing at an easel on which the rules of the race were printed, taking questions from an audience of "reporters." The race contestants were all chained to a long wall, waiting. Some were facing the wall; others looked at the camera. A couple were lapping up something from bowls with their names on them.

"This is just—" Giovanni said, before I cut him off with a chopping motion of my right hand.

The tape rolled on, as predictable as a fixed fight, then suddenly became a plain gray screen with white lines of static running horizontally. Another few seconds passed; then . . .

A long corridor, mostly dark, with a few pools of reflected light. Looked like an industrial building, maybe an old factory. Abandoned, or maybe just closed for the night. A figure flitted past the far corner, then disappeared—all I could see was some kind of black robe, with a hood.

And a long knife.

A woman zipped across the screen. She was dressed in white shorts and a white T-shirt, white sneakers and white socks. A white hair-ribbon flamed from her dark hair as she ran.

Another black robe popped out of a doorway.

The only sound was breathing. Two, three separate tracks, as distinctive as voices would have been.

The woman in white turned a corner. Stopped when she spotted a ladder. Hesitated, as if making up her mind, then started to climb. The camera filled the frame with her from the waist down, coming in tight on her buttocks and thighs, frantic, in sync with her high, frightened breathing.

Somewhere behind her, confident, in-control breathing. Low-register grunting. Getting louder.

The woman made it to a higher floor. A more open space than what she'd left, but still mazelike from the play of shadow against lighter pockets of dark.

The images chased each other for what seemed like a long

time, sometimes running, sometimes creeping. It was half-ass-surrealistic, black-and-white-in-color "symbolism." A bad movie with a worse script.

Suddenly, the woman in white turned a shadow corner and ground to a stop in a puddle of diffused light. The black robes, two of them, had her bracketed. The camera rushed in on her face as she opened her mouth to scream, her eyes wide with shock.

Vonni.

I turned to the handcuffed twin, said "Where was the—?" just as Giovanni put his pistol against Heltman's temple and blew skull fragments all over the room.

"The shell casing," I said. "*Find* it, Giovanni."

"I . . ."

"We don't have time!" I snapped at him, and ran for the back bedroom.

The sodomized woman hadn't even twitched. The drugs they'd fed her must have been near-terminal.

"They were the ones," Giovanni said. "It was them who . . ."

I didn't say anything.

"Burke, he had to go."

"I'm not arguing."

"But I shouldn't have . . . gone off like that, right? We should have made him tell us—"

"It's done," I said, as I slid the Plymouth through wide streets, past landscaped lawns. "Get Felix on the phone, tell him we're coming in."

"**T**here!" Giovanni said, pointing at a substantial brick Tudor, barely visible from the street.

Even as he spoke, the garage door started going up.

"**T**hat was slick, that pull-off stuff you got," Giovanni said. He was talking to keep from going jagged, and I let him run with it. "When I yanked it off, it looked like a different car."

"I must have swapped paint with that Mustang somewhere," I said. "I'm going to need a whole new front end clip."

"I'm good for—"

"I know," I told him. "That's not the problem now. Thing is, can I leave my car here?"

"Felix?" he asked his partner.

"For a couple of days, no problem. I can have someone come by, flat-bed it out, get it to the crusher."

"No way!" Giovanni said. "You should have seen how this—"

"It doesn't have to be disposed of," I told Felix. "Just worked on. The people you're talking about, they're trustworthy?"

"*Mi famiglia,*" he said.

We pulled out in the late afternoon, me and Max in Giovanni's BMW, Felix and Giovanni in a cream-colored Infiniti Q45. By Exit 12 on the Jersey Turnpike, we lost sight of them.

The Mustang driver's wallet had nothing in it but cash, a few credit cards, and assorted ID, all in the name of Brett Heltman.

But his gym bag was the other side of the legit coin—a

red-zone pharmacy. Dozens of clear plastic sheets of pop-out Dianabol pills, a half-dozen dark little rubber-topped bottles of Testovit, and a huge assortment of different kinds of alleged "andro," flies just under the FDA's radar. Inside the bag's flap pockets were a Rambo knife, a cell phone, a handful of syringes, individually wrapped. And one of those "personal digital assistants," a Palm m105.

I ran through the cell phone's menu. All the stored numbers were 609 area codes, local. The last number the twin had dialed was to a gym.

That left the PDA. "He liked gadgets," I told the crew, remembering his remote-starter trick. "I don't even want to turn this damn thing on. Maybe he's got it passworded or something, nuke everything if you do it wrong."

"Give it to me," the Mole said.

It's an emergency, Pepper."

"Leave your number, chief. And not a wireless."

That one's an NV, too?" Cyn said, tilting her head in the direction of the cassette I'd brought back from New Jersey.

"Yeah."

"Burke . . . Burke, what does it mean?"

"I think I know, now," I told her. "The NV tapes, for some of the people in them it's an acting job, and for some it's the real thing."

"But the guy making the movies . . . ?"

"For him, it's *all* real," I said. "And he's in charge."

"*H*ow many?" Wolfe, on the phone.

"A hundred and seventy-seven, total," I told her, the results of the Mole's invasion of the Palm Pilot spread out in front of me. "But—"

"You're joking."

"But I only need the 516 and 631 ones."

"And that's . . . ?"

"Seventy-one."

She made a sound of disgust. Asked, "The names on each bill?"

"Names and addresses. But if any one of them made calls to or received calls from *these* numbers," I said, giving her the number from the cell phone in the gym bag, and the one I'd copied off the wall phone in their kitchen, "that's the only one I need."

"This could take—"

"Price no object," I said. "Even a few hours could mean the difference."

I became a news junkie: print, radio, and TV going simultaneously, scanning for "Twin Brothers Found Murdered in New Jersey!"

Nothing.

There was always the chance that the cops hadn't connected what they thought was a hit-and-run with what had to be a deliberate homicide—maybe the Mustang's plates dead-ended instead of taking them to the address we'd pulled from the driver's license. Or maybe the woman in the back bedroom gave them enough likely suspects to keep them working local for a long time.

Or maybe they were keeping the media lid down until they tightened the noose.

"Y ou understand it's not like the City out there," Wolfe said, on the phone. "You've got 516 for Nassau, 631 for Suffolk, but 516 is also the area code for *all* the cell phones on Long Island. There's no separate cell prefix, like our 917."

"And you can't get into cell phone records because there's so many different . . . ?"

"We got one hit," she went on, like I hadn't said anything. "Out of all seventy-one numbers, only one call was made to either of the Jersey numbers. It went to their house phone."

"When?"

"About six weeks ago."

"Do you have the—?"

"I don't think you're getting this," she said. "What I did, I had . . . some people do a back-check. Instead of pulling all the records for seventy-one customers, they focused on matching any of those numbers with the phone records for the *Jersey* numbers . . . the two you gave me, understand?"

"Yes," I said, wondering how my brain had gone so numb. Grateful that Wolfe's never did.

"And what we found was a cluster of calls," she said, crisp to the edge of impatience. "A pattern. Mostly from the cell, a few from the house. All to the *same* number in Suffolk County. And when we looked at *that* customer's records, we found that single call to the house in Jersey I just told you about. Clear enough?"

"Perfect."

"Not so perfect," she said. "The calling number's a cell phone. The customer's name is Robert Jones. And the address is a PO box. The credit card's a dud, too."

"B yron, can you do something for me? With the studio?"

"I only paid the interest, brother." A honeyed baritone voice on the phone. "Just say what you need."

"The Lloyd Segan Company. How may I direct your call?"

"To Mr. Segan, please," I said, pronouncing the name with the accent on the first syllable, like Byron had said to.

"May I tell Mr. Segan who is calling?"

"My name is Burke. I was told he'd be expecting my—"

"Mr. Burke, yes. Hold, please."

A short pause, then . . .

"Lloyd Segan."

"Mr. Segan . . ."

"Lloyd."

"Lloyd. My name is Burke. Byron said you'd—"

"What can I do for you?" the man said, his voice friendly with warmth and sharp-edged at the same time.

"What I need, Lloyd, is a favor. A number someone can call, and someone to answer it, do a little routine. And some . . . coaching, I guess you'd call it. So I can play my role."

Two-thirty in the afternoon. Half past eleven in Hollywood.

I pointed across the room, where Michelle was poised at the desk, a headset buried somewhere in her hair, only the mouthpiece at the end of the wand visible.

She nodded, blew me a kiss, and dialed.

I tried to hear the phone ring at the other end in my mind—we couldn't risk putting it on speaker.

"Good afternoon, I have Mr. Chenowith, from Acidfree Productions, for Mr. Vision."

. . .

"Oh, certainly, sir. We're at area code 323. . . ."

"What's he *doing*?" Cyn asked, pacing anxiously.

"Checking out Acidfree Productions," I told her. "Or getting across a border."

When the direct line rang, I knew Lloyd had come through. Now it was time to see how good a coach he was.

"Acidfree Productions," Rejji answered the bounced call.

. . .

"Mr. Vision, is Mr. Chenowith expecting your call?"

. . .

"Hold, please," she said, sliding out of the chair as Michelle slid in, giving Rejji a "Nice job!" pat on the bottom.

"Mr. Chenowith's office," Michelle said.

. . .

"Oh, Mr. Vision. Thank you so much for calling. May I give you to Mr. Chenowith?"

. . .

Michelle pointed at me. I took a centering breath, picked up the extension, said, "This is Stan Chenowith. Do I have The Vision himself?"

Rejji dropped to her knees in front of me, hands clasped. Not playing. Praying.

"I can get word to him," the voice said.

"Oh. All right. Can you tell him we would like to take a meeting with him, concerning backing one of his projects?"

"What do you mean, backing?"

"Well, financing, actually. I don't know what you know about our—"

"I know how it works," the voice said, as if I'd offended him. "How did you . . . I mean, have you seen any of . . . the work?"

"To be honest, I have not," I said. "But you know how this industry works. The buzz is that The Vision is going to be *very* hot. And if you think the elevator's going up, *way* up, the ground floor's the best place to get on."

"People are talking about . . . the work?"

"Oh, *everybody's* talking about it. Word is, he's on the edge. New concepts. I've heard *Blair Witch* meets *Fight Club;* is that outrageous? But, I have to tell you, your client isn't the easiest man to get hold of."

"Where would this meeting be?"

"That would be up to him, of course. I'm only calling now because I have to red-eye in tomorrow, and I'd hoped we could get together in the evening. But if that's not convenient . . ."

"You'd meet in New York?"

"At the Helmsley Park Lane. On Central Park South," I said, underlining that I was a Holy Coaster. A New Yorker would have said "Fifty-ninth Street." "If that would be all right. It's where I always stay."

"What time?"

"Any time The Vision wants. We bring more than money to our projects. We bring *flexibility*."

"Like nine o'clock?"

"You got it! Just have The Vision come to the front desk and ask for my suite. One of my people will come down to get him. Or would you like us to send a car . . . ?"

"Okay."

"Okay, you'll ask The Vision?"

"No. Okay, he'll be there. I can . . . I have the authority to make commitments for him."

"Will you be coming, too, Mr. . . . ?"

"Just him," he said.

"I was afraid you were going to lose him," Cyn said. "Why didn't you tell him you'd actually seen his 'work'?"

"Way too risky," I told her. "Next thing, he asks me *which* of the tapes I've seen. And, in his mind, he's wondering how I got them. Besides, it would make sense to him that the 'word's out' without anyone actually seeing product."

"You've got him hooked, honey," Michelle assured me.

"I would have felt better if he'd let us send that car for him," I said.

"I know why Vonni had those tapes now. This Vision—he gave them to her. Let her in on his high-concept idea. Because he knew he had her."

"She wanted it," the Prof agreed.

"Wanted what, then?" Clarence.

"Wanted to be a star," Michelle put in. "Or maybe that's not fair to her. Wanted to be in the movies, anyway. Remember, she was in the drama club. . . ."

"And she left that morning, she told the little boy she was going to be famous," Cyn put in.

"That tape? The one of her running into nowhere?" I said to them all. "I know what it was now. A rehearsal. Vision wanted her to prove she could *act* frightened to death. That was her role."

Nobody said anything.

"That was her role," I went on. "And right up to the end, she thought she was playing it."

I was connected to Vision as close as if we shared an artery. Desire and fear warring in both of us, pumping our blood. I could feel him. He *wanted* it to be true, a Hollywood production company discovering him, making him rich and famous. *Power,* spreading long sweet shapely legs for him.

But had they *really* heard of him? And what had they heard? Come or run?

And me? What if he didn't show? What if I'd spooked him, given him a head start? How much money did a guy like that have? Did he already have a backup plan, a place to run to?

The door opened. Cyn. Dressed in a black sheath. And Rejji. Nude.

"We couldn't sleep, either," Cyn said.

"N o!"

"It'll be subtle," Giovanni promised me. "I've been in plenty of places like this before. The guys who work the desk, they're *used* to a little grease."

"Forget it."

"You say we don't know what he looks like . . . and that's right. But he doesn't know us, either. We'll be in the lobby, just hanging. We scoped it out. The registration desk's way over to one side; he won't even *look* where we'll be, okay? The desk man gives us the high sign, and . . ."

"And what? You jump him right there, in front of fifty witnesses, minimum?"

"Come on! I just want to—"

"You just want to fuck this up," I said, very quiet and calm. "One, he could send someone else. Like a point man, see if this whole thing's for real. So we have to talk to him, see if *he* is, understand? Two, you pay a man for a service, doesn't mean someone else can't pay him, later, to talk about it. You get all anxious now, you're going to blow it up."

"I've got to be there," he said, adamant.

"So you can lose it? *Again?* You're putting me in a cross, Giovanni. We needed a public place to meet, the ritzier the better. You see how the joint's laid out, how many people we're going to need to make it work. You think you can bang a guy out in a hotel lobby in *that* neighborhood, and just fade?"

"I'm not going to—"

"You're not going to be there, period. You said I was driving the car, remember?"

"Burke, listen to me," he said urgently. "He's the one. Not the feds, him. I was blind insane to ever think it could be . . . but who could have ever . . . I . . . Burke, he fucking made a *movie* of my . . ."

"The only way we're going to know for sure is if he talks. That's what I do. What I'm good at. You're not. You only know the one way," I said.

"So?" he demanded. "You think he could—?"

"Who are you talking to, Giovanni? Some *Godfather* fan? You stick a gun in a guy's mouth, cock the trigger, *maybe* he spills, that's right. And maybe he panics. Goes catatonic. Has a heart attack. Who knows? Thing is, *you* don't. Nobody does.

"And you can't ever trust what someone says, a situation like that. He's going to say whatever he thinks you want him to say. A nine-millimeter's not a lie detector.

"If all you want to do is take him off the count, you do it away from me. Far away. But you can't even do *that* until you know he's the right guy, because if you do the wrong guy *this* time you'll never get another chance."

Giovanni bowed his head, clasped his hands, as if asking for strength. When he opened his eyes, they were clear and calm. "You be the lie detector, Burke," he said. "Soon as you know for sure, you just ring me. I'll be right downstairs."

"I've been with you on this?" I put it to him. "Right down the line?"

"You have," he said, no hesitation.

"Then listen to me now," I told him. "Because I've got a better idea."

"**A**lways it is the black man who is the chauffeur," Clarence mock-complained. Trying to lighten the fear we all shared.

"So who should drive?" I asked him, playing along. "The *Mole*?"

"Schoolboy's telling it true," the Prof added. "I was still doing banks, I'd rather have Ray Charles for a wheelman."

"Any of us could have been seen," I said. "During all those 'interviews' we did. And maybe he's got a pipeline—maybe more than a couple of those kids we spoke to were in one of his little movies. But I don't think they were looking at anything besides the camera."

"Without the patch, you look *very* different, honey," Michelle assured me. "And once I add those streaks to your hair, and you put on a suit . . ."

"I've got a *dynamite* maid's uniform," Rejji said, grinning.

"I don't want to overload it," I said. "The way this suite's laid out, we can keep him isolated. And if we do have to go to Plan B, the credit card we put it all on won't tell them anything."

They all nodded silently. Plan B was the Mole. In another room. On a higher floor. If he went into action, nobody was going to pay any attention to our two suites. Not with a fire raging through the hotel.

"**D**o I look all right?" Michelle asked. For maybe the tenth time in the last hour.

"You look *gorgeous,*" Rejji told her. "So in control. I love it."

"You slut." Michelle laughed.

I refused to look at my watch.

The phone rang.

Michelle started to fly across the room, stopped, smoothed her skirt over her hips, walked over, and picked it up just past the second ring.

"Yes, please?"

. . .

"Please tell the party that someone will be down to collect him directly. Thank you."

She hung up.

"Oh God," Rejji said.

"Keep it together, now, bitch," Michelle said. "You're up next."

"**D**o you think it's really going to be—?"

"No more," I told Rejji, holding my finger to my lips.

A soft double rap at the door.

"Danielle!" I called out.

Rejji practically trotted over to the door. She stepped to the side as she held it open, one hand gently waving an invitation.

He was older than I thought he'd be, from the vague descriptions we'd gathered. Late twenties, early thirties. A bit taller than medium height, light-brown hair, cut into a neat sculpture. His face was narrow, with fleshy lips over the perfect teeth the NHB girl had remembered, large dark eyes the most prominent feature. Wearing a safari jacket, with a briefcase-sized red nylon bag on a strap over his shoulder.

Michelle stayed next to him, one hand on his arm, steering him over to me as I stood up to greet him.

"Mr. Chenowith . . . The Vision," she made the introduction.

"Vision!" I said, extending my hand.

He took it, returning my moderate squeeze with a firm one of his own. His palm was as dry as statistics.

"Sit down, sit down," I said, indicating the best chair in the room.

"Thanks, Mr.—"

"Stan, please. It's me who's honored to meet you, Vis . . . Can I call you 'Vision'?"

"Yeah, sure. It's my . . . it's my name, for professional purposes."

"It has real strength," I congratulated him. "And, from what I've heard, it's a perfect fit, too."

"You've never seen my work, is that right, Mr. . . . Stan?"

"Not a single frame of your reel," I assured him. "But that's . . . Ah, excuse me, I'm a little excited. Would you like something to drink?"

"Sure. Whatever you're—"

"When you're with us, Vision, it's whatever *you* want. Danielle . . ."

Rejji sashayed over, bent forward just enough to show off a little, said, "What can I get you, sir?" to him.

"Uh . . . vodka rocks."

"Yes, sir. Is Absolut all right?"

"Sure," he said.

"I'll have what The Vision is having," I told her.

Michelle handed me a sheaf of papers, FedEx'ed over from Lloyd's office, tapping one spot on the top page with a red talon.

"I don't want to put any pressure on you," I told him, "but I don't want to insult you by not putting real cards on the table, either. As Alana just reminded me, we're looking for a three-picture commitment."

"A three-picture . . . ?"

"With escalators, of course," I assured him. "But you can understand why we don't want to commit substantial development money to you if you're free to just walk after the first one."

"But you haven't—"

"This isn't about what you've done; it's about what you're *going* to do. Do you know what Hollywood runs on, Vision? *Buzz!* And you've got it going on. You're all *over* it. The word's out. Hot hot *hot*. Don't get me wrong. We'll want to see everything. But it's not your reel that's driving the car, it's your *concept*, are you with me?"

"I didn't realize word got out so—"

"This business is all about high-stakes gambling. Today becomes yesterday like *that*!" I said, snapping my fingers.

"The winning bettors are the ones who can see *tomorrow*."

Rejji put down coasters, handed us our drinks. I took out a red box of Dunhills, offered it to him. He took one, gratefully. Rejji reached in her apron, caught my slight shake of the head just in time. I wanted to see if he had his own lighter, and if a cigarette would calm him a little.

Yes. To both.

"So," I said. "Tell me all about your concept."

"Mr. Chenowith . . ." Michelle, pointing to the papers.

"All right, Alana," I said to her. "It's up to you," I said to the target. "Do you want to see our offer first?"

"Well . . ."

"This is really just boilerplate," I told him. "The blank spaces are where the numbers get filled in. I mean, some things are industry-standard, five points on the gross, separate card for the director's credit. . . . You're a writer-director, yes?"

"Absolutely. The way I—"

"Look, Vision, I won't jerk you around. I've got a ceiling. A limit I can go to. But I promise you, *promise* you, that if your concept is as revolutionary as we've heard it is you'll *hit* that ceiling. Right in this very contract. Fair enough?"

"I . . . I'd have to . . ."

"Well, of *course,* your people would have to look it over. I'm not a lawyer, either. My game's finance; your game's creativity. But that's a marriage, am I right? Financing and creativity? That's the way movies get made."

"But when you said *Blair Witch,* I thought you—"

"You thought we were looking ultra-low-budget?" I said, in disbelief. "No *way*! I mean, look, I won't deny that this is a business. We're here to make money. But we know you have to bring some to get some. Our company can't finance some hundred-million-dollar *spectacle*. And we don't want to. We were thinking of a moderate investment. Say, two and a half to, maybe, four. All on digital."

"That's . . ."

"What? Not enough? Listen to me, Vision. It's *more* than

enough, believe me. We've got the distribution contacts, the overseas market—this isn't some straight-to-video pitch I'm making here."

"No. I mean, that *could* be . . . it could be plenty, if it was handled right."

"Take the contracts with you," I told him. "But, first, tell me about your concept. Tell me *everything*. So we can fill in some of those blanks."

"My inspiration," he said, leaning back, "my original inspiration was seeing one of those convenience-store holdups on videotape—not a re-enactment, the actual robbery—on one of those surveillance cameras they keep in those stores? I was struck by the . . . *immediacy* of it."

He leaned forward to light another cigarette, then leaned back again for the first drag, keeping the interviewer on "Pause," just as he'd rehearsed it in front of his mirror a thousand times.

Rejji came over, removed his near-empty tumbler, and deftly replaced it with a fresh drink, giving him a little extra wiggle, now that it was clear he was a VIP for real.

"There's a power to that kind of . . . performance," he intoned. "An impact never duplicated in conventional cinema. I became a kind of connoisseur of the entire . . . genre, if you will. There was something about those tapes that was absolutely special. Unique. So I decided to deconstruct the tapes as a totality. Not in the formal sense, of course," he said, breezily, "more in the way of disassembling the mechanism . . . isolating the elements to understand the gestalt.

"From that work came my vision," he said, in the solemnly portentous tone a pop star uses when explaining that global warming isn't a cool thing.

"And your name," I said, saluting him with an upraised glass.

"That wasn't until later," he corrected me. "Those surveillance tapes, the closest label you could put on them, artistically, would be a kind of *cinéma vérité*. But they're not actually *creations;* they're not even documentaries. Why? Because there's no *control*—the filmmaker isn't *directing;* it's nothing more than the camera itself. Now, for some, that *is* the goal . . . to make the director disappear, so that the audience 'sees' directly into the life. But without control, there is no art. You might capture something fantastic on tape, but that's just a question of being in the right place at the right time. That's not art. It's not even skill. Just dumb luck. The Zapruder film is world-famous, right? A piece of history. But nobody ever talks about his . . . gift. Or his art. And," he said, in a tone of finality, "he never made anything else."

"But you can't direct real life," I said, gently fanning the flame.

"No?" he said complacently.

"Well, how could you?" I asked. "I mean, if you direct it, then it's . . . acting."

"That's what I thought, too," he said, his voice getting tumescent with confidence. He segued into full lecture mode. "I remember watching that robbery tape. Over and over. Thinking how much better it could have been if they'd positioned themselves differently. Or said different words. Because just because something's real doesn't mean it's even interesting. Much less art. That's when I began scripting. Before that, all my work was just . . . *filming*. Without any real . . . vision," he said, chuckling at himself. He shifted his shoulders, positioning himself to deliver another dose of insight. "For a while, I did straight *vérité*. Have you ever seen a dogfight?"

"No," I said. "I've *heard* about them, but . . . they're . . . I mean, only hillbillies do them, isn't that true? Like cockfights being a Hispanic thing?"

"No . . ." He was starting to educate me, then caught himself before the topic veered too far from his favorite one. "Anyway, I filmed one. It was *incredible*. I filmed other things, too. Things you'd probably never see on tape in your life. But I couldn't *control* any of it. So what I had was a lot of amazing footage, but none of it—even *all* of it together—would add up to a movie.

"It all . . . evolved," he said. "It took a long time. Years. My next stage was when I used actors to 'be' real. I'd put them in situations, and whatever happened, happened. Kind of *vérité* cranked up. And what I saw was that I had a *lot* of control but it cost me the realism. Like, have you ever seen a trial on Court TV?"

"OJ," I replied. "And when Frank Dux sued Jean-Claude Van Damme." A safe Hollywood answer.

"Do you think *any* of them would have behaved the same way if they hadn't *known* the cameras were on them every second? The lawyers, the witnesses, even the judge? And those 'reality' TV shows. *Survivor?* Right! *Big Brother?* Sure! That Jenny Jones thing, where the guy thought he was going to meet someone who had a secret crush on him, and it turned out to be another guy? But on camera, what happens? Not so much. Off camera? He fucking *kills* the queer. Blows him away. You see what I mean? What if I'd had *that?*"

I nodded, unwilling to interrupt the flow of something so important with speech.

"Don't you *see?*" he said. "Even if all I did was set the . . . boundaries, like, it *still* wasn't real. Because, if they knew the camera was rolling, that changed everything. I threw most of that crap out. You know what I called it, finally? *Faux vérité!*"

"Wow," I said softly, overawed.

"Everybody's a screenwriter," he said caustically. "They want to write 'realism' and call it their 'creation.' But they don't *get* it. If you *create* the realism, it isn't real!"

"That is heavy," I said. *CV for* cinéma vérité; *FV for* faux vérité. *And NV . . . ?*

"That's when it came to me," he said. "Can I show you something?"

Without waiting for a response, he opened the flap on his shoulder bag and took out a cassette. I felt Michelle freeze next to me.

"You've got a VCR here . . . ?"

"Of *course,*" Michelle assured him. She stood up and took the cassette from him, walked over to the console, turned it on, inserted the tape. She came back and handed the remote to Vision.

"Thanks," he said. Without further preamble, he pointed the remote at the console and kicked the tape into life.

Darkness.

The camera's eye picked up a synagogue.

"Jews!" a harsh, off-camera whisper. "Fucking Jews."

Figures running across an expanse of lawn.

Heavy breathing.

Swastikas springing from spray cans.

"Heil Hitler!"

"The white man is coming, kike bastards!" A different voice.

Fade to black, deeper than darkness.

In the silence, I said, "How did you know they'd be—"

"What you've just seen," he interrupted, "is a very early example of what I call *noir vérité.*"

"I *love* that name!" Michelle.

He bowed slightly, taking his due, but not finished opening our eyes. "With *cinéma vérité,* I had realism but not control," he said. "With *faux vérité,* I had control but not realism. But with *noir vérité,* I finally had *both.*"

"How is that . . . I mean, how is what we just saw . . . both?" I asked him, my tone a study in confused admiration.

"How many actors did you see?"

"Uh . . . four, I think, right?"

"No," he said. Waited a beat. "You saw *one*. One of them knew this was a movie. The other three, they thought they were going on an 'action.'"

"You mean they were set up to . . . ?"

"Not set up! They *wanted* to do exactly what they did. It was the actor's assignment to get them to do it *when* they did it, and *where* they did it, that's all. For the actor, this was a role. But for the others . . ."

"I think I under—"

"That was just the beginning," he said. "The first step."

"**N**ow, who was acting in *that* one?" he asked, eyes on Rejji, who he'd spotted sneaking peeks at the screen.

"It can't have been the one *doing* the paddling," I said. "Why would the others have just gone along and—?"

"This is the final stage," he said. "Or *nearly* it, anyway. Because they were *all* acting. But only one of them knew the script."

"I don't . . ."

"Okay, look," he said, leaning forward, intense. "They all *thought* they were acting. In a movie. The script was this sorority thing . . . like you saw for yourself. But the girl *doing* the paddling, she was told that this was a *different* movie. And the plot of *that* movie was a girl who wants to get even with another girl, so she makes up this whole 'movie' thing."

"Unreal!" I said.

"*Completely* real," he corrected. "The concept is that everyone knows they're on camera, but only *some* of them know that the script isn't really the script. But even the ones who *think* they know, they don't understand that their role is *another* role. One that only the director knows. And when it all comes together, *at that perfect moment,* it's totally real. And totally under my direction."

"Oh my God!" Michelle said.

"*Noir vérité,*" he said proudly. "That's why it's always done with a single camera. The last thing I want is a *Rashomon* effect. Here, each of the actors has his or her own reality, but the only truth is what goes *into* the camera. And there can be only one truth. That," he said, pausing, the way he'd rehearsed this moment before his mirror so many times, "was my vision."

"That's . . . amazing," I said. "So, in each movie you make, the star—"

"The catalyst," he said. "Not the star. In *noir vérité,* there are no stars. Because there are no limits, do you see?"

"Not . . . really."

"The ultimate control is the director's. In *noir vérité,* the director *directs.* Not just the lines, or the sets. He directs reality. The catalyst—there can be more than one—their job is to create the opportunity for conduct. But the conduct itself is real."

"So if you let the . . . person *think* they're the catalyst, but they're really playing the *role* of catalyst . . . ?"

"Exactly," he said.

"Everything I heard about you was gospel," I told him, admiringly. "This *is* a new concept. Nobody's got this one. And it truly has no limits. You could do . . . anything with it."

"No limits," he agreed.

"Couldn't it ever get . . . I don't know, out of hand?"

"Even if it did," he said, shrugging his shoulders, "whatever happened, it wouldn't be real. It would be something else entirely. My creation. *Noir vérité.*"

Before he left, he inked the deal memo Michelle handed him.

"I'll just sign it 'Vision,' if that's all right," he said. "It's the name I'll be known by."

"Oh, you already are," I promised him. "We just need your Social Security number for the accounting department. You know, the tax boys. You better get used to a *lot* of attention from them, Vision."

He put his copy of the contract into his briefcase, as Michelle tapped a single digit on her cellular.

"Please bring the car around," she said. "You are to take our guest wherever he directs."

"Better ring Fong, too," I told her. "A little security wouldn't hurt, considering . . ."

"Considering what?" The Vision asked me.

"Considering your signing bonus isn't a check," I told him. "Alana . . ."

Michelle handed me a Gucci bag of soft blue leather. I unzipped it, so Vision could see the banded stacks of bills. Then handed the bag to him.

He took it in both hands, torn. Then he made his decision and zipped it closed without counting. All class. Or maybe he wanted to keep the bag.

I'd expected a man so driven, he'd be almost vibrating with barely contained power. A psychopath, radiating evil *ki*. Not this. Not this lethal little cliché.

We shook hands.

Michelle took him downstairs, to the waiting limo.

"What if he—?"

"There's no way," I said to Rejji. "Not now."

"Burke . . ."

"They heard it all?" I asked Cyn.

"Every word. I was right there."

"I stationed Max behind Giovanni, just in case."

"He didn't *move*, Burke. Not a muscle. I don't see how he did it. I wanted to . . . just . . ."

"How do you think *I* felt?" Rejji said to her. "And I was close enough to do it."

"Why isn't Michelle with you?" Cyn asked.

"She stayed behind to clean up anything he might have touched. And to check out. She's going to ride over with Mole and the Prof."

"And he can't possibly . . . ?"

"There's some reality he doesn't get to direct," I promised her.

I pulled up to the barbed-wire-laced chain-link gate, flashed my brights three times.

The gate swung back from both sides. I drove the Plymouth through. The gate closed behind me.

"Watch those spike heels," I told the women. "The ground here is all busted up."

We got out. Made our way over to a small building with a single gas pump in front.

"You wait over there," I told them. "Next to the car."

The white stretch limo ghosted up to the gate, flashed its brights three times.

I watched as the gate swung back.

The limo pulled into the shadows.

The back door opened. The Vision climbed out, Max right behind him. The driver's door opened, and Clarence stepped out, his semi-auto aimed at the ground.

I slipped back into the shadows, got to the shack before they arrived.

When the door opened, The Vision saw me sitting on an old office chair.

"Have a seat," I told him, pointing to the chair's mate.

"What . . . what are you *doing*? I thought we had—"

"Sit down, Vision," I said gently. "I'll explain everything."

"People know where I am!" he said.

"*You* don't even know where you are," I told him. Words I'd said to another man, years ago. Another man like him. "That's part of all this. Your own concept, right?"

His mouth opened, but he didn't speak. His eyes were dull.

"Come on, sit down," I said. "I have one more thing to show you."

"**I** didn't do anything," he said, fear spiderwebbing his voice like a rock against a windshield.

"I know you didn't," I said, my voice wafting through the lattice of the professional interrogator's faked empathy. "It was those insane twins, wasn't it?"

"*That's* what this is about? *Those* psychos? They're steroid abusers. You know what that does to people. I never meant for them to—"

"Oh, I know, Vision," I told him. "It's not your fault that you're a genius."

"I'm not saying I'm a—"

"Well, even if you're not, *I* am. Because you are, my friend. *Noir vérité*. It's so strong, it just takes over. You never filmed the actual killing, did you?"

"No! I'm telling you, it wasn't *supposed* to be . . . real. It's . . . it's like you said. They just got out of control. I wasn't the director anymore. I wouldn't film *that*."

"I know."

"You're not a . . . producer, are you?"

"That's exactly what I am," I assured him. "And your concept, it just killed me. In fact, we're going to be doing one of your projects, and that's a promise."

"Then all this . . . like, kidnapping stuff, you're just . . . ?"

"Making a movie," I said. "Getting the feel of what you told us. Sorry if it looked scary. But I just wanted to see for myself."

"Oh! Oh, I get it. So when do I—?"

"Just sit here for a few minutes, Vision. I'll have the car brought around for you."

He expelled a long breath, said, "I thought—"

"Five minutes," I promised him, and stepped out the door.

It took less than that for the limo to vanish.

I piloted the Plymouth carefully across the waste ground, the moon's cold glare lighting the way.

Rejji was sitting next to me, her trembling thigh pressed against mine. She pointed at the shadow-shrouded building. "For real," she whispered.

Giovanni and Felix didn't come with us. The last I saw of them, they were putting on long black robes, adjusting the hoods over their heads.

Andrew Vachss has been a federal investigator in sexually transmitted diseases, a social services caseworker, and a labor organizer, and has directed a maximum-security prison for youthful offenders. Now a lawyer in private practice, he repre sents children and youths exclusively. He is the author of numerous novels, including the Burke series; two collections of short stories; and a wide variety of other material, including song lyrics, poetry, graphic novels, and a "children's book for adults." His books have been translated into twenty languages, and his work has appeared in *Parade, Antaeus, Playboy, Esquire,* the *New York Times,* and numerous other forums. A native New Yorker, he now divides his time between the city of his birth and the Pacific Northwest.

The dedicated Web site for Vachss and his work is www.vachss.com.

A NOTE ON THE TYPE

The text of this book was composed in a typeface called Bookman. The original cutting of Bookman was made in the 1850s by Mssrs. Miller & Richard of Edinburgh. Essentially the face was a weighted version of the popular Miller & Richard old style roman, and it was probably at first intended to serve for display headings only. Because of its exceptional legibility, however, it quickly won wide acceptance for use as a text type.

Composed by Stratford Publishing Services,
Brattleboro, Vermont
Printed and bound by Berryville Graphics,
Berryville, Virginia
Designed by Virginia Tan